MINARET

MINARET

LEILA ABOULELA

BLOOMSBURY

First published 2005

Copyright © 2005 by Leila Aboulela

The moral right of the author has been asserted

Bloomsbury Publishing Plc, 38 Soho Square, London W1D 3HB

A CIP catalogue record for this book
is available from the British Library

ISBN 0 7875 7626 2

10 9 8 7 6 5 4 3 2 1

Typeset by Palimpsest Book Production Ltd, Polmont, Stirlingshire
Printed by Clays Ltd, St Ives plc

All papers used by Bloomsbury Publishing are
natural, recyclable products made from wood grown
in well-managed forests. The manufacturing
processes conform to the environmental regulations of
the country of origin.

Bism Allahi, Ar-rahman, Ar-raheem

I've come down in the world. I've slid to a place where the ceiling is low and there isn't much room to move. Most of the time I'm used to it. Most of the time I'm good. I accept my sentence and do not brood or look back. But sometimes a shift makes me remember. Routine is ruffled and a new start makes me suddenly conscious of what I've become, standing in a street covered with autumn leaves. The trees in the park across the road are scrubbed silver and brass. I look up and see the minaret of Regent's Park mosque visible above the trees. I have never seen it so early in the morning in this vulnerable light. London is at its most beautiful in autumn. In summer it is seedy and swollen, in winter it is overwhelmed by Christmas lights and in spring, the season of birth, there is always disappointment. Now it is at its best, now it is poised like a mature woman whose beauty is no longer fresh but still surprisingly potent.

My breath comes out like smoke. I wait to ring the bell of a flat; the number is written down in my notebook. She said eight. I cough and worry that I will cough in front of my new employer, implant in her the anxiety that I will pass germs on to her child. But she might not be the anxious type. I do not know her yet. The only time I saw her was last week when she came to the mosque searching for a servant. She had an aura of haste and grooming about her. Her silk scarf was rolled casually around her head and neck and, when it slipped and showed her hair, she didn't bother to tug it back on again. A certain type of Arab woman – rich student, late twenties, making the most of the West . . . But I still did not know her. She was not herself when she spoke to me. Few people are themselves in mosques. They are subdued, taken over by a fragile, neglected part of themselves.

I hope she hasn't forgotten me. I hope she hasn't changed her mind and put her little girl in a nursery or found someone else. And I hope that her mother, who has until now been the baby-sitter, has not extended her stay in Britain and made me unnecessary. St John's Wood High Street is busy. Men in suits and young women wearing the latest fashions get into new cars and drive off to good jobs. This is a posh area. Pink hues and the expanse that money blesses people with. The past tugs but it is not possessions that I miss. I do not want a new coat but wish I could dry-clean my old one more often. Wish that not so many doors have closed in my face; the doors of taxis and education, beauty salons, travel agents to take me on Hajj . . .

When someone picks up the entry-phone, I say, my voice edgy with hope, 'Salaamu alleikum, it's me, Najwa . . .' She is expecting me, alhamdullilah. The sound of the buzzer is almost thrilling. I push the door open and enter to find everything in wood; the past preserved and cared for in good taste. This is a beautiful building, dignified and solid. Old, cautious money polished by generation after generation with love and care. Not like my father's money, sequestered by a government, squandered by Omar. I was silly too with my share, I did nothing useful with it. There's a mirror in the lobby. It shows a woman in a white head-scarf and beige, shapeless coat. Eyes too bright and lashes too long, but still I look homely and reliable, the right age. A young nanny might be careless, an older nanny complains about her back. I am the right age.

The elevator is the old-fashioned type so that I have to yank the door. It clatters in the elegant quiet of the building. I reach to press the button for the second floor but find that the first button says one to three, the second three to four, and the third four to six. I try to work it out, stare at it but I am still confused. I decide to climb the stairs instead. A door slams above me; quick footsteps descend the stairs. When he comes within sight I see a youth who is tall and gangly with the start of a beard and curly hair. I stop him and ask about the elevator.

'It's the flat numbers, not the numbers of the floor.' He speaks English as if it is his mother tongue but the accent is not local. It is difficult guessing people's origins in London. If he were Sudanese, he would be considered light-skinned but I have no proof that he is.

'Right, thanks.' I smile but he does not smile back.

Instead he repeats, 'You just have to press the number of the flat you want.' His eyes are liquid brown; they shine not with intelligence, not at all like Anwar's, but with intuition. Perhaps he is sensitive but not particularly bright, not quick and sharp like young people nowadays.

I thank him again and he ducks his head a little, shrugs his shoulders to adjust the strap of his bag. I have heard the saying that you can smell Paradise on the young. When he backs away and walks out of the building, everything goes back to normal again.

I ascend and open the door of the elevator to an elegant, vacuumed carpet, take hopeful steps towards the flat.

3

I will take the little girl to the square across the road. I will take her to the mosque, time it so that I can pray with everyone else and afterwards feed the ducks in Regent's Park. It is very likely that the flat will have satellite TV and I will be able to watch an Egyptian film on ART and the news on al-Jezira. Last week I heard a talk and these were the lines that stayed with me, that touched me the most: *The mercy of Allah is an ocean. Our sins are a lump of clay clenched between the beak of a pigeon. The pigeon is perched on the branch of a tree at the edge of that ocean. It only has to open its beak.*

Part One

Khartoum, 1984–5

One

'**O**mar, are you awake?' I shook his arm that lay across his face, covering his eyes.

'Hmm.'

'Get up.' His room was wonderfully cool because he had the best air conditioner in the house.

'I can't move.' He put his arm down and blinked at me. I moved my head back, wrinkling my nose at his bad breath.

'If you don't get up, I'm going to take the car.'

'Seriously, I can't . . . can't move.'

'Well, I'm going without you.' I walked to the far end of his room, past his cupboard and the poster of Michael Jackson. I switched the air conditioner off. It died down with an echo and heat surrounded the room, waiting to pounce into it.

'Why are doing this to me?'

I laughed and said with glee, 'Now you'll be forced to get up.'

Downstairs I drank tea with Baba. He always looked so nice in the morning, fresh from his shower and smelling of aftershave.

'Where's your brother?' he grumbled.

'Probably on his way down,' I said.

'Where's your mother?'

'It's Wednesday. She goes to Keep Fit.' It always amazed me how Baba deliberately forgot my mother's schedule, how his eyes behind his glasses looked cautious and vague when he spoke of her. He had married above himself, to better himself. His life story was of how he moved from a humble background to become manager of the President's office via marriage into an old wealthy family. I didn't like him to tell it, it confused me. I was too much like my mother.

'Spoilt,' he now mumbled into his tea, 'the three of you are spoilt.'

'I'll tell Mama you said this about her!'

He made a face. 'She's too soft on your brother. It's not good for him. When I was his age, I was working day and night; I had aspirations . . .'

'Oh no,' I thought, 'not that again.' My feelings must have shown on my face because he said, 'Of course you don't want to listen to me . . .'

'Oh Baba, I'm sorry.' I hugged him and kissed his cheek. 'Lovely perfume.'

He smiled, 'Paco Rabanne.'

I laughed. He cared about his clothes and looks more than any father I knew.

'Well, time to be off,' he said and the ritual of his departure began. The houseboy appeared from the kitchen and carried his briefcase to the car. Musa, the driver, leapt out of nowhere and opened the car door for him.

I watched them drive off and there was only the Toyota Corolla left in the driveway. It used to be Mama's car but last month it became mine and Omar's. Mama had a new car now and Omar stopped using his motorcycle.

8

I looked at the garden and the road beyond. There were no bicycles on the road. I had an admirer who kept riding his bicycle past the front of our house. Sometimes he came past three or four times a day. He had hopeful eyes and I despised him. But, like now, when the road was empty, I felt disappointed.

'Omar!' I called from downstairs. We were going to be late for our lecture. At the beginning of the term, our very first in the university, we used to go well ahead of the time. Six weeks into the term, we discovered that the sophisticated thing was to appear at the last minute. All the lecturers turned up ten minutes past the hour, and swept grandly into halls full of expectant students.

I could not hear any sound from above so I ran upstairs. No, the bathroom was empty. I opened Omar's bedroom and the room was, as I had expected, an oven. Yet there he was fast asleep, sprawled snoring. He had kicked the covers off and was drenched in sweat and listlessness.

'That's it. I'm going to drive, I have nothing to do with you.'

He stirred a little. 'What?'

I sounded angry but I was also afraid. Afraid of his sleepiness that did not stem from any illness; afraid of his lethargy that I could not talk to anyone about.

'Where are the keys?'

'Ha?'

'Where are the car keys?' I yanked open his cupboard.

'No, in the pocket of my jeans . . . behind the door.'

I pulled out the keys; coins fell to the floor, a box of Benson & Hedges.

'See what will happen when Baba hears about this.'

'Put the air conditioner back on.'

'No.'

'Please Nana.'

His use of my nickname softened me a little. The empathy of twins gripped me and for a moment I was the one who was hot and unbearably sleepy. I switched on the air conditioner and marched out of the room.

I rolled up the window of the car so that dust wouldn't come in and the hot wind wouldn't mess up my hair. I wished I could feel like an emancipated young student, driving her own car with confidence. Was I not an emancipated young woman driving her own car to university? In Khartoum only a minority of women drove cars and in university less than thirty per cent of students were girls – that should make me feel good about myself. But I preferred it when Omar was with me, when Omar was driving. I missed him.

I drove slowly and was careful to indicate and careful not to knock down anyone on a bicycle. At the Gamhouriya Street traffic light a little girl knocked on my window, begging with tilted head and unfocused eyes. Because I was alone I gave her a note. If Omar had been with me, I would have given her a coin – he hated beggars. She clutched the five pounds with slow disbelief and ran back to the pavement. When the light changed to green, I drove on. From the rear-view mirror, I could see her engulfed by other children and a few desperate adults. Dust and the start of a fight.

My hands were sweaty when I knocked on the door of lecture room 101. I was fifteen minutes late. I could hear Dr Basheer inside delivering another chapter on Accounting, my least favourite subject, but my father wanted Omar to study Business and, after years in a girls' school, I wanted to be with Omar. I knocked again louder and gathered courage to turn the knob. It was locked. So Dr Basheer had been true to his announcement that no latecomers would be allowed in his lectures. I turned and walked to the cafeteria.

My favourite cafeteria was at the back of the university. It overlooked the Blue Nile but the water couldn't be seen because of the dense trees. The morning shade and the smell of the mango trees began to soothe me. I sat at a table and pretended to read my notes. They meant nothing and filled me with emptiness. I could foresee the hours I would have to spend memorizing what I couldn't understand. When I looked up I noticed that Anwar Al-Sir was sitting at the next table. He was in his last year and known for the straight As he got. Today he was alone with his cigarette and glass of tea. In a campus where most were scruffy, he always wore clean shirts, was clean-shaven and his hair was cut short even though longer hairstyles were in fashion. Omar had his hair just like Michael Jackson on the album cover of *Off the Wall*.

Anwar Al-Sir was a member of the Democratic Front, the students' branch of the Communist Party. He probably hated me because I had heard him speaking in a *nadwa* with wit and scorn of the bourgeoisie. Land-owning families, capitalists, the aristocracy; they were to blame, he said, for the mess our country was in. I talked to Omar about this but Omar said I was being too personal. Omar did not have time for the likes of Anwar; he had his own set of friends. They lent each other videos of *Top of The Pops* and they all intended to go to Britain one day. Omar believed we had been

11

better off under the British and it was a shame that they left. I made sure that he didn't write these ideas in any of his History or Economics essays. He would surely fail because all the books and lecturers said that colonialism was the cause of our underdevelopment.

It would have been childish to move from where I was sitting. But I felt uncomfortable sitting facing Anwar. He smiled at me and this took me aback. He kept looking at me. I felt that my blouse was too tight and my face too hot. I must have exhaled because he said, 'It's hot, isn't it? And you're used to air conditioners.' There was a teasing in his voice.

I laughed. When I spoke, my voice sounded strange to my ears, as if it were not me. 'But I prefer the heat to the cold.'

'Why?' He threw the butt of his cigarette on the ground and, with his feet, covered it with sand. His movements were gentle.

'It's more natural, isn't it?' There were two tables between us and I wondered which one of us would make the first move, which one of us would get up and move over to the other table.

'It depends,' he said. 'Someone in Russia might regard the cold as natural.'

'We're not Russians.'

He laughed in a nice way and fell silent. His silence disappointed me and I thought of different ways to revive the conversation again. I scrambled different sentences in my head, fast, 'I heard you have a brother studying in Moscow', 'The air conditioner in my car broke down', 'You know, Dr Basheer wouldn't let me in'. I discarded them all as foolish and unbecoming. The silence grew until I could hear my heart above the sound of the birds. I got up and left the cafeteria without a glance towards him or a goodbye. It was nearly ten o'clock and time for Macroeconomics. The lecturer passed the attendance sheet. I wrote my name, then changed pens, made my handwriting more upright and wrote Omar's name.

I walked out of the Macro lecture room to find him waiting for me.

'Give me the car keys.'

'Here. Don't forget we have History at twelve. Show your face, please.'

He frowned and hurried off. I worried about him. It was there, nagging at me. When I was young my mother said, 'Look after Omar, you're the girl, you're the quiet, sensible one. Look after Omar.' And year in, year out, I covered for Omar. I sensed his weakness and looked out for Omar.

Two

I took my wallet, notebook and pencil case out of my straw bag and left it on the shelf near the library door. Two girls from my class were leaving the library and we smiled at each other. I was not sure of their names. They both wore white tobes and one of them was very cute with deep dimples and sparkling eyes. They were provincial girls and I was a girl from the capital and that was the reason we were not friends. With them I felt, for the first time in my life, self-conscious of my clothes; my too short skirts and too tight blouses. Many girls dressed like me, so I was not unusual. Yet these provincial girls made me feel awkward. I was conscious of their modest grace, of the tobes that covered their slimness – pure white cotton covering their arms and hair.

In the basement of the library the air coolers blew heavily and the fans overhead twirled. I put my things on the table and looked at the shelves. Something Russian, to come close to him, to have something to say to him. Marxist theory, dialectics. No, I wouldn't understand anything. At last I took a fat book off the shelf and sat down to read from a collection of translated poems.

I understood the line 'I've lived to bury my desires'. But I did not know from where this understanding came. I had a happy life. My father and mother loved me and were always generous. In the summer we went for holidays in Alexandria, Geneva and London. There was nothing that I didn't have, couldn't have. No dreams corroded in rust, no buried desires. And yet, sometimes, I would remember pain like a wound that had healed, sadness like a forgotten dream.

'I like Russian writers,' I said to Anwar next time, for there was a next time, a second chance that was not as accidental as the first. We walked together, past the post office and the university bookshop.

'Who?'

'Pushkin,' I said. He was not impressed with my reply.

'Look,' he said, 'if I gave you some leaflets, would you help me pass them out?'

'I can't. I promised my father I wouldn't get involved in student politics.'

He shrugged and raised his eyebrows as if to say, 'Why am I not surprised?'

'What are your own political views?' he asked.

'I don't know. I don't have any.'

'What do you mean you don't know?'

'Everyone seems to blame everyone else.'

'Well, someone has to take the blame for what's happening.'

'Why?'

'So that they can pay the price.'

I didn't like him saying that. Pay the price.

'Your father is close to the President?'

'Yes. They're friends too.'

'Have you met him?'

'Of course. He telephones my father at home and I answer the phone.'

'Just like that.' He smiled.

'Yes, it's nothing. Once, years ago, when I was in primary school, he phoned and when I answered I said "hello" in a very English way.' I held an imaginary receiver in my ear, mimicked myself saying, 'Hello, 44959.' I liked the way Anwar was watching me, the amusement in his eyes. 'Then,' I continued, 'the President got angry and he said, "Speak properly, girl! Speak to me in Arabic".'

Anwar burst out laughing. I was pleased that I had made him laugh.

'I like talking to you,' he said, slowly.

'Why?' That was the way to hear nice things. Ask why.

Years later, when I looked back, trying to remember the signs of hidden tension, looking behind the serenity, I think of the fights that I took for granted. The smell of dust and sewers fought against the smell of jasmine and guava and neither side won. The Blue Nile poured from the Highlands of Ethiopia and the Sahara encroached but neither was able to conquer the other. Omar wanted to leave. All the time Omar wanted to leave and I, his twin, wanted to stay.

'Why Samir and not me?' he asked Baba as we ate lunch. We ate from china and silver. We wiped our mouths with napkins that were washed and ironed every day.

'Because Samir didn't get good enough grades,' Mama said. She had just come back from the hairdresser and her hair curled over her shoulder. I could smell her hairspray and cigarettes. I wished I were as glamorous as her, open and generous, always saying the right things, laughing at the right time. One day I would be.

'So, is it fair,' I said, in support of Omar, 'that the one who gets the poor grades gets to go abroad and the one who gets the good grades stays here?' Samir was

16

our cousin, the son of Uncle Saleh, Mama's brother. Samir was now in Atlantic College in Wales doing the IB, which was like A levels.

'You too?' Baba glared at me.

'No, I don't want to go anywhere. I want to stay here with you.' I smiled at Mama and she smiled back. We were too close for me to leave her and go study abroad.

'Najwa is very patriotic,' Omar said sarcastically.

'As you should be,' said Baba.

'Eat and argue later,' said Mama but they ignored her.

'I want to go to London. I hate studying here.' Omar meant it. I could tell from his voice that he meant it.

'It's good for you,' Baba said. 'Roughen you up a bit. All this private schooling you've had has spoilt you. In university you're seeing how the other side lives. You'll understand the reality of your country and the kind of work environment you'll be facing one day. When I was your age . . .'

Omar groaned. I began to fear a scene. I swallowed, afraid of Baba shouting and Omar storming out of the house. I would have to spend the rest of the day phoning round searching for him.

I stood alone at the bottom of the garden. My admirer passed by on his bicycle. His clothes were awful and his haircut was terrible. It wasn't flattering to be admired by someone like him. I felt the familiar anger rise in me. But it was fun to be angry with him. I frowned at him, knowing well that any response would only encourage him. He grinned hopefully and pedalled away. I actually knew nothing about him.

'Come with me, Najwa', Mama said. She was wearing her plain blue tobe and her black high-heeled sandals. They

17

made a tapping noise on the marble of the front terrace. She carried a plastic bag full of lollipops and sweets.

Musa, the driver, came round with the car, gravel churning in the stillness of the afternoon. He opened the car door for her and went to bring out from the house more plastic bags bulging with old clothes and two pails of homemade biscuits. I recognized Omar's old Coca-Cola T-shirt and a pink dress that I'd stopped wearing because it was out of fashion.

'Where are you going?' I guessed from Mama's subdued clothes that it wasn't anywhere fun.

'Cheshire Home,' she said, getting into the back of car. She said 'Cheshire Home' gaily as if it were a treat. Only Mama could do that.

I hesitated a little. The thin twisted limbs of the children disturbed me and I preferred it when she took me to the school for the deaf. There the children, though they could not speak properly, were always running about care-free, with sharp intelligent eyes taking in what they couldn't hear.

But I got in the car next to her and, when Musa started the car, she opened her bag and gave me a spearmint gum.

'If you could see the orphanage your Aunt took me to yesterday!' she said. 'In comparison Cheshire is Paradise. Dirty, dirty, you wouldn't believe it.'

I wrinkled my nose in disgust. I was relieved they had gone in the morning when I was in university and so had not been able to drag me along.

'And they have nothing,' she went on. 'But is this an excuse not to keep the children clean?'

She did not expect a reply from me. Musa was smiling and nodding in the driver's seat as if she was talking to him. That's how she was. That's how she talked. There were times when she was animated and other times when she would be low and quiet. And it was strange that often at parties and weddings she would be sober, preoccupied, yet in crises she had the strength to rise to whatever the situation demanded. I knew, listening to her talk about the orphanage, that she was not going to let it rest. She would pull every string, harass my father and harass His Excellency himself until she got what she wanted.

Cheshire Home was cool and shady, in a nice part of town with bungalows and old green gardens. I envied my mother's ease, how she swept in with her bag of sweets and her biscuits, with Musa walking behind her carrying the rest of the things. The nurse, Salma, welcomed her like an old friend. Salma was very tall and dark, with high cheekbones and white dazzling teeth. Her drab white uniform did not hide her lovely figure: she looked dignified, with crinkles of white in her hair. 'Congratulations,' she said to me, 'you got into university.' She had not seen me for a long time.

'You keep this place very clean.' Mama started to praise Salma.

'Oh, Cheshire was even better in the past.'

'I know. But it's still good. I went to this orphanage yesterday and it was dirty, dirty, you won't believe it.'

'Which one was that?'

The room was large with a blackboard to one side, a few child-sized desks and stools. Cots lined the wall and a few balls and toys were scattered here and there. They looked familiar – maybe Mama had brought some of them in an earlier visit. There were a few posters on the wall about the importance of immunization, and a frightening picture of a baby with smallpox. Salma brought Mama and I chairs but she sat on one of the children's stools. The children clambered towards us in zimmers and some dragged themselves on the floor. One Southern boy was very fast, able to move around the room freely with his arms and one leg.

'One by one and I give you your lollipops,' said Mama. A faint attempt at forming a queue was abandoned in a confused flurry of outstretched hands. Mama gave them a lollipop each.

'John!' Salma called to the Southern boy. 'Stop this roaming around and come and get a lollipop.'

He casually heaved himself towards us, grinning, his eyes bright.

'What colour would you like?' Mama asked him.

'Red.' His eyes darted here and there, like he was scanning everything or like he was thinking of something else.

'Here. A red one for you,' Mama said. 'The last red one, all the rest are yellow.'

He took the lollipop and started to unwrap it. 'Is this your car outside?' he asked.

'Yes,' Mama replied.

'What's it to you!' Salma scolded him.

He ignored her and kept looking straight at Mama, 'What kind of car is it?'

'Mercedes,' Mama smiled.

He nodded and sucked his lollipop. 'I'm going to drive a big lorry.'

'Look at this silly boy,' Salma laughed, 'How are you going to drive?'

'I will,' he said.

'With one leg?' Salma raised her eyebrows, sarcastic, amused.

Something changed in him, the look in his eyes. Salma went on, 'You need two legs to drive a car.' He pivoted and dragged himself away.

'There are special cars in Europe,' I said, 'for people without . . . for disabled people.' It was the first time I had spoken since we arrived; my voice sounded stupid, everyone ignored me.

Suddenly John overturned a desk, dragged a stool round the room banging everything with it.

'Stop it, John, stop being rowdy!' Salma yelled.

He ignored her. He pushed the stool straight across the room. If it hadn't collided with another stool, it would have hit Salma straight on.

'I'm going to call the the police.' Salma stood up. 'They'll come and beat you up.'

He must have believed her for he stopped and became very still. He leaned against the wall. His leg was sticking out at an awkward angle, his head against the wall, lollipop in his mouth. Suddenly still.

In the silence we heard her weeping. She might have been eleven or even twelve; she was very thin, with callipers on both legs and a pink dress that was too small for her. How would she get married, how would she work . . . ? I must not ask these things, Mama always said, there is no point thinking these things, we just have to keep visiting.

'Why is she crying?' Mama asked Salma.

'I don't know.'

'Come and have a lollipop.' Mama called out to the girl but the girl continued to cry.

'Get up now and come and have a lollipop,' Salma shouted at the girl.

'Leave her, Salma. In her own time.' When the girl didn't move, Mama walked over to her and gave her sweets, patted her dishevelled hair. It didn't make any difference. She remained whimpering, with the sweets on her lap, until

21

the end of our visit. Only when we were getting up to go did I see her quieten and start to unwrap the lollipop. Hunched over, she squinted, mucus dribbling from her nose over her mouth. It was a struggle for her to unwrap the lollipop, aim it at her mouth. I had thought that her legs were the problem but there was something wrong with her hands too.

Three

The party at the American club was in full swing when Omar and I arrived. We walked into the tease of red and blue disco lights and the Gap Band's 'Say Oops Upside Your Head'.

'Where were you?' my best friend Randa screeched above the music. 'Come with me to the bathroom.'

'But I just got here.' I tried to protest but she grabbed my arm and pulled me.

'You look amazing,' I said to her. She was wearing a black halter-neck T-shirt and a longish swirling skirt. I hadn't made half the effort she had made. The bathroom was smelly and hot. Randa put on strawberry-flavoured lip gloss and smoothed her eyebrows. She had glitter in her hair and on her bare shoulders.

'Have you been to the hairdresser?'

'Yes I've been to the hairdresser.'

'My trousers are too tight.' An awkward twisting around to see my hips in the mirror.

'Your trousers are fine – how did you get them on?'

'Aaah . . .'

'Just joking.'

'Is he here?'

23

'Yes, His Highness has just walked in two minutes ago and I've been here since seven!'

His Highness was the unreadable Amir whom she had been going out with for the past six months. He had lately been acting strangely.

'Tonight,' she said, 'I'm going to get some response from him.'

I avoided her eyes. There were rumours that Amir had become friendly with a girl from the Arab Club. I didn't have the courage to tell Randa. Instead I said, 'You really look nice today.'

'Thanks, my love.'

'Let's get out of here, I'm suffocating.'

'Wait.' Out of her handbag came the inevitable mint spray. She opened her mouth and sprayed, then turned towards me. I hated the taste but opened my mouth anyway.

Outside the bathroom, the air was fresh and some children were still in the swimming pool. Delicious smells of kebab and French fries came from the kitchen.

'I'm hungry,' I said.

'Is this a time for food?'

I caught her excitement and we giggled arm in arm down the steps and back to the tingling darkness of the party. It was my favourite song, Boney M's 'Brown Girl in the Ring'. I started to sing along. In the middle of the dance floor the Indian girl Sundari was dancing with her marine. Her black straight hair swung all the way down to her waist and when she turned it flew up and fell down. I couldn't take my eyes off her. She had a way of dancing where she moved far away from her partner and with sharp high heels skipped back towards him again. He looked so like a Sudanese you could easily be fooled, but Randa and I had analysed him deeply and decided that you could tell he was American just by the way he held himself – conscious of this unglamorous part of the world he had been posted to.

I did not have to wait for long. One of Omar's friends asked me to dance and, leaving Randa, we made our way to the centre of the dance floor. White smoke rose up from the floor just like in *Saturday Night Fever*. I twirled around so that my earrings swayed and the arms of the others dancers brushed against mine.

Unfortunately, after Boney M came the Bee Gees with 'How Deep is Your Love' and the numbers on the dance floor dwindled to no more than five couples. Warm from dancing, I went and bought myself a Pepsi then I searched the tables exchanging 'hi's until I found Randa sitting with Omar and the ever-serious Amir. His glasses flashed in the darkness, hiding his eyes; Randa was smiling hopefully.

'So how's the university?' she was asking him.

'All right,' he drawled.

'When do you get to carry that T-shaped ruler?' I asked. The Architecture students were always a striking sight on the campus, walking around with that ruler.

'Next year.' His boredom was infectious. I gave up and sat back in my chair, poured Pepsi in my glass and watched the dancers. Some couples danced very close, others moved awkwardly at arm's length. Sundari and the marine were of the very close type – his hands locked around her small waist, brushed by the fall of her hair. She lifted her head from his shoulders, moved her head back and said something to him. He smiled. I imagined myself dancing with Anwar and then told myself not to be stupid, this was exactly the sort of thing he despised; Western music, Western ways. I had not told Randa about him. She would not understand. Yes, she would agree that he was handsome, but he was not one of us, not like us . . . And a member of the Democratic Front; she would not even know what the Front was.

Omar offered Amir a cigarette. A gust of wind suddenly blew, ruffling the tablecloth. It would be winter soon, we'd wear cardigans and it would be too cold to swim.

Randa suddenly blurted out, 'I'm leaving next month.'

'What!' from me and Omar, simultaneously. 'Where are you going?' Question after question from me and Omar.

Amir didn't raise an eyebrow or speak. She answered us while her eyes were on him, watching his reaction, testing him.

'I'm going to England to do A levels.'

'But I thought you were going to sit your O levels again and try to get into Khartoum University . . .'

'My parents want me to leave.'

'Just like my cousin Samir,' said Omar. 'He didn't make it and gets to go abroad. And we get stuck here.' He looked at Amir for support or at least an acknowledgement of the irony. There was no response.

'Oh Randa, I'm so upset.' All through secondary school, I had hoped we would be together in university. When her grades weren't good enough, I had hoped she would try again and join me next year. I had made dreams that we would be together, that she would meet Anwar; that she would learn what the Front was.

'I can come back after A levels.' A hardness was in her voice. And suddenly her hair glitter and lip gloss weren't as nice as before.

'What do you think Amir?' She turned to him again, voice a little sharp, focused.

He shrugged. 'Why not?'

'Exactly, why not?' She sat back in her chair.

That was it then, he didn't care. I hurt for her and that was mixed up with the shock that she was going away. Would she want me to go with her to the bathroom now, would she cry? There was a distracted expression on her face.

'Come on Omar, let's dance,' she said.

There was a pause as my brother registered what she was saying, and hesitated, deciding between extinguishing his cigarette or taking it with him. I looked down at the ground. They walked to the dance floor, blocking my view of Sundari and her marine. I did not watch them dance and instead surrendered to the Bee Gees' sickly lyrics. Amir didn't speak and I finished my Pepsi, crunching every bit of ice. I was waiting for the slow songs to end, waiting for Omar and Randa to come back.

After the party, I went to her house. Omar dropped us and went off to another party, a private one this time – some seedy affair he didn't want to take me too. They were getting more frequent these mysterious outings of his, and so were the places and new friends I was not part of.

At Randa's house, her parents were having a dinner. To avoid them, we went in through the kitchen door, past frantic servants and a floor sticky and slippery with frying oil and discarded vegetable peel. Randa's room upstairs was neat and the air cooler blew softly. She put on a long-sleeved shirt over her halter-neck T-shirt. 'So that we can go and get some food,' she said. I pulled my blouse out of my trousers and, though the bottom part was all crumpled, at least that way it hid my hips and made me a little bit more respectable.

Randa's parents were a little mad according to my parents. Ever since they had studied in England, where Randa

27

was born, they had come back with eccentric English habits. They went for walks, invited people to dinner with cards and kept a puppy. Randa's mother was one of the very first women professors in the country. For this reason, Randa's inability to get into university was a sore disappointment. Now they were going to send her to England to study – another bold move as not many girls went on their own to study abroad.

The grown-ups had finished eating and were in the garden so we didn't have to say hello and chat. Just before the servant started to clear up the dining room, we heaped plates full of food and went back to Randa's room. I think she was heartbroken about Amir so she didn't eat much. I finished my plate and ate the rest of hers.

'Did you see Sundari with her marine?' I laughed. 'Things are getting serious . . .'

'You know, the other day I saw her car parked in front of the Marine House.'

'You're joking?'

'I'm not and it was siesta time!'

I shrieked and Randa laughed. She became herself again and we were soon giggling together, gossiping about everyone in the disco (except Amir of course) – what they wore, who they danced with and how close. I waited for her to speak about Amir but she didn't. She took the empty plates to the kitchen and said she'd bring back dessert.

Alone in her room, I did what Mama had tried over the years to stop me doing but never succeeded. I snooped around. I opened Randa's cupboards, looking through her drawers. I found a photo of both of us at school, wearing identical uniforms – the navy pinafore and white belt. We were arm in arm and smiling at the camera. It was nice in those days to see Randa every day, every single day; to

28

sit next to her in class, to chat during lessons and annoy the teachers, to swap sandwiches and drink from the same bottle of Double Cola.

I leafed through a *Jackie* and found it childish – why did Randa keep having them sent from London? I turned the pages of an old *Time* magazine. Khomeini, the Iran-Iraq War, girls marching in black chadors, university girls . . . A woman held a gun. She was covered head to toe, hidden.

Randa came in with bowls of crème caramel, apples and bananas.

I put the magazine on the floor and reached for my bowl.

'Totally retarded,' she said looking at the picture and handing me a spoon. 'We're supposed to go forward, not go back to the Middle Ages. How can a woman work dressed like that? How can she work in a lab or play tennis or anything?'

'I don't know.' I swallowed spoonfuls of crème caramel and stared at the magazine, reading bits of the article.

'They're crazy,' Randa said. 'Islam doesn't say you should do that.'

'What do we know? We don't even pray.' Sometimes I was struck with guilt.

'I do sometimes,' said Randa.

'Yeah, when?'

'In exam time . . . A lot of good it did me.' She laughed.

'When I fast in Ramadan, I pray. A girl in school told me that fasting doesn't count unless you pray.'

Randa raised her eyebrows. 'You spend half the month saying you've got your period and can't fast!'

'Not half the month. I cheat a bit but not half the month.'

'Last year we were in London and we didn't fast at *all*.'

'Really?' I couldn't even imagine Ramadan in London, London in Ramadan.

'How can anyone fast in London? It would spoil all the fun.'

'Yes it would.' I looked down at the picture and thought of all the girls in university who wore hijab and all the ones who wore tobes. Hair and arms covered by our national costume.

'Would you ever wear a tobe?' I asked her.

'Yes but a tobe is different than *this*.' She jabbed the *Time* magazine. 'It isn't so strict. With a tobe, the front of your hair shows, your arms show.'

'It depends how you wear it, what you wear underneath it. The way some of the girls in the university wear it, they're really covered.'

'Huh,' she snorted and I realized I should not have mentioned the university, a sore point. I put the magazine away and finished my bowl of crème caramel.

'I didn't study enough,' she said glumly. 'I just didn't take these exams seriously.'

'It's so unfair. You're smarter than me.' The only reason I was able to get into Khartoum University was because I could sit on my fat bum for hours memorizing.

'I suppose I should be happy,' she said quietly. 'I suppose I am happy that I'm going to London, though I might not be going to London. I might go somewhere outside London.'

I waited for her to talk about Amir, to complain about how he had ignored her the rest of the evening. She did and I told her the rumours about him and the girl from the Arab Club.

✳   ✳   ✳

It was past three in the morning when Omar picked me up. I had started to worry and phoned round asking about him. Everyone in Randa's house slept and we stayed up watching videos of *Dallas*. It was lucky that Mama and Baba were away in Cairo; otherwise he would have got into trouble. When he finally came to pick me up, he looked tired and smelled of beer and something else, something that was sweet.

'You drive,' he said and I didn't like that. I drove home and he didn't put Bob Marley in the tape recorder like he usually did. He just sat next to me, quiet and distant, but he wasn't asleep. I smelt him and guessed what the smell was. But I didn't want to believe it. Hashish? Marijuana?

We heard the dawn azan as we turned into our house. The guard got up from where he was sleeping on the ground and opened the gate for us. The sound of the azan, the words and the way the words sounded went inside me, it passed through the smell in the car, it passed through the fun I had had at the disco and it went to a place I didn't know existed. A hollow place. A darkness that would suck me in and finish me. I parked the car and the guard closed the gate behind us. He didn't go back to sleep.

'Omar, we're home . . . Omar.' I leaned and opened the car door for him. He opened his eyes and looked at me blankly. We got out of the car and I locked it. There was not a single breeze. The night tight, no coolness, no flow. Still I could hear the azan. It went on and on and now, from far away, I could hear another mosque echoing the words, tapping at the sluggishness in me, nudging at a hidden numbness, like when my feet went to sleep and I touched them.

The servants stirred and, from the back of the house, I heard the sound of gushing water, someone spitting,

31

a sneeze, the shuffle of slippers on the cement floor of their quarters. A light bulb came on. They were getting ready to pray. They had dragged themselves from sleep in order to pray. I was wide awake and I didn't.

Four

It no longer surprised my friends that Anwar waited for me after lectures. We usually went to the Department of Science cafeteria because there were fewer people there who knew us, although Anwar was a familiar face because of his political activities. He didn't speak to me a lot about politics but sometimes he asked me strange questions.

'How many servants do have in your house?'

I started to count something I had never counted before. 'The cook, the Ethiopian maid, the houseboy, the guard and Musa the driver. That's all. No, then there's the gardener, but he doesn't come every day.'

'Six.'

'Yes . . . six.'

'And there's four of you?'

'We have a lot of guests.' This I said defensively. The campus was nearly empty. This was lunchtime, naptime, everyone was indoors away from the sun, but it was winter now and the sun was bearable. At four or five o'clock the light would start to soften and the campus would fill up again for the evening classes.

'Does it not strike you that it is wrong for such wide discrepancies to exist between people? There's famine in the west. This country is one of the poorest in the world.'

I fidgeted in my seat, said, 'There is nothing I can do about it.'

His voice softened a little and so did the way he looked at me. 'But this isn't true. It's up to us to change the system. It's always up to the students and the workers to change things.'

I told him what I'd read about the Iranian revolution in *Time*. He seemed amused that I read *Time*. Perhaps because it was in English and my English was very good because I had gone to a private school. Or perhaps because *Time* was American.

I wanted to know what he thought about the revolution. He talked about it for a while, approving of the deposing of the Shah but unsupportive of an Islamic government. He echoed Randa's words – 'We have to go forward not back' – and was contemptuous of the black chadors.

'You're very progressive then, where women are concerned?' I smiled, pleased with the turn in the conversation that followed, the chance to flirt and prove to myself again and again that, in spite of all his disapproval of my background, he liked me.

Anwar wrote for one of the student newspapers, the one for the Front. Every week the newspapers were handwritten and stapled on to the board in the cafeteria. There would be quite a rush for it at first, many students crowding round, standing on tiptoes to read the top pages, sitting on their heels to read the bottom. After a day or two when the crowd subsided I would go and have a look. Most of the articles bored me, but I always read his and tried hard to appreciate them. Most times though, the colours of the letters and the beauty of the handwriting distracted me from the meaning of the words. Titles in large flowing script, red shaded with black, a bold 3-D effect. There were sometimes illustrations too, a leaf to mark the end of an article, a flying dove. Cartoons too, sketches and a cynical joke. Within the walls of the university, free speech was allowed. The walls of the university were sacred and even the police were not allowed to go in. But everyone knew that there were spies. With pride, Anwar told me that the secret police had a file on him.

The way he said my name. The way he said, 'You have an effect on me.' Sometimes he hurt me, said I was stupid, sometimes he made me laugh.

I told Mama about him. She said, 'Don't risk your reputation and waste your time on someone who is never going to be a suitable husband for you.' She could see I was not convinced and her argument became tense. 'Your father would never approve. And you wouldn't be able to live that kind of life, no servants, no travelling. Believe me, you'd feel bad in front of your friends and the family. It would be such a humiliation for you and us.'

'OK,' I said, my voice too loud, 'OK.'

Her voice became smooth, trying to explain. 'I brought you up so that you can have a position in society, so that you can live at a certain standard.'

I walked out of the room catching a glimpse of the genuine alarm in her eyes. She was afraid that I would disobey her, afraid that I would do something rash. But I was held back by the rhythm of going day after day to the university, sometimes seeing him, sometimes not. I didn't know if I had a place in his future plans; he gave no hint. As for me, I dreamt dreams shaped by pop songs and American films. Then I would shake my head and tell myself that these were the sorts of things he despised.

His English was good in terms of vocabulary and grammar, but his accent was, I had to admit, poor. His clothes were tidy and in nice colours – but they were old-fashioned and he wore sandals instead of socks and trainers. He had not gone to a private school, he had not had private tutors, he was clever just by himself, just reading and going to talks and debates. His father was a senior technician with the railways. His two uncles, one a qualified architect, had been imprisoned for membership of the Communist Party. He had seven brothers and sisters; the eldest, a policewoman, was married with one child, one brother was studying in Moscow, one brother in the Khartoum Branch of Cairo University, then Anwar, then two younger girls in primary school. One of his younger sisters was ill but he didn't like talking about it. His mother was a qualified nurse but she didn't work anymore. He had an aunt who struck lucky and went with her husband to Saudi Arabia. He lived in the hostels and rarely went home, even though his house was across the bridge in Safia. He smoked every day but drank occasionally. He smoked only cigarettes and didn't pray. He never fasted in Ramadan; he did not see the point of it. He had never been abroad but he had travelled around the country, he had been to Port Sudan and the Nuba mountains, El-Obeid and as far south as Juba. I had never been out of Khartoum.

'Why do you go to Europe and not want to see your own country? Our country is beautiful,' he said, striking a match, lighting a cigarette. When no one could see us, in the evenings when the university was poorly lit, we would hold hands or sit close together so that our arms touched.

The speaker stood on an overturned Miranda crate, under the tree. A soft wind blew and the sun was gentle but still

I held my copybook over my head and squinted. The crowd was thick around me. There were girls in white tobes and a few like me holding copybooks over their heads. Some of the boys sat on the grass, others on the ledge that separated the paths from the garden. In the distance a sprinkler twirled, shooting out gusts of water at the flowerbeds and the grass. There was a good microphone today and that made a difference. It drew a bigger crowd, and the echo of Anwar's voice reached the cafeteria and inside the library.

He spoke steadily at first, almost coolly and then with a kind of controlled passion. He held himself back, waiting for the challenges and provocations that came with the questions. Only then would he give his best lines, the sharpest argument, the sarcasm, and the punch line, after which he would grin and raise his eyebrows as if to say, 'I rest my case'. A joke, a good joke to ridicule his opponent, make those sitting on the grass chuckle and those at the back smile. I felt proud of him, and the pleasure of looking and listening to him was like a treat – like ice cream when I was a child, a chocolate sundae with cream on top and wishing it would not end. But then he hurt me, and I should have expected it. I should have seen it coming, the inevitable dig at the bourgeoisie. It was his favourite word. But even worse, he was explicit now, using my father's name – my surname, so familiar, so close – and it was like a punch in the stomach, high in my stomach. My breath caught and I went cold but my cheeks were burning. A roar in my ears – the laughter rising around me – blocked out the rest of his sentence. He did not once look at me. I was invisible but that was my name in the direct accusation of my father. That was my name that made everyone laugh. I was an aristocrat, yes, from my

37

mother's side with a long history of acres of land and support for the British and hotels in the capital and bank accounts aboard. And if all that wasn't bad enough, my father stood accused of corruption.

I pushed my way out of the crowd, deaf and not knowing if anyone was looking at me. I knew that I mustn't cry, that I must walk with dignity to my car. I sat in the car, on the hot sticky plastic seat. I released the handbrake, twisted the key in the ignition. As I started to drive off, there was a knock on the window. Omar. Omar in a good mood, smiling. Not Omar of the seedy parties and suspect smell but Omar fresh in a white T-shirt and jeans, smiling. I rolled down the window.

'What's wrong, Nana?'

How did he know? Once long ago we were asleep inside Mama's stomach together, facing each other, twisting and kicking. I would like to go back to that time. The stupid tears come now.

'What's wrong, Nana?'

'Nothing.'

'OK, let me drive.'

'But you don't want to go home now.'

'It's OK, I can come back.'

'That's silly.' I wiped my face with the back of my hands, sniffed.

'Come on, move over.'

I got out and moved around the car to the passenger's seat. I felt floppy and I didn't want to talk.

We saw an accident on the way home. We heard the glass smash as the two cars hit each other: one was a taxi, the other a blue Datsun. People crowded round and all the traffic came to a standstill. Omar turned into a side street to get away from the jam. The side street had a ditch, houses with metal doors. On one of the doors was a design of aces, diamonds, hearts and clubs. Omar put Bob Marley on the tape recorder and sang along to 'Misty Morning'.

Five

I dived into the pool and the January water was a shock. I surfaced with a catch in my chest, out of breath. 'Freezing,' I spluttered.

'You're mad,' Randa shouted from under the umbrella of a poolside table. She had on glamorous sunglasses and was eating a grilled cheese sandwich. My only choice was to swim, keep swimming until I warmed up. The surface of the water was warm where the sun had been hitting it all morning. It was much colder below and so I didn't swim underwater. I reached the shallow end, turned and pushed my legs against the wall, started to breaststroke to the deep end. Some foreigners were on deckchairs sunbathing, slathered in Ambre Solaire reading Sidney Sheldon, but I had the whole of the pool to myself.

It took three lengths before the stiffness of the cold melted away and I began to enjoy myself. My eyes tingled with chlorine, the familiar taste of it in my mouth. My arms and legs separated the water, making a way for me to go ahead. Yesterday I walked right past Anwar without saying hello – he was with some friends pinning up the latest newspapers. It made me feel good to ignore him. He was waiting for me when I came out of the Accounting lecture all nice and smiling as if nothing had happened. He expected me to go walking with him but I just went off with some girls to the cafeteria. I could still feel, moving in the water, a dull anger towards him.

When I got out of the pool, I wrapped a towel around my waist and sat next to Randa.

'The lifeguard couldn't take his eyes off you,' she said.

'Very funny.' I stole a quick look at him. He was wearing a yellow polo shirt over swimming trunks. He was Eritrean.

I took my comb out of my bag and started to tug at my hair. I did not have nice, smooth hair like Mama's.

'Aren't you going to have a shower and shampoo it?'

'No.' After what she had told my about the lifeguard I felt too shy to go and stand under the showers which were just next to him.

'He'll get a good view of you then,' she giggled.

'Exactly.' I felt uncomfortable for no reason. Mama didn't object to me swimming as long as I didn't wear a bikini but, ever since I started university, I had begun to feel awkward, even in my black full-piece.

'My dad booked my ticket today,' Randa said.

'No!'

'Yes. I'm leaving next Saturday. Monday the term will start.'

I counted the days. Ten more days.

'We'll have a goodbye party for you,' I said.

'That will be nice.'

I tried to imagine where she was going. She was not going to London. She was going to Wales. I said, 'My cousin Samir is there too, at Atlantic College. You know, he said they have to do mountain climbing and outdoors stuff like that. It's part of the syllabus. He can tell you all about it. He's here now for the Christmas holidays.'

I pushed my chair back from under the umbrella so that

the sun could dry my hair. Chlorine-streaked hair. I had to go home, wash it and set it fast because I had an evening class.

I wore my denim skirt that evening. It was my favourite, tight and longish, with a slit at the back. It had two side pockets and a zipper in front just like trousers. I wore my red short-sleeved blouse with the little blue flowers on the collar. My hair turned out nice that day, wavy and not crinkling up into curls. I cared that day about how I looked, more than usual. As if by looking good I would annoy Anwar or show him that I didn't care.

He wasn't there when I got to the university at five. I was late for my lecture because Omar had gone out with Samir and I had made the mistake of waiting for him. A breeze blew around the trees as I took a short cut across the lawn. The boy from the canteen was spreading out a big palm-fibre mat on the grass. He unrolled it and was shifting it around, getting the angle just right.

The Economics class was good that evening – Rostow's Take-off, which I understood and it made perfect sense to me. Our country was going to take off one day like an aeroplane, we just needed to keep jogging, to accelerate our development and then we'd move, slowly at first but then much quicker, from our backwardness, faster and faster until lift-off, take-off. We would become great, become normal like all the other rich Western countries; we would catch up with them. I was understanding all of this crystal clear, writing in my notebook, wishing Omar was with me, knowing that he would have loved Rostow. But then the professor pushed his glasses up his nose and said, 'And now the Marxist criticism of Rostow's explanation for underdevelopment.' So it wasn't true after all.

42

We were not going to take off. Around me the students began to shuffle their feet and fidget, murmur that it was time to pray. The professor ignored them. 'History shows that not all developed nations have followed Rostow's model . . .' The murmurs increased and two brave boys just walked out, some girls started to giggle. The professor gave in and said, 'We'll have a ten-minute break.'

A rush for the door. 'Because he's a communist, he's not bothered about the prayers,' smiled the girl next to me, the pretty one with the dimples. She passed me in a hurry to go out, calling out to her friends, her high-heeled slippers slapping her heels. She wore a blue tobe today and looked even more cute. All the girls wore white tobes in the mornings and coloured ones in the evening. I liked watching the change in them, from the plain white in the morning to blue and pink flowers, patterns in bold colours.

I was one of the last to leave the class. Outside, I found Anwar chatting warmly with the professor as if they were old friends. I walked past them to the garden outside and sat on the steps of the porch watching those who were praying. Not everyone prayed. Girls like me who didn't wear tobes or hijab weren't praying and you could tell which boys were members of the Front, because they weren't praying. The others lined up on the palm-fibre mat but it was too small to take everyone. The ones who came late made do with the grass. Our Maths lecturer, who belonged to the Muslim Brothers, spread his white handkerchief on the grass. He stood, his shoulder brushing against the gardener's. The student who was leading recited the Qur'an in an effortless, buoyant style. I gazed at all the tobes of the girls, the spread of colours, stirred by the occasional gust of wind. And when they bowed down there was the fall of polyester on the grass.

'Why are you ignoring me?' Anwar's voice next me. I felt as if he was interrupting me – from what, I didn't know. I didn't reply. I got up and walked away in the direction of the lecture room. I couldn't see the students praying anymore and I felt a stab of envy for them. It was sudden and irrational. What was there to envy?

Anwar followed me. We were alone in front of the lecture room. He held my arm, above my elbow. 'Don't play with me.'

'I am the one who is angry.' I tugged my arm away but he still held on.

'Is it what I said that day at the talk?'

'Yes it is what you said that day at the talk.'

He let go of my arm. 'It has nothing to do with you . . .'

'It's my name. It's my father.'

'You're taking it personally. Broaden your mind.'

'I don't want to broaden my mind.'

'Do you know what people are saying about him?'

'I don't want to know.'

'They call him Mr Ten Per Cent. Do you know why?'

'Stop it.'

'You can't bury your head in the sand. You have to know what he's doing. He's taking advantage of his post in the government. He takes commissions on every deal the government makes with a foreign company.'

Anwar said the word 'commissions' in English. It sounded to my ear formal and blameless. 'So!' I said, sarcastic.

He lowered his voice, but it was sharper. 'He's embezzling money. This life you're living – your new car, your new house. Your family's getting richer by the day . . . Can't you see, it's corrupt?'

My anger was like a curtain between us. 'How dare you say these lies about my father! My father is me. My family is me.'

'Try and understand this. My feelings for you and my politics are separate. It's bad enough I'm laughed at for going with you.'

'Then leave me alone. Just leave me alone and no one will laugh at you.'

He blew impatiently, turned and went. I walked into the lecture room and, instead of emptiness, found a girl wearing hijab sitting filing her nails. She looked smug and carefree, filing her nails. She had probably heard all the conversation between me and Anwar. What was she doing here anyway instead of going out to pray? She probably had her period. I sat down in my seat and, to prove to myself that I wasn't upset, I took my pen and started to make an invitation list for Randa's goodbye party.

Six

Pizza, Pepsi, chips and tomato ketchup. Cupcakes and *ta'miyah*. Samosas and chocolate éclairs from the GB. Sandwiches made of tuna, egg, sausage, white cheese mashed with tomato, white cheese with olives. Vanilla ice cream in small paper cups. I passed them round in the dark and ended up dropping plastic spoons in the flower-pots. Grey-dark on the porch, mauve shadows on the cars. We were all beautiful in the moonlight.

'Sorry guys, the generator just isn't working . . .'

'I couldn't get the bloody thing to work.'

'Why are they cutting off the electricity in the middle of winter? What's wrong with these people.'

'Watch it, their father is the government.'

'Don't you have batteries for the tape recorder?'

'Batteries. Omar find batteries. Go.'

'I'll go buy some.'

'No . . . no.'

'She's gone to Nairobi for the wedding.'

'Five minutes in the car . . .'

'You have the most perfect white teeth, did anyone ever tell you that? I can *see* them in this dark!'

'You're embarrassing the guy.'

'This is my going away party. *This?*'

46

'Randa!'

'I'm glad I'm leaving you . . . if this is the best you can do.'

'Look at that girl!'

'Day after tomorrow, no power cuts. Civilization.'

'Have a sandwich! That looks like egg . . . I can't tell. Smell it . . . This one is sausage for sure . . .'

'It might come back . . .'

'What wrong with your generator anyway? Why couldn't you get it to work?'

'Let's go . . .'

'*No one* is going anywhere. Don't you dare move. *Samir* . . . You'll just spoil the party.'

'If we just had the music . . .'

'What's he doing? No, you can't go. Please don't go.'

'Samir, you can't leave us.'

The car light shone on Samir, on his Afro and new moustache. He sat on the passenger seat, one leg still outside, the door open. He looked down at the car radio, turned knobs and then there was the sudden blare of the tape recorder with Heatwave's 'Boogie Nights.'

He started to dance towards us. Randa laughed out loud.

'Samir you're a genius!' I shouted above the music.

'Put the engine on, man. Put the engine on . . . your battery will die out.'

I didn't feel well after they left. I sat on the porch while the servants cleared up. It was still dark because the lights hadn't come on yet, but by then my eyes had adjusted to the darkness and I could see the neighbouring houses and the swing in the garden. The party had been

47

a flop. And now Omar and most of the others had gone off somewhere else. Randa had gone home to pack. She thanked me and said the party was great, but she didn't mean it. I could tell she didn't mean it. It was the power failure that spoilt everything. One minute we were indoors dancing with the music loud and the atmosphere just right. Next minute it was the dark silence of outdoors, the intimidating sky. The lights never did come on and the generator was useless. They would talk about this, say we were so rich and yet too stingy to have a generator that worked properly. I knew they would say this because I would have said it if I were in their place.

I thought about Anwar and how separate he was from the party. He did not know Randa or my cousin Samir. Now when I met him in university, he said hello and I said hello, that's all. Sometimes he looked at me as if he was going to say more, but he didn't. He seemed busy these days with a lot of Front activities. I still thought of the things he had told me, tried to make sense of them; why I felt frightened when he said, 'The situation in the country can't last,' or when he said, 'This system is bound to fall.' He had told me that his youngest sister was blind and if they had the money she would be able to go to Germany and get an operation. Every year we went to Europe, every summer we stayed in our flat in London or in hotels in Paris and Rome and did all our shopping. If one summer we stayed at home, Anwar could take the money we had saved and send his little sister to have an operation. When I was young, before secondary school, I used to get into serious trouble with Mama and Baba over things like that. I gave all my Eid money to a girl in my class. I gave my gold earring to the Ethiopian maid. The maid was fired and the girl got into trouble at school with the headmistress. There are rules, Mama always said, you just can't give charity based on whims – you will be despised, you will be thought a fool.

I learnt these rules. Only give away clothes you have worn. Give fairly. Give appropriately. Give what is expected. You can offend people by giving them too much. You can confuse people. You can embarrass people by giving them expensive gifts they will feel obliged to reciprocate. Never give one person something and ignore their colleague, their sister/brother. Think. Think before you give. Is it expected of you?

I stayed up until Omar came home. One of his friends dropped him at the gate and he walked slowly up the drive, stumbled up the steps to the porch, once nearly falling. He didn't see me until I spoke out. On one side of our porch was a bench built in the wall. He lay down on it, staring up at the sky, his hand dangling to the ground. The smell came from him again, sweet and smoky, distinguishable from beer.

'You're in big trouble,' I said to him. He didn't even turn to look at me. 'I saw a packet full of powder in your drawer.'

'Did you take it?' He sounded calm but more alert.

'No, but I'm going to tell Baba about it.'

'It's nothing, Najwa.' His words were spaced out. 'It's only *bungo*. It's not addictive – a bit stronger than a cigarette, that's all.'

'You think Baba is going to be happy his son is smoking hashish?'

'Will he be happy his daughter is going out with a communist?'

'It's finished between me and Anwar.'

'You just had a fight, you'll make up.' He shifted sideways, looked at me in the dark. 'And when you do, do you know what Baba will do to him? Send him some thugs to beat him up. Make sure when he graduates, no one gives him a decent job.'

I breathed out. 'You're talking rubbish – that stuff has messed up your head. Baba wouldn't do that.'

He laughed. 'He'd do anything to protect his precious daughter.' He turned again on his back and we were quiet. He started to breathe steadily as if he was beginning to fall asleep.

'You better go inside before they come back.'

He grunted.

'Here, take the torch.' I put it in his hand.

While he was heading inside, I saw the headlights of Baba's car coming towards the house. The car horn sounded and our night watchman got up to open the gate. There was the sound of the wheels on the gravel, then Mama's voice as she got out of the car. 'How long have these lights been out?'

I went over to Baba and hugged him like I was afraid of something and he was going to make the fear go away. He smelled of grilled meat and supposedly banned whisky. I moved away from him. Mama looked tired, her shoulders stooped. Even in the moonlight I could see the mascara smudged around her eyes. We climbed up the steps of the porch. They didn't ask about the party and continued the conversation they'd been having in the car.

'He'll weather it out,' Baba said, 'he's faced opposition before.'

'I hope so,' she said. 'Whatever hurts him will hurt us.'

I opened the door of the house. The lights came on and hurt my eyes.

Seven

Baba didn't often share his wishes with us but he did that day. We were at the farm and he was wearing a safari shirt. He was irritated a little because he did not like the family gatherings that my mother organized. He preferred meetings with business friends, useful contacts, to day-long picnics spent playing cards and eating non-stop. Leaning back on his deckchair, he looked up as a small plane flew past, spraying pesticide. 'One day,' he said, 'I'm going to have my own private jet. Three more years at the maximum – I've got it all planned!'

'Wow,' Omar and I said at the same time. We were sitting on a picnic rug on the grass.

'Think of your father, kids. I started out with nothing, not a father, not a good education, nothing. Now I'm going to have my own private jet.'

'I'll learn to drive it,' said Omar. 'I'll take lessons.'

Baba looked at us over his gold-rimmed glasses and asked, 'So how old are you now?'

'Nineteen,' Omar chanted.

'Nineteen, already? And you too, Najwa?'

'Yes,' I smiled.

He was teasing us. 'I thought you were eighteen.'

'That was last year,' said Omar. I laughed. It rarely

happened but today Omar and I were dressed in identical colours. We were both wearing Wrangler jeans and I was wearing a beige polo neck and he had on a long-sleeved beige shirt. Mama came and took a photo of us. Years later, after everything fell, that photo remained. Omar and I smiling, a pink flower wedged in my hair, my legs crossed, my elbow on my knee and hand on my chin. Omar close, his back against my arm, his eyes bright, legs stretched out, hand resting lightly on the tape recorder, the cassettes scattered on his lap and on the red-check rug. Years later, when everything fell, I would narrow my eyes and try to distinguish by colour and words the tapes on the rug, tapes we used to buy on our summer holidays in London: Michael Jackson, Stevie Wonder, Hot Chocolate and my own tapes of Boney M.

Everything started to fall that night, late after the picnic, after the barbecue, after the guests had gone home and we also had gone home. After grilled kebab and peanut salad, boiled eggs, watermelon and guava. We drove back home and we were quiet, we were all tired. I washed my hair that night because of all the dust that had got into it. I examined an ant bite on my elbow. It was swollen and raised and I could not stop scratching it. The telephone call came late at night, close to dawn. I heard it and I thought someone had died. It had happened before, someone dying, a close friend or relation and Mama and Baba having to leave the house in the middle of the night. Over the next days of mourning they would say, 'We came as soon as we heard the news . . . we came at night.'

I didn't get out of bed. I was not curious enough. I heard Baba's voice on the phone but I could not distinguish his words. I could hear his voice and something about it was not right. There wasn't the bite and shock that came with death. I sat up in bed, saw the outline of the room slowly come to focus as my eyes adjusted to the dark. The nights were still cool; we did not need air conditioners. If they had been on, I would not have heard the phone.

The door to Omar's room was closed. I walked down the corridor to my parents' room. Their light was on and the door was ajar. I saw the suitcase on the bed. I saw Mama tucking some of Baba's socks in the suitcase, which was already nearly full. He was getting dressed, buttoning his shirt. He turned and looked at me as if he couldn't see me, as if it was the most natural thing in the world for him to be going out in the middle of the night.

'Are you going away?' I asked but neither of them answered. Mama continued to stalk the room, packing, distracted, as if she was listening to a voice in her head, a voice that was listing things for her, telling her what to do. 'Go back to sleep,' she said to me.

Wide awake, I went to the bathroom. I stared at myself in the bathroom mirror, smoothed my eyebrows, admired how the yellow of my pyjamas suited my skin and forgot about Baba.

When I got out of the bathroom, I heard him starting the car. It had to be him starting the car because Musa didn't sleep over. Musa went home every night. I wondered where Baba was going, where was he travelling to. Why didn't they tell me that someone important had died abroad? I went into Omar's room and started to wake him up. He woke but didn't come with me to the window. I looked through the curtains. I saw Baba easing the car out of the garage, over the pebbles towards the gate. I saw the night watchman drag open the gates for him. Then I saw the headlights of a car coming fast down our road. It stopped with a screech in front of our gate, blocking Baba's car. Two men got out. One hovered near the gate and the other went and opened Baba's car door, like Musa opened it for him every day but not like that, not exactly like that. Baba turned the ignition off and got out of the car. He spoke with the man, gestured towards the boot of the car. The man said something to his friend and the friend opened the boot and took Baba's suitcase out. They started to walk towards their car and just left Baba's car beached in the parkway, neither in the house nor out of it. Baba took out something from his pocket, probably money or the car keys, and gave it to the night watchman. Then he got into the car with the two men. He sat in the back seat and that was wrong, I knew. He shouldn't be in the back seat. I had never seen him sitting in the back seat, except in taxis or when Musa was driving. And Mama was next to me; she frightened me. The way she ground her teeth, stopping herself from crying, and banged the window softly with her fist frightened me. Omar came and put his arm around her, led her away from the window.

'What's wrong?' he said. 'What's wrong, Mama?'

His voice was calm and normal. I looked out at the dark empty street, at Baba's abandoned car, at the watchman trying to close the gate and realizing that he couldn't. He couldn't move the car because he didn't know how to drive. It would have to wait for morning, for Musa to come.

'What's wrong, Mama?' Omar's voice was patient. They both sat on his bed.

'There's been a coup,' she said.

Eight

Our first weeks in London were OK. We didn't even notice that we were falling. Once we got over the shock of suddenly having to fly out the day after Baba was arrested, Omar and I could not help but enjoy London. We had never been there before in April and the first thing we did was go to Oxford Street and buy clothes. It was fun to do all the things we never did back home; grocery shopping, pushing the Hoover around, cooking frozen food. It was fun to do all the things we usually did in the summer. Omar went to the cinema in Leicester Square and I don't know how many tapes he bought from HMV. I went through Selfridges trying the perfumes and getting my face made up at the Elizabeth Arden counter.

But Mama was not herself at all; she was in a daze, sometimes crying for no reason, muttering to herself in the middle of the night, immune to the excitement of London. She refused to go out shopping and constantly followed the news of the coup; surrounding herself with all the Arab papers as well as *The Times* and the *Guardian*, phoning round and leaving the TV on all the time. Our flat in Lancaster Gate was constantly filled with other Sudanese: businessmen passing through London, anxious Embassy staff who were awaiting the inevitable changes that would come about with the new government. They all reassured Mama about Baba. 'They'll soon let him go and he'll join you here,' they said. 'It will all die down,' they said, 'be patient, they'll flex their muscles at the beginning and then they'll slacken.' She listened to them quietly and I helped her serve coffee and tea. Her face was harsh without make-up, her hair out of the way in a bun because she no longer went to the hairdresser; the jumpers she wore under her tobe were in sombre colours.

Randa called me from her college in Wales. 'I can't believe it, you're really here!' she shrieked.

'I can't believe it either – I was just saying bye to you a while back . . .'

'What are you going to do now?'

'We're waiting for Baba to join us – we're worried about him.' I swallowed and there was a burning in my fore-head.

'And then what, how long will you stay here, what about your university?'

'I don't know Randa. I brought all my notes and books with me . . .'

'But this new government seems like it's here to stay, the coup was a success. I suppose you'll just stay here on political asylum . . .'

'They might allow us to go back. I don't know.' I had not thought things out.

'You can come here you know.'

'Here where?'

'Here in Atlantic College with me.'

The idea for some reason horrified me. 'Omar would love that – but Randa tell me about you. Tell me what's it like for you. Do you like it in Wales? Is the work hard? Have you done the mountain climbing?'

'I'll tell you all about it in a letter. I can't stay on the phone for long.'

'OK. Give the letter to Samir, he's coming down to see us at the weekend.'

'Yeah, OK I will. I do bump into him frequently.'

'Randa I forgot to tell you – Sundari's pregnant . . .'

'Whaaat!' she hissed.

'It's a big scandal; even the American Embassy is involved. This is not why marines are posted to Sudan.' I tried to laugh at my own joke but the sound that came out was more like a lumpy cough.

Samir came at the weekend, wearing faded jeans and a leather jacket. He had on a new pair of glasses. He hugged Omar hard and I felt again that burning in my forehead that had started to come to me from time to time. He kissed Mama and she started to cry, embarrassing us all.

'Any news?' Samir sat down in one of the armchairs, Omar in the other. I sat on the sofa with Mama. The TV was on, as we sometimes had it these days, pictures without sounds.

'They are going to try him,' Omar said. Mama dabbed at her eyes with a handkerchief, her mouth stretched open.

'Insha' Allah it will all be OK.' Samir shifted in his arm-chair. He looked smothered by the deep, soft cushions.

But what if it didn't turn out to be OK, I wanted to say. What if they found him guilty, what if he *was* guilty, what then? As if I understood what they were trying him for . . . Corruption. What did that mean? How could that word have anything to do with my father? We shouldn't have left him, we should have stayed with him. What were we doing here? It was Uncle Saleh who decided that we should come here. He had sorted everything out, all in a few hours, getting us on the last plane out before they closed the airport. But maybe he was wrong, maybe we should have stayed, maybe us running away would make Baba be found guilty. Weren't we acting as if he were guilty? But I didn't say anything; I stared at ITV – ads for chocolate biscuits, coffee, a new drama serial. Whenever I watched television, I forgot all about Baba, the bad food he must be getting in that 'special' house he was held in, the coming trial. The President was now in the US. He had called last night and spoken to Mama. 'It's all his fault,' she said afterwards, 'it's all his fault.' But on the phone she had been all nice, respectful in the same way she had always been with His Excellency.

'Samir, will you drink tea or something cold?' I smiled at him, happy to see a familiar face.

He said, 'I've got a letter for you from Randa.' I took it from him and went to read it in the kitchen.

'Where's that tea?' Mama called out. I stopped in the middle of a description of Randa milking a cow (how absurd that that was part of her course!) and switched the kettle on.

Pizza Hut was warm and they played all the latest songs, songs we were just getting to know. The three of us shared a large seafood pizza and Samir ordered something I had never had before – garlic bread with cheese. It was very nice. Outside in the cold, Leicester Square was full of lights and so lively that I forgot it was night. People were coming out of the theatres heading towards the restaurants and the tube station, bouncers stood in front of nightclubs wearing check waistcoats. In one of the smaller cinemas *Saturday Night Fever* was still playing. We stood in front of a disco. We could hear the beat of Michael Jackson's

'Billie Jean' and the glimmer of red and flashing lights.

'Are you mad? How can we go to a disco?' I glared at Omar.

'Why not?' He did his imitation of a moonwalk. It was good but I was not in the mood to praise him.

'Tell him why not.' I looked at Samir but he shrugged and moved away from us. He seemed guarded, stiff with a new formality.

'We can't go to a disco because of Baba,' I said to Omar. 'What do you want people to say? The man's on trial for his life and his children are dancing in London.'

'What people? Who do you think is going to know us in there? Don't be silly.' He turned to Samir to get support but he was busy examining a shop window.

'There just might be someone in there who knows us. It might just happen. Why take the risk?'

'You're obsessed with what people think of you!'

'I'm not obsessed. I am just sure that if we were in Khartoum, we wouldn't be at a disco.'

'We are not in Khartoum. Look, just go home.'

'Right, I will go home.'

Omar turned and started to walk towards the disco. 'Samir, come on,' he called out.

'Look, I'll take you home first,' Samir said. He didn't want to take me home. It struck me that he was bored with us. As if something had happened to make us less than him. As if he was all grown up and we were still little.

'No,' I said, 'stay with Omar. I'm OK by myself.'

Our flat was only a few stops away by underground. The floor of the train was littered with cigarette butts and empty cans. The passengers were sleepy and tense, I felt as if we were moving in stale, unfulfilled time. Baba was going to be found guilty. Why else would they try him? That would be the justice the papers were crying out for. The new regime was supported by the Democratic Front. It was a populist regime, a regime of the people: no more old feudal ways, no more accumulation of wealth and power in the hands of an élite. Members of the Front were now offered places in the new government. My communist lecturer who had taught us about Rostow's take-off was now the Minister of Finance. I read all that in the papers, after Mama discarded them. I read an article about Baba's trial written by a student – because the students were the vanguards of the revolution. The article said that justice would be met and nothing was a fairer punishment for corruption than sequestration and the noose. The article was written by a student I knew well. The article was written by Anwar.

There are all kinds of pain, degrees of falling. In our first weeks in London we sensed the ground tremble beneath us. When Baba was found guilty we broke down, the flat filling with people, Mama crying, Omar banging the door, staying out all night. When Baba was hanged, the earth we were standing on split open and we tumbled down and that tumbling had no end, it seemed to have no end, as if we would fall and fall for eternity without ever landing. As if this was our punishment, a bottomless pit, the roar of each other's screams. We became unfamiliar to each other simply because we had not seen each other fall before.

Part Two

London, 2003

Nine

Lamya, my new employer, stands holding open the door of her flat. There is a light above her head and she is more relaxed than when I saw her at Regent's Park mosque. Her voice, when she returns my greeting, is thick as if she has just got up. She is wearing jeans and an attractive cardigan. Her face is not pretty but her figure, clothes and hair compensate. I keep my eyes and head lowered like I trained myself to do. This is not my first job; I know how deferential a maid should be. I take off my shoes and leave them near the door. I take off my coat, fold it and put it over my shoes – it wouldn't be polite to hang it over the family's coats on the coat-rack. I know I must be careful in everything I do; I mustn't slip. The first day is crucial, the first hours. I will be watched and tested but, once I win her trust, she will forget me, take me for granted. This is my aim, to become the background to her life. She closes the door behind me and I hear the television; the sound of a toddler and an older woman's voice.

I follow Lamya down the corridor towards the television sounds. The flat is modest, subdued – I had expected it to be more luxurious given the posh area and the fine building. Lamya pushes a door open, a thick wooden door. It is stiff and rubs against the wool of the carpet. The living room is spacious, with large windows overlooking the autumn trees of the park. Shadows of leaves flicker over the carpet and the light in the room is orange. It glows on the green upholstered furniture, on the mahogany dining table and sideboard. I try and stop my eyes from wandering too much. Surveying is disrespectful and likely to give the impression that I am the type who steals. I take in as much of the room as I can with lowered eyes. A little girl with soft curly hair is sitting on the floor surrounded by bricks and dolls, her eyes fixed on the television. A large middle-aged lady is sitting on one of the armchairs, eyeglasses sliding down her nose; she is reading the characteristic green pages of *Asharq Al-Awsat*. She looks up and studies me, her eyes bulging and serious above her glasses. The newspaper rests on her lap. Her hair is short and severely cut, but softened with the colours of henna.

'Salaamu alleikum,' I say

'Mama, this is Najwa,' Lamya says, and then to me, 'Doctora Zeinab,' introducing her mother.

'*Ahlan*, Najwa,' the Doctora says lightly, 'I'm leaving tomorrow for Cairo, insha' Allah, and the responsibility of all this house is going to be on you.'

I smile, slightly taken aback by her husky smoker's voice. I go towards my prime responsibility. I kneel and sit next to her on the floor.

'Mai,' I say, 'Mai, how are you, what are you watching?' She doesn't respond.

Lamya's sleepy voice. 'Mai, say hello to Najwa. She's here to play with you.'

The little girl looks at me once without interest and then back to the *Teletubbies*. She has her grandmother's eyes.

'Leave her,' the Doctora says, 'she's concentrating on the television. It's a sign of intelligence when a child

66

concentrates so well.' And as if to demonstrate concentration, she goes back to reading her paper.

'Come, let me show you the rest of the flat before I leave,' says Lamya.

Another room, a bedroom also overlooking the park. It is in ivory with two beds and a cot. 'This is my room and Mai's,' says Lamya. 'My husband works in Oman and comes every six weeks or so for a holiday. He just left so it will be some time before he comes again.'

'Were you living before in Oman?' I venture, curious but aware that I have no right to ask her questions. She intrigues me, as does her mother. The mother's accent is clearly Egyptian and she is going tomorrow to Cairo but Lamya's accent has traces of the Gulf and she is much darker than her mother.

'Yes, we were in Muscat . . . Let me show you Mai's clothes.'

She shows me Mai's clothes and where the nappies are kept. 'Change her on the bed,' she says. 'I'm trying to toilet-train her but she still wears nappies. She just turned two, she really should be toilet-trained.' Her voice trails in a dreamy way as if she is thinking of other things. She must be clever, I think, to be doing a PhD.

'Here is the kitchen.' It is slightly dark, with a large rectangular table in the middle, cluttered with Mai's high-chair.

'You have to put on this tape for Mai when she eats, otherwise she won't eat.' She gestures vaguely towards a tape recorder on the kitchen counter. 'Unfortunately we don't have a dishwasher.' A pile of dishes stands up in the sink.

She shows me the washing machine, which is also a

dryer. She shows me how a slim kitchen drawer opens out into a folding ironing board. Underneath is a cupboard full of clothes waiting to be ironed.

She shows me where the vacuum cleaner is kept, the brooms and mops. 'This floor,' she trails her toes on the clay-red plastic tiles, 'is so difficult to clean. Me and Mama are fed up with it.'

We walk down the hall. There is a washroom and a bathroom. The bathroom is all in brown tiles, 'These brown tiles are troublesome,' she says. 'We have to wipe every drop of water, otherwise the stains show.'

At the end of the corridor is a small dark room. We need the light to see. There are two beds, a dressing table and a small washbasin in the corner. 'Mama's room and my brother Tamer's,' she says. 'You won't see him much. He has lectures early in the morning and he comes home late.'

Something in her voice makes me guess that her brother is younger than her, rather than older. I wonder if he is the youth I met in the lobby.

'When Mama leaves tomorrow, Tamer will probably turn the dressing table into a desk. So far we've both been using the dining table in the evening. He's so untidy,' she says, her eyes falling on a T-shirt discarded on the floor. I smile, remembering a young Omar, the Omar of Khartoum, not the one he became in London.

When she leaves to go to her university, I spend a long time in the kitchen, washing the dishes, tidying up and then tackling the ironing. Doctora Zeinab and Mai remain in the sitting room until eleven o'clock.

'Oh, you've done a lot of ironing, very good,' she says when she sees the ironed clothes draped all over the kitchen chairs. 'Go get hangers from the cupboards, so you can hang them up.' I go back and forth between the bedrooms and the kitchen in some confusion, until all the clothes are in the correct cupboards. Mai's clothes are of course the easiest to sort out. I can tell which are Lamya's clothes and which are Doctora Zeinab's, but the men's shirts confuse me. It turns out that some belong to Lamya's husband and need to go to her room. Some belong to Tamer and need to go to his room. And a few shirts belong to the father who had not been in London for several months. Their ironing has certainly been piling up!

Doctora Zeinab shows me the airing cupboard where clothes, damp from the dryer, are hanging up. It is right outside her room, in front of the bathroom. She stands with the cupboard wide open and starts to pull the clothes out while I sit on the floor folding them as fast as I can, sorting them into piles. They fall around me as she pulls them out one by one. Mai has trailed after her grand-mother. She messes up the pile of clothes I have folded. I smile at her and move the clothes out of her way. Doctora Zeinab scolds her but I know better than to object to any-thing the little one does. I know from experience that employers don't like maids scolding their precious chil-dren, no matter what damage the child does. So I keep on smiling and folding. 'Look Mai, this is how you do it,' I say. I show her how to fold a T-shirt.

'Ta-ma, Ta-ma,' she says urgently, patting the shirt on the carpet.

'Yes, it's Tamer's shirt,' her grandmother says. 'You're a clever girl. And whose is this?'

'Ma-wa, Ma-wa,' she says reaching out for her own red jumper with a picture of a bear on the front.

'Now that pile, which needs ironing, goes to the

cupboard in the kitchen. Take it there but you did enough ironing today, leave it for tomorrow.'

Back in the kitchen, she announces, 'It's time for my coffee,' in such a way that I move to make it for her, but she is already pressing the button on the kettle and scooping Nescafé into a mug.

'Now it's time for Mai's nap. I give her juice and take her to the bedroom and she sleeps for about an hour and a half, sometimes two. While she's asleep, you should do the cooking. Later in the afternoon she gets a bit trouble-some and you won't have time. Also in the afternoon, if the weather is good, you must take her out to the park. She enjoys playing on the swings and seeing other chil-dren. What can you cook? Tamer loves macaroni.' She says her son's name with fondness.

In the afternoon, the three of us go to the park – Doctora Zeinab grand in a dark coat and bright lipstick, her hair the perfect autumn colour; Mai bundled up in her pushchair. I had thought park meant Regent's Park and that we would cross the big roundabout with the statue of St George slaying the dragon, pass the mosque, and turn left into Regent's Park. But by park Doctora Zeinab means the small park across the road. It also has a children's play-ground, but is quiet, more relaxed. We walk under the same trees that are visible through the sitting-room window. It is slightly windy but not too cold. The early morning sun has given way to greyness, but still the autumn leaves on the ground are dry and crunchy.

I have been trying to draw close to Mai and win her trust. It is difficult because of the presence of her grand-mother. They are attached and Mai does not even let me push her pushchair. So Doctora Zeinab pushes and I walk along feeling sheepish and anxious that come evening time, the verdict to Lamya will be, 'she wasn't any good with Mai'.

'Are your family here or in Sudan, Najwa?'

'I have a brother here.' I try to sound open, natural. Yesterday I received a visiting order from Omar. He is allowed to write letters but he rarely writes to me.

'Do you have children?'

'No, I'm not married.'

'Were you living in Khartoum?'

'Yes, in Khartoum.'

'Lamya was born in Khartoum,' she says. 'Her father is Sudanese.'

'Really?' My heart starts to pound as it always does when there is the threat that someone will know who I am, who I was, what I've become. How many times have I lied and said I am Eritrean or Somali?

'My children are Sudanese in name only,' she goes on. 'They don't remember the Sudan. We spent years in Oman – my son, Tamer, was born there, and now we're in Cairo.'

'Do you go back to the Sudan for holidays?'

'My husband doesn't have any brothers or sisters, maybe that's why we don't go back often.'

Her words reassure me. Their ties to Sudan are obviously fragile. Even if I were to reveal my last name, they might not know it. They might not remember my father. At any rate, Doctora Zeinab is much younger than my father's generation. She must be no more than ten years older than me – even though I feel she is older. If I feel young it is because I have done so little. What happened stunted me.

'Who were you working with before us?' She stops walking and silently gives me the pushchair to push. I am grateful to end the embarrassment of walking next to her, swinging my arms while she pushes. However Mai is sensitive, she looks back, sees me and starts to holler. Doctora Zeinab takes hold of the handle of the pushchair again.

'I worked with a Lebanese lady who lived near Swiss Cottage tube station. She had two children. She was a second wife to a Saudi businessman who lived with his first family in Riyadh. He came for visits and it was then that she needed me most. They entertained regularly or they went out in the evening and she left the children with me. Her husband eventually got her a Sri Lankan maid from Saudi Arabia.'

An elderly couple smile and stop to admire Mai. I look beyond the park and see, between the trees, the Humana Wellington Hospital. I have never seen it before from this angle. It looks unfamiliar, yet I had stayed there with Mama for weeks. I remember the colour of the carpet, the telephone in my hand, the way the television was high up on the wall. If I tell Doctora Zeinab that my mother died in such an expensive hospital would she believe these words coming from her granddaughter's new nanny?

Near the children's playground, Mai sees the swings and starts to get excited. She points and babbles and wants to be taken out of her chair. I undo her seatbelt.

'Shall I take you to the swing Mai, shall I?' I sound desperate as I crouch near her chair trying to meet her eyes.

'Mai, I will go for a walk,' the Doctora says, 'and Najwa will take you to the swing. OK?'

The plan succeeds. The pushchair is parked near a bench, Doctora Zeinab strides off and Mai allows me to put her on the swing and push her. We are soon having a fun time.

* * *

Rain drives the three of us back home. The flat is cosy and, with the curtains drawn, the light in the sitting room is mellow. I read Mai a story while Doctora Zeinab goes to her room to finish her packing. But Mai's concentration is limited and she wants to run out of the room to her grandmother. It becomes a battle between us with me doing my utmost to keep her in the room and she wanting to leave. I try the television, a make-believe game with her teddy bear and her Rugrat doll, a snack, but all these things succeed for only a few minutes. She is very irritable.

The sound of the key turning in the lock is a relief. Lamya is home, a little breathless, her jacket splashed with rain but her eyes merry. She kisses and hugs her daughter, saddles her on her left hip and walks around with her. Mai is beaming now and Lamya is livelier than she was in the morning. She asks me lots of questions, inspects the dinner I cooked, lifting up saucepan lids. She seems impressed, her heavy features alive. Is this how a young affluent woman feels, fulfilled in her work, coming home to a young child? I owe myself an absence of envy; I owe myself a heart free of grudges.

Ten

It being a Monday, I have my Qur'an Tajweed class at the mosque. So, instead of going home, I go to the halal restaurant on the other side of the road from the mosque and eat my dinner there. Their dal tastes good and the pitta bread is warm. Always new places and new people make me tired. It is a good job, I tell myself. Once I get into the swing of things, it will not be too much work. They seem to be nice people. Tomorrow Doctora Zeinab will leave and I will have more control over Mai. I will be alone and that will be less stressful. I eat quickly so that I can get to the mosque and lie down a bit before the lesson starts. I need to stretch out.

The ladies' area is empty when I arrive. It doesn't surprise me. Soon the others will come for the class, and later more sisters will come accompanying their husbands for the Isha prayer. I put on the lights and pray two rakas' greeting to the mosque. Then I roll my coat like a pillow and stretch out. My legs burn slightly; my back aches but not too badly. I roll my ankles, stretch my toes and flex them. *Alhamdullilah*, it's a good job, I tell myself and people take ages to complete their PhD. It is a job that can last me a number of years, insha' Allah.

I close my eyes. I can smell the smells of the mosque,

tired incense, carpet and coats. I doze and in my dream I am small and back in Khartoum, ill and fretful, wanting clean, crisp sheets, a quiet room to rest in, wanting my parents' room, wanting to get up and go to my parents' room. Men's voices come from downstairs, a low rumble, a cough. I wake up and the cough reminds me of my father, the dream of my parents' room. I don't want to be vulnerable today. Fatigue does this to me. I sit up and feel utterly relieved to see Shahinaz come in, carrying her baby, surrounded by her three children.

I stand up to hug her, bend down and kiss her children, help them take off their coats. The eldest girl sits away from us with a Game Boy. The two boys run off, the whole mosque is their playground.

'Are we the only ones?' asks Shahinaz. Her eyes are bright black, round. She hands me her baby, takes off her coat, and underneath it she is wearing green.

'You're starting to get your figure back.' Her face is still puffy from pregnancy, her stomach still bulging, but every week she is slimmer, more and more like her old self.

She pulls the material of her dress against her stomach. 'Not yet,' she says, 'it's taking longer this time.' She sits cross-legged next to me, our backs against the wall.

'Shall I take off Ahmed's coat, it's warm here?'

She nods and I begin to unzip the baby's jumpsuit.

'I should have got his chair,' she says.

'Don't worry, I'll hold him for you.' I put him sideways on my knees. He is so sweet, fast asleep with a finger against his cheek, as if he is serious and thoughtful. I push his hood away from his head. His hair has recently been shaved, but it is growing thick again, straight and black. I run my finger over it.

'*Ya habibi ya* Ahmed,' I say to him. I feel that I know

him. I've known him since Shahinaz was pregnant, I saw him at the hospital the day he was born. Every week I see the changes in him.

'*Ya habibi*,' says Shahinaz rummaging in her bag, 'you Arabs always say that.'

'Wait till Um Waleed comes,' I say, 'she says it more than me.' Um Waleed is our Syrian teacher. Everyone is '*ya habibi*' or '*ya habibti*' to her. Even the Prophet, peace be upon him, is, '*ya habibi ya Rasoul Allah*', said in such a heartfelt way.

'I smell of oil, don't I?' Shahinaz sniffs at her sleeve. 'I was frying and there wasn't time to change.'

'No, you don't, you're imagining it.' I am mesmerized by her baby. I hold his hand and his fist curls around my finger. He is so deeply asleep. 'His hair is growing.'

'I know. We didn't really give him a close shave. A zero with the hair clippers.'

Um Waleed bustles in now with her twins. She always looks alarmed, I don't know why. I've stopped expecting her to impart any dramatic news, as her excitement seems to come from within her or from perhaps a turbulent domestic life I know nothing about. Her twin daughters are neat, pretty-looking girls, their brown hair fashionably cut. They copy their mother and automatically hold out their cheeks for me to kiss. I am taken aback at how businesslike they are.

'Two of you only for the class – where are the others? What am I going to do? What happened to them?' Um Waleed glares at the two of us as if the absence of the others is somehow our fault.

Shahinaz rolls her eyes.

I shrug my shoulders. 'It's still early.'

'No, it isn't early. This is the time. And I'm in a hurry

thinking I'm late.' She starts to take her notes and books out.

Suddenly five young ladies stroll in.

'*Masha' Allah*,' beams Um Waleed, transformed. 'I thought you'd never come'.

The next few minutes are taken up with more kisses and laughs, squeals of admiration for Shahinaz's baby. He is taken from my arms and passed around. One of the young girls, who is still holding her car keys, says something about 'pass the parcel' and laughs. Another comments on the new way Um Waleed has tied her headscarf. Always the teacher, she unties and starts to demonstrate. 'The usual square folded into a triangle but when you put it over your head leave one end longer than the other. See. You pin it under your chin. Then you take the longer side – hold it like this under the pin, lift it sideways over the pin and tuck it under your ear.'

'It's that simple?'

'It's how the Hizbullah women tie their scarves,' says Um Waleed. 'I see them on the satellite.'

'Cool,' says the girl next to me. She has rosy cheeks, dreamy eyes. I like the way she wears her hijab, confident that she has the kind of allure worth covering. Usually the young Muslims girls who have been born and brought up in Britain puzzle me though I admire them. I always find myself trying to understand them. They strike me as being very British, very much at home in London. Some of them wear hijab, some don't. They have individuality and an outspokenness I didn't have when I was their age, but they lack the preciousness and glamour we girls in Khartoum had.

I leave the gathering and go downstairs to the bathroom because I need to renew my wudu. Sitting on the row of stools that face the taps, there are a few women whom I never met before. They look Malaysian but one looks like she is Sudanese. She reminds me of a girl I once knew in Khartoum University. A girl who was not my close friend, but only a mild acquaintance, someone I said hello to as we passed each other to and from lectures. She was cute, with dimples. I don't know if I ever told my father how much I loved the university he chose for me. I don't think I spoke to him much. I know he didn't think a lot about me, not because he didn't love me but because I was a girl and Mama's responsibility. He had detailed, specific plans for Omar's future, while I was going to get married to someone who would determine how the rest of my life flowed. I am glad Baba didn't live to see what happened to Omar. Or even to me.

There's the sound of rushing water and I realize that I am alone in the wudu area. I am staring at my wet feet, facing a gushing tap. I close the tap and, not finding any paper towels to dry myself, walk upstairs, leaving damp footsteps on the carpet. The lesson has already started; everyone is sitting in a large circle. Um Waleed in sitting on her knees, which makes her a little bit higher than the others; her voice is clear and loud. She is someone else now, someone I love, my teacher, specific in everything she says, sharp and to the point. The Qur'an is open on her lap; she pulls her scarf over her forehead, and pushes back strands of hair that have escaped. She is in her element and she doesn't look alarmed any more.

I take a copy of the Qur'an from the shelf and Shahinaz shuffles sideways and makes room for me. She is breast-feeding Ahmed and, with a free hand, helps me find the correct page, points to the verse Um Waleed is now discussing. The Tajweed class is my favourite. I learn how to pronounce the letters correctly, when to blur two letters together, when to pronounce the n in a nasal way, for how many beats to prolong a certain letter. This concentration on technique soothes me; it makes me forget everything around me. Um Waleed is a qualified teacher, with a degree in Sharia Law. Many of the sisters say that her other classes on Law and History are more interesting – they generate a lot of discussion and the sisters, especially the young British-born ones and the converts, like to discuss and give their opinions. But I become fragmented and deflated in discussions; I never know which point of view I support. I find myself agreeing with whoever is speaking or with the one I like best. And I become anxious that someone's feelings will get hurt, or worse take serious offence, as sometimes happens, and stop coming to the mosque. Here in the Tajweed class, all is calm and peaceful. We practise and practise until we can get the words right. I want to read the Qur'an in a beautiful way.

After the class, I have a new energy. Shahinaz's baby is awake and I hold him, my hand supporting his head. I talk to him, nod and smile. He rewards me with a lop-sided twitching of his lips; he is only six weeks old, too young to smile.

Shahinaz carries him when we all pray Isha. She puts him down on the floor whenever she bends down and then picks him up again. I stand next to her and I realize in the middle of the prayer that I don't know who is next to me on the other side, whose arm is brushing my right arm, whose clothes are brushing my clothes. I pull my mind back and concentrate.

Outside the mosque, the night air is cold and crisp. Shahinaz offers me a lift. 'It's late for you to be going home on your own.'

I shake my head. I think of their car. Shahinaz and her husband in front, Ahmed in his baby seat at the back plus the other three children – it will be a crush.

'I'm not on your way.'

She protests but the children demand her attention. I leave her and walk to the bus stop. Cars swish fast on the relatively empty roads, taxis brake at the traffic lights with that peculiar whistling sound that London taxis make. The first bus I take is the old-fashioned kind with the permanent open door and a conductor. He is glum but I feel safer in his presence and in the knowledge that I can hop out at the traffic lights if I need to. The second bus has no conductor. I show my bus pass to the driver and the doors swing shut behind me. I stifle the feeling of being trapped. At the next bus stop, three young men stagger in. I know just by glancing at them that they are not reliable, they are not harmless. I start to recite *Say: I seek refuge in the Lord of Daybreak*. I recite it again and again.

As they walk past to the back of the bus, one of them looks at me and says something to the others. I look away out of the window. I tell myself that Allah will protect me so that even if they hurt me, I won't feel it too badly; it will be a blunted blow, a numbed blow.

Laughter from behind me. Something hits the edge of the seat next to me and bounces down the aisle; I don't know what it is. He has missed his target this time. Will they move closer, and what if they run out of things to throw? I look up at the bus driver's face in the mirror. His eyes flicker and he looks away. I stare out of the window but I see my reflection staring back at me. It is best to look down at my shoes. The smooth night traffic means that the bus moves fast. It shouldn't be long now, a couple more stops. I hear footsteps come up behind me, see a blur of denim. He says, 'You Muslim scum', then the shock of cool liquid on my head and face. I gasp and taste it, Tizer. He goes back to his friends – they are laughing. My chest hurts and I wipe my eyes.

The bus stops and the doors swing open. A couple walk down the stairs and towards the exit. I make a quick decision and follow them out of the bus. The wind hits against my wet scarf, it makes my scalp feel cold. I use the dry edge of the scarf to wipe my face. I breathe in and out to make the anger go away, to let it out through my nose. My cheeks are sticky. I bite my lips and they taste sweet. It could have been beer but I've been lucky. I blink and that's uncomfortable because my eyelashes are twisted and stuck together. I didn't know that eyelashes could ache. I walk the rest of the way home thinking about my eyelashes and that I will have to wash my hair. I don't like washing it at night. My hairdryer doesn't work anymore and I don't sleep well with wet hair. It irritates me, damp and sprawling over the pillow.

Eleven

M y second day of work and I almost arrive late. I reach the door of the flat to find Lamya already on her way out. Doctora Zeinab is at the door too, wrapped in a dressing gown, bright blue under the light of the hall. Lamya lifts her hair out of her jacket, bends to pick up her umbrella. I stand outside the doorway, waiting for her to leave so that I could enter. She has those same sleepy eyes and slow movements I remember from yesterday morning. Her eyes flicker over me, without expression. It must be that she is an evening person, not at her best in the morning. She kisses and hugs her mother, rubs her back in a friendly way. I remember that Doctora Zeinab is leaving this afternoon for Cairo.

'When Tamer takes you to the airport,' Lamya says to her, 'don't forget to give him your set of keys.'

'I will. He shouldn't be missing his lectures. I can go on my own.'

Lamya shrugs. 'Don't forget to order the taxi. Early.' She kisses her mother again and sweeps past me. Doctora Zeinab stands still for a few seconds watching her daughter walk down the stairs. The goodbye seems to have made her subdued, flabby. 'Come in, Najwa,' she says and shuffles back to the sitting room.

I close the door of the flat behind me, take off my shoes and put them near the side of the door. I roll my coat and put it over my shoes. The day begins, less daunting than yesterday, the tasks more familiar. Mai remembers me in a grudging sort of way. I smile and act the clown for her. My work will be easy when I win her trust. I talk to her about going to the park, jog her memory of how yesterday I pushed her on the swings. She is still in her pyjamas so I change her, take her to the toilet and cajole her into brushing her teeth. I discover that, unlike yesterday, Lamya hasn't given her any breakfast. I pour hot milk over Weetabix and sprinkle a bit of sugar. The Weetabix softens into a smooth paste and I scoop one teaspoon after another into her mouth. She drinks milk by herself from a special cup.

Yesterday's dinner plates are piled high in the sink – no one had bothered to wash them. If they had at least rinsed them, it would have been a help. Instead, bits of food are congealed and sticky on the plates. I run the hot water over them a long time, till they become unstuck. I enjoy being in a home rather than cleaning offices and hotels. I like being part of a family, touching their things, knowing what they ate, what they threw in the bin. I know them in intimate ways while they hardly know me, as if I am invisible. It still takes me by surprise how natural I am in this servant role. On my very first day as a maid (not when I worked for Aunty Eva – I didn't feel like a maid with her – but later when I started working for her friend) memories rushed back at me. All the ingratiating manners, the downcast eyes, the sideway movements of the servants I grew up with. I used to take them for granted. I didn't know a lot about them – our succession of Ethiopian maids, houseboys, our gardener – but I must have been close to them, absorbing their ways, so that now, years later and in another continent, I am one of them.

I remember an Ethiopian maid who told me that her friends called her Donna Summer because she resembled the singer. She laughed when I too started to call her Donna. Donna put eggs yolk in her hair, egg white on her face, rubbed her legs with BP petroleum jelly. She wore a short pink corduroy skirt on her day out. She was a refugee in Sudan. She would talk about Ethiopia, about the cool mountains and the rains and the good schools they had there. She said she would go with her boyfriend to the States and, once she got there, escape from him at the airport, run. Why? I asked her and she said because he was not qualified, he wasn't even a mechanic she said; he just washed the glasses in a juice counter. She was fun to be with – sparkling, pretty, swinging her hips in the kitchen. She always wore a necklace, a little bronze cross shining between her collar-bones. One day she was ill and Mama and I visited her. Her home was a wretched mud house, wide and sprawling, almost like a compound. It was full of men and women, all young, all Ethiopian, all refugees. We didn't know if they were related or not. Donna was lying, thin and feverish, on a low cot. I didn't know if she was glad to see us or not. When she recovered, she stole Mama's Chanel No 5, a nightdress and a pair of sandals Mama had never worn. We never saw her again. Mama could have called the police and told them where Donna lived but she didn't – she liked her too much – and, feeling hurt, she even hid the theft from Baba. We got another Ethiopian maid – dull and untalkative, she took no pride in her looks or her figure. I like to think that Donna made it to the States; made it to that better life she felt she deserved. I wish I could meet her now, hug her with my dripping gloves which I wear because, like her, I pride myself in keeping my hands smooth. I would tell her, 'Look what happened, I'm washing dishes like you did,' and we would laugh together.

'It's time for my coffee,' Doctora Zeinab says as she puts the kettle on, scoops Nescafé into her mug. I know now that I am expected to continue ironing – I push a button and steam heaves out, I manoeuvre the iron around the buttons.

She surveys the kitchen. 'I took that chicken out of the freezer last night so that it would have time to melt. Otherwise, how would you cook it? I told Lamya she has to remember every night before she sleeps to take out meat or chicken so that you can cook it the next day. I hope she remembers.'

'Insha' Allah,' I murmur.

'My children grew up in Oman where we always had maids. They're very spoilt and can't look after themselves. Tamer can't even make himself a cup of tea! I wouldn't mind if he ate out, McDonald's or at his college, but none of that is halal here and he's always been strict. He will only eat halal meat. I don't know where he got his religiousness from, none of us is as observant as him.'

I don't know what to say to that – so I continue ironing.

'Anyway, *alhamdullilah*, Lamya found you. It was a good idea to ask in the mosque.'

'Yes,' I say.

She pours the hot water over the coffee granules in her mug. 'I would stay with them longer but I need to go back. I came to settle them in and they seem to be settled now. Tamer didn't like it here at first but his father wants him to study like he did in England. As soon as Tamer finished

85

school last year, his father applied for him to come here.'

I am flattered that she is chatting to me; I hang on to her every word, enjoying her Egyptian accent. Mama and I used to watch the Egyptian soaps every day – even when we were out visiting we would ask our hosts to please, put on the TV.

It is the first time for me to put Mai down for her nap and it is a challenge. I follow Doctora Zeinab's instructions – the ritual of carrying her to the kitchen, pouring sugar-free Ribena in her favourite cup, adding Evian (none of the family, to my surprise, drinks tapwater). Then carrying Mai to the bedroom, closing the curtains, settling her in her cot, giving her the cup to suck on. I sit on the floor next to the cot. She bounces up and stands in the cot, wide awake. 'Lie down, Mai, go to sleep.' I take the cup away from her. 'Lie down, then I'll give you your cup.' She starts to scream. I have no choice but to give her back the cup, afraid that her cries will bring Doctora Zeinab to the room.

'Lie down, Mai, see, like me.' I stretch out on the floor and close my eyes. In a while, I hear a gentle thud on the cot mattress. I open my eyes and find her lying with a foot resting on one of the bars of the cot. One hand holds the cup, the fingers of the other twists and plays with the tassels of her cover. She seems content. Her eyes meet mine and she lifts her head, perks up. I quickly close my eyes again, telling myself I must remain perfectly still so as not to disturb her. Soon I began to hear her steady breathing. I agonize over whether to remove the empty cup from her sleeping fingers or leave it. Perhaps, in the middle of her nap, she will want another sip but then she might knock her cup against the bars of the cot and wake up. I take the risk and ease the cup away from her grasp. She stirs and rolls over. I freeze, afraid that any movement, any sound will wake her up. But I am safe, she is deeply asleep.

In the afternoon, Doctora Zeinab sits in the armchair in the living room, waiting for the taxi she has called. She looks elegant in a brown two-piece suit, full make-up and shiny high-heeled shoes. Earlier I carried her two suitcases from her bedroom to the door of the flat.

Now I sense a tension in her as she waits, rustling the newspaper, an impatience to be off. Her good clothes make her reluctant to hold Mai and so my role is to occupy and amuse Mai, prevent her from messing up her grandmother's clothes. It is raining outside and that is why Mai and I can't go to the park. I hold Mai up to the window to watch the rain. The ledge is wide enough for her to stand on and the window is safely closed with a child lock. The trees in the park sag under the weight of water and the leaves have lost their crisp shine. Below us, people hold up strong umbrellas, the windscreen wipers of the cars swish back and forth. The room darkens and Doctora Zeinab puts on the light. The telephone rings and she picks it up.

Her hoarse hello softens into, 'Tamer, *habibi*, what's wrong, you're late?' A pause. 'Of course I don't mind. I told you this morning that you needn't come. I can go to Heathrow on my own – you never listen to me.' I sit on the window ledge and Mai settles in my lap – we are becoming friends now.

'No, it isn't a problem getting my suitcases downstairs. Of course not.' A pause and she smiles. 'I'm glad you're not going to miss your lecture.'

I hear the key in the door of the flat, it opens and the

young man I had met in the lobby walks in. I can see him down the corridor in the hall, but Doctora Zeinab can't. He is talking into a mobile phone and his voice reaches me in a whisper. 'So Mama, you're sure you don't need me to come home? You're going to manage going to Terminal 4 all by yourself?'

He walks into the sitting room as she is saying, 'It's too late now anyway for you to come home . . . Tamer!' They both start to laugh. He switches his phone off and puts it in his pocket. I notice that he resembles her; those large slightly protruding eyes, the curve on the nose, but these features are handsome on him. His mother stands up and they hug. She is shorter than him and he is languid in his show of affection. They laugh; there is an ease in their relationship, a carelessness I did not notice between mother and daughter.

Mai squeals, 'Ta-ma, Ta- ma.' And he turns towards her. He notices my presence for the first time and is a little embarrassed, more restrained. I look away, out of the window. He must have made a face to his mother, for I hear her say, 'Come, let's go to my room.' But Mai slips from my arms, rushes to him. He is on his knees now, arms wide open. She is lifted high up. The whole room is different. Some people do that, they can enter a room and change it.

From the window, I see a black taxi park; the driver gets out and rings our bell. Tamer heads towards the entry-phone. His accent strikes me as being slightly American. It must be the kind of school he went to in Oman.

'I'll take the suitcases downstairs,' he calls out to his mother who had gone into the bathroom. I hold the door open for him, run and call the lift. He picks up his mother's suitcases, both at the same time. I almost laugh at the effort he makes to pretend that they are not heavy. He is

heading towards the stairs, but I call out that the lift is
here. I stop Mai from walking into the lift after her uncle.
She is charged with the excitement of too many things happening all at the same time. The elevator descends and I
catch a glimpse of a small smile aimed at me, a vivid picture of him standing between the two suitcases; jeans and
Nike trainers, his light green jacket spotted with rain.
'He'll come back,' I tell Mai. She is totally confused. One
minute Tamer was tossing her in the air; the next minute
Doctora Zeinab is kissing her goodbye.

In a while, he is leaping up the stairs again. Now that
the suitcases are in the taxi, he is impatient to get going.
I dither at the doorway with Mai in my arms, wondering
if it would be presumptuous to kiss Doctora Zeinab
goodbye. She puts her coat on slowly. He is almost bouncing
up and down. 'Come on Mama, come on.'

'Tamer,' she says, 'Lamya told me to give you my set of
keys but how would Najwa get back into the flat if she
takes Mai to the park?'

He looks at me when she says my name and back at
his mother. He is bored with what she's saying.

She continues, 'My set of keys has to remain in the flat
– for Najwa to use whenever she goes. There it is.' She
plonks the set of keys on the shelf near the door. The key
chain is a flat green picture of Harrods.

'Don't forget Najwa, to take it with you if you go out.'

'I don't need it today,' I say. 'Today we won't go out
because of the rain.'

'*If* it stops raining.' She is irritated now. 'And tomorrow
and the day after – *if* you don't take the key with you,
you and the girl will be stranded outside.'

Tamer groans and heads for the stairs. They are both
obviously fed up with my stupidity.

'Look after the house,' Doctora Zeinab says more gently, 'I will be coming back again, insha' Allah, and I will be phoning. This girl is your biggest responsibility.'

'Insha' Allah, you will come back to us soon, Doctora,' I say knowing I will not kiss her goodbye, knowing she does not expect me to.

I watch her walk briskly down the stairs. Only when she is out of sight do I close the door of the flat.

I take Mai to the window and we watch Tamer and Doctora Zeinab get into the taxi. They look up at us and wave. Tamer pushes down the window and grins up at us. Mai starts to cry. She bawls and stamps her feet on the ledge and, though I am propping her, she loses her balance and tumbles. I grab her in time and hold her up again to the window. We must be a sight – Mai having a tantrum, and me with a dumb expression on my face, incompetent.

Twelve

The train comes out of the underground tunnel. There is sunlight and grass now, the houses of outer London. Every time the train stops more people get out and hardly anyone boards. We are nearing the end of the line. I am closer to Omar now.

A bus takes me from the station to the prison. It is an ordinary building set well back from the road with spacious grounds and a car park. Omar has not always lived here. There were other prisons before, ones that were darker and rougher. Now this benign one is a graduation. Inside the building I show my VO to the guard. He takes my handbag and keeps it. I am on time. Already a small group has started to gather: a blonde women with her two black sons, several middle-aged couples, another woman with a baby. We are ushered into a lift by a jolly guard in a dark blue uniform. He chats with the small boys and their mother laughs. She is excited, looking forward to seeing her man. As I do every visit, I reach out for a sense of shame, for a sense of guilt or even sheepishness but there is nothing. Everything is ordered and ordinary – we might as well be visting innocent patients in an asylum or teenagers in a boarding school.

The room we are led to has a snack shop along one

side. The little boys and their mother head there. There are round tables surrounded by immovable stools – three white stools for the visitors and one blue stool for the prisoner. We sit on our white stools and wait; the guards stand in pairs along the doors, chatting. It is only a few minutes but it feels like a long time. They come out individually, not in pairs nor in clusters nor in single file but aloof as if there is neither camaraderie nor shared experience between them. Yet they all wear the same pale blue shirt, slight variations in trousers. A man in dreadlocks struts into the arms of his sons. He and the mother kiss. This family is noisy while the rest of us are more subdued.

When I see Omar I know I must have aged too. Time has passed, taken us by surprise. 'Hey, Nana,' he says, the only one in the world now who still uses my nickname. We shake hands, pat each other on the back and eventually hug. Over the years his hair has thinned, his hairline receded. Now he is almost bald and I can remember luxuriant curls greased in imitation of Michael Jackson on the cover of *Off the Wall*. He wears glasses now – unfashionable ones that the prison services have given him. His health isn't very good. He has stomach ulcers, kidney problems, colds that take ages to clear up.

'It's been ages since you sent me an invite. You know I would come and see you every weekend. You know that.' It irks me that I cannot visit him whenever I want to, that the initiatives have to come from him.

He shrugs, 'It's too far away for you.'

'I don't mind.'

'You were here a couple of weeks ago, weren't you?'

'No, a whole month.'

'Has it been a whole month?' He looks confused. His memory is not as accurate as it used to be. Sometimes I think he is not well, not himself, will never be. As if to reassure me, he leans forward. 'So, what's your news?' His interest in me is highest at the beginning of the visit. It will dwindle as if I disappoint him, as if I don't bring him what he needs. I tell him about my new job. I describe St John's Wood High Street where the clothes in the shops are so expensive that they don't even display the prices in the windows. I tell him about Doctora Zeinab, Mai and Lamya. 'Her brother,' I say, 'is only nineteen and is so devout and good. No cigarettes, no girlfriend, no clubbing, no drinking. He has a beard and goes to the mosque every day.'

'What a wimp!'

'No, he isn't a wimp!' I sound possessive.

Omar shrugs as if it doesn't matter to him either way. He changes the subject. 'Do you have any news of Uncle Saleh?'

'I've just got a letter from him. He sends you his regards.'

'How is he?'

'Fine, *alhamdullilah*, getting used to being a senior citizen in Toronto.'

'And Samir? He's dropped us like a hot potato.'

'He's not the only one, Omar.' But I wonder if our old friends have dropped us or merely drifted off, lost touch.

'I expected more of him, being a cousin and all.' His voice is a little bitter, only a little.

Once, when Samir was still in Britain, Omar had sent him an invite. Samir had not visited him, nor sent an apology, nor written.

'Well, he's very high up in ICI now. His children are getting big – Uncle Saleh sent me a few photos. The eldest girl looks like Mama so much you wouldn't believe it.'

We talk of the past, before Mama died. We talk of the

pop music we liked and how nowadays the new bands are no good. We remember a Bob Marley concert we went to in Earls Court. We remember buying vinyl records and the evening Baba took us to see the musical *Oliver* in Shaftesbury Avenue.

'Do you remember ice skating in Queensway?' Omar smiles. 'I loved that place. There was a jukebox in the cafeteria. The first jukebox I had ever seen. We would put in ten pence and press a button, choose the song we wanted.'

'How did we learn how to skate? I can't remember!' I laugh – children from hot Khartoum coming to London every summer – walking into an ice-skating rink in Queensway as if they had every right to be there. Money did that. Money gave us rights.

'I wanted to stay here the whole year,' he says, 'I wanted to stay in London for ever.'

I am relieved that he is relaxed today and talkative. Sometimes he never unwinds, stays moody until the end of the visit. I say, 'You used to get ill on the last day of the holiday when we were due to fly back to Khartoum.'

'Did I? I don't remember.' There is pleasure in his voice as if he admires his childhood love of London.

'You would get a stiff neck. You wouldn't be able to move your neck. Mama said it was psychological.'

He laughs a little and starts to tell me the prison library has improved and he spends more time reading books. He likes books about pop music and the biographies of film stars. I tell him he should read the Qur'an. It is the wrong thing to say. He shrugs and says, 'These religious things – they're not for everyone.' He takes his glasses off to clean them on the edge of his shirt. One of the guards turns to look at him and then away.

I start to speak but he interrupts me. 'Don't nag me, Najwa.' There are dark shadows under his eyes.

'I'm not nagging.'

'Every time you visit me you go on about the same thing.' He is right. For twelve years now I have been trying to tell him the same things in different ways. Ever since I started to pray and wear hijab, I have been hoping he would change like I've changed. He puts his glasses back on. The guard's eyes flicker over him again.

'Look,' I say, 'I know how you feel. We weren't brought up in a religious way, neither of us. We weren't even friends in Khartoum with people who were religious.'

'The servants,' he says, 'I remember them praying. Musa, the driver, and the others – they would be praying in the garden.'

Our house was a house where only the servants prayed. Where a night-watchman would open the gate for our car arriving late after a night out, then sit reciting the Qur'an until it was time for the dawn prayer. I remember him sitting cross-legged in the garden, dark as a tree.

'If Baba and Mama had prayed,' I say, 'if you and I had prayed, all of this wouldn't have happened to us. We would have stayed a normal family.'

'That's naïve . . .'

'Allah would have protected us, if we had wanted Him to, if we had asked Him to but we didn't. So we were punished.' I cannot talk fluently, convincingly. Always I come on too strong and fail.

'Don't be daft. You make it sound like Baba did something wrong. They lied about him. Where were the millions they claim he embezzled and took abroad? We came here and there was nothing.'

'You're right but that is all in the past now. It's you I'm worried about. I care.'

'I know,' he says but he sounds distant.

'Those people who put you in prison – they don't care about you. You think that if they forgive you they will let you out of here, but it's more important that Allah forgives you. Then He will do wonderful things for you and open doors for you. Doors you didn't even know existed.'

'This is way over my head Najwa, way over my head.' He shakes his head from side to side. 'I don't have a clue what you're on about.' He puts on an accent now, continues to shake his head, pretends to look awed. 'Doors I didn't know existed. This is deep, man, real deep.'

'You're hopeless.' I can't help but laugh. He wants me to laugh.

Then he looks straight at me. 'Najwa, listen, you obviously feel happy being devout – that's your business. But I'm fine as I am.'

How can he be fine as he is? His youth wasted and he tells me he's fine.

Thirteen

I like my new job. As the days pass, Mai warms to me. She takes my hand as we walk from her room to the bathroom, she smiles when she first sees me in the morning. The days follow a rhythm. Lamya's grumpiness in the morning, her barely whispered greetings, and how she comes home in the evening radiant, refreshed. She must love her studies. I take pride in ironing her elegant clothes, in arranging the bottles of lotions on her dressing table. She has many necklaces, which she hangs on a special stand shaped like a tree with bare branches. I hold up a string of multi-coloured beads and admire them. I hold her pearl necklace in my hand. I once had one too but Omar took it and sold it to buy drugs. Her silk scarves are for her neck not her hair – but sometimes I try them on as headscarves, look at my face in the mirror. There was a time when I looked good and it didn't matter whether I was ill or not or what time of the month it was. Now my looks are inconsistent as if they are about to slide away.

Every morning I face a mess in the kitchen. It has worsened since Doctora Zeinab's departure and a considerable part of my day is spent cleaning up the kitchen from the misuse of the night before. It saddens me when they leave cooked food out all night. More often than not it spoils and I can't eat it. I have been eating their leftovers ever since Lamya said, 'We don't eat food unless it's freshly cooked – you can have it.'

The light in the sitting room changes every day as the trees in the park become more bare. When Mai has her nap, I sit on the armchair where Doctora Zeinab used to sit and enjoy the light in the room or watch the Arabic channels on TV. I see the Ka'bah and pilgrims walking around it. I wish I were with them. I see teenage girls wearing hijab and I wish I had done that at their age, wish there was not much in my past to regret. The religious programmes make me feel solid as if they are telling me, 'Don't worry. Allah is looking after you, He will never leave you, He knows you love Him, He knows you are trying and all of this, all of this will be meaningful and worth it in the end.' I learn from these programmes. Bits and pieces: everyone in Paradise will be thirty-three years old regardless of what age they were when they died. Eve was the most beautiful woman Allah created; the second most beautiful woman was Sarah, Abraham's wife. The Prophet Muhammad, peace be upon him, stopped in the street to chat to a mad woman. They spoke for a long time and everyone was surprised that he had time for someone as insignificant as her.

This kind of learning makes sense to me. That's why I go to talks and classes at the mosque. It surprises me that what I learn stays with me. At school I used to forget everything immediately after the exams. Once at an Eid party in the mosque there was an Islamic knowledge quiz – I got all the answers right and I won a box of Cadbury's Milk Tray.

There are books about Islam in Lamya's flat but I doubt that they belong to her. She does not strike me as religious and there is not even a prayer mat or tarha in her room. The books are in Tamer's room so they must be his. Books about Sufism, early Islamic history, the interpretation of the Qur'an. He reads them; they are not just there to fill shelves. I can tell that he reads them because he sometimes leaves them open on his mother's dressing table, which has now become his desk, or they are stacked on the table next to his bed.

His room disturbs me. It is dark; the only window looks out over the service stairs and brings sounds of cluttering on the metal steps, voices of workmen and the garbage collector going about his work. I have to put on the light in order to clean the room. He folds his prayer mat neatly on the chair but leaves the bed unmade. Empty cartons of juice and chocolate wrappers lie around the wastepaper basket as if he has thrown them and missed. I pick up his clothes off the bed; they smell of him and make me feel self-conscious. I wipe his desk. I stack his university books in one pile, his other books in another. I put his Amr Khalid tapes in order. I always leave cleaning his room last, after all the other chores. I read that piece of advice long ago in *Slimming* with regard to exercise. Save your favourite stretch for last so you can be motivated to start with the ones you don't like and get them over with. Sometimes, I take one of his books out of the room to read. While Mai naps, I read what he has been reading. The flat becomes quiet without the TV. Not all of the books are easy for me to read. I sift through them and if I understand them I keep reading, if I don't I put them away.

I hardly ever see him in the mornings. He is out before I arrive. It is in the evenings that we usually meet. Sometimes he arrives just I am leaving. In the hallway he takes off his shoes while I put on mine. He is always polite, always smiles when he says, '*Salaamu alleikum*'. There is a modesty in him which his sister doesn't have. Sometimes I meet him on the stairs. He takes them two at a time and perhaps I walk too softly because he always seems taken aback to see me. I step to the right to let him pass, while at the same time he moves to his left. I then step to the left only to block him again and we both laugh. The silliness of it and the laugh stays with me until I reach the bus stop.

Sometimes we meet on the landing, our reflections in the mirror making it seem as if there are four of us. The mirror in the landing is compassionate: it makes me look young, makes me look better than I feel though I always feel uplifted when I see him. It is natural; a beautiful, devout youth with striking eyes.

One day the weather is exceptionally warm and Mai and I spend a long afternoon in Regent's Park. On the way home, in front of the mosque, we meet Tamer. He comes up to us, greets me and ruffles Mai's hair. For a few seconds, she does not recognize him. She has been dozing in her pushchair, tired out from playing in the sandpit and the slides. 'It's me – Tamer,' he says bending down, sitting on his heels. He picks up her hand and kisses it. The three of us are blocking the pavement and around us people start to get irritated. I push Mai again and he falls in step with us.

'I wanted to take Mai to the zoo on Sunday,' he says, 'but it was raining.' His voice is a little loud and, as we walk towards St John's Wood, I sense the slight unease he inspires in the people around us. I turn and look at him through their eyes. Tall, young, Arab-looking, dark eyes and the beard, just like a terrorist.

100

He disarms me by suddenly saying, 'Your cooking is very nice. Thank you for cooking for us.' His sister has never thanked me. But she pays me well and on time, which is more important than words of thanks.

Instead of acknowledging his compliment I say, 'At night please put any leftovers in the fridge. Because the kitchen is warm, the food sometimes goes bad and that's a waste.'

He looks ashamed. He ducks his head and says, 'Yes, it's a sin to waste food.'

Perhaps I have spoken too harshly. To make amends I start to speak to him as I imagine an aunty would speak: 'How are you getting on at university?'

'I don't really know many people.'

'Well, you're still new. In no time you'll make friends.' We stop at the zebra crossing.

'I've joined the Muslim Society. They organize Friday prayer at the college so we don't have to go far and skip lectures.'

'That's nice. And the course itself – how are you getting on with your studies?' I don't usually talk like that to my employers. I would never talk like that to Lamya.

'I don't particularly like what I'm studying,' he replies. 'It's my dad – he wants me to study Business.'

A silver Peugeot and a taxi come to a stop. We cross.

'What would you have liked to study?'

'I wanted to study Islamic History.'

'That's nice that you have this interest'. We start to walk down St John's Wood High Street.

'That's what my mom and dad say – it's an interest, a hobby. They say I have to be practical and study something that would get me a proper job.'

'I am sure Allah will reward you for trying to please your parents.'

101

'Insha' Allah,' he says and smiles as if I had paid him a compliment.

My hands don't tremble when I make his bed, when I smooth his pillow, when I empty the pockets of his jeans before I put them in the washing machine. In his pockets I find receipts from the university cafeteria, a piece of gum, coins, a leaflet about a rally in Trafalgar Square for Palestine. I tidy his desk, pick up pencil shavings, wipe a smudge of ink. I unfold a piece of paper. It is his timetable with the room numbers of his lectures. Perhaps he has forgotten to take it or now knows where to go. On the corner he has written, 'Studying sucks'. I smile as if I can hear him breathing the words. I leaf through the books he studies from: Economics, Accounting, Business Management. Once a long time ago in Khartoum University, I struggled with these subjects. I was in university to kill time until I got married and had children. I thought that was why all the girls were there too but they surprised me by caring about their education, forging ahead with jobs and careers. I surprised myself by never getting married.

Fourteen

It is rare to have Shahinaz in my living room. I prefer to go to her house, to be surrounded by her four children, her mother-in-law, the photos of cousins and uncles on the shelves. I prefer the voices of her children calling each other by their nicknames to my own dry flat. Mama bought this flat before she died. She sold the large one in Lancaster Gate and bought this smaller one, on the top floor of a house in Maida Vale. She hardly had time to live here. Some of her things are still in boxes and suitcases, not yet unpacked from the move. I would have liked to keep the television but the licence is a luxury.

'You're lucky,' Shahinaz says, 'you don't have a television – it only brings horrible news.' Her children would not have agreed but only baby Ahmed is with her today. He is wide awake and holding a red rattle.

'*Habibi ya* Ahmed – you've grown!' I kneel on the floor to kiss him and kiss him again. He is too young to mind. I lift him off his chair and put him on my lap. He smells lovely.

Shahinaz takes off her headscarf and sits back in the armchair, running her fingers through her hair. It is a treat to see her hair, long and black like Pocahontas in the Disney film that Mai likes to watch. Shahinaz wants to cut it but her husband says no. I am on his side.

'I told him I had to go out,' she says. 'I had to get out of the house. The kids have been driving me mad.'

'Were they on holiday today?' Ahmed drops his rattle on the ground. I pick it up and give it back to him.

'Teacher training. And it was raining so they couldn't go out to play. So as soon as Sohayl came in from work I said to him, please, let's leave the children with your mother and go eat out. Then we can go to that talk at the mosque. He said yes, that's a good idea but let's take Ahmed, he might be too much for my mother. And I said fine, we'd take Ahmed and leave the others. Then he goes off to her room to say goodbye.'

I can't help but smile at the way she talks, how pretty she looks and how unaware. I kiss Ahmed's head; hide my smile in his hair.

'I started to get dressed,' she continues, 'then he came back from her room and said we're not going out. I asked why. He said his mother doesn't want us to. Just like that.'

'What's her reason?'

'I don't know. She hates anyone eating out – she thinks restaurant food is a waste of money or she doesn't feel up to looking after the children today or just to spite me!'

'Shahinaz, you don't mean that!'

'I'm so annoyed.'

'Your mother-in-law is a sweetie.'

'She is, yes. It's just . . . difficult sometimes.'

It is difficult with their house being small and the seven of them sharing one bathroom (though thankfully there is another toilet with a washbasin). They are the kindest people I have ever met in the mosque, kind enough not to ask me questions or expect confessions in return for their favours. Why Shahinaz chose me as a friend, and how Sohayl approved her choice, is one of those strokes of good

104

fortune I don't question. We have little in common. If I tell her that, I think she will say, very matter-of-fact, 'But we both want to become better Muslims.'

Now I say about her mother-in-law, 'Look, we've talked about this before. If she lived somewhere else, Sohayl would spend hours away from you visiting her.'

'While I'm stuck home with the kids!'

'Exactly. It's so much more convenient for you all to live together. This way you and the children get to see him more. And think of all the reward from Allah you're getting.'

'You're right. Poor Sohayl, I shouted at him and he said, "Why don't you go to Najwa?" I know it is the Islamic thing for a man to obey his mother and I should support him in this – but sometimes it just gets too much.' Her voice becomes soft. She is more herself now.

'Look,' I say, even though I feel that the day has already been long enough, 'we can go to that lecture at the mosque if you want to. What's it about?'

'An American has translated a really old book written by a famous scholar.' She sounds keen.

'It might be boring, don't you think?' I stand Ahmed on my lap; he pushes with his feet, bounces.

'Oh no, the speaker's come all the way from the States; he must be good. Did you eat?'

'I did at work. Lamya gave me the rest of a quiche she'd bought over the weekend from Harrods. I asked her if it was halal and she glared at me.' I glare at Shahinaz in imitation.

She laughs. 'Well, it was a bit cheeky of you to ask her that!'

'I know.' I laugh, remembering Lamya's face. 'Then she said to me Tamer ate from it as if that's supposed to mean it's all right.'

'Oh, Sohayl thinks so highly of him. He said to me, "I hope our boys grow up to be as committed to the Islamic movement as Tamer."'

'Did you hear this, baby Ahmed?' I tickle him and he smiles back at me, dribbles saliva down my shirt. 'Why does Sohayl think that?' I ask Shahinaz. 'What does Tamer do?' I want to know another side of him.

'Not much really. They play football together and every week Tamer brings a big container of juice for the whole team.'

I laugh. 'You call this commitment to the Islamic movement?'

'Well, Sohayl says he's polite and respectful to people older than him – he hasn't got that "attitude" that so many of these young brothers at the mosque have.'

'That's true. I just thought, when you said that Sohayl thinks well of him, that he's active.'

'Well, he's had a cushy upbringing, hasn't he, so I guess he's not really used to active work.'

I can tell her about the way he leaves his bed unmade, the pyjamas he steps out of and leaves as a heap on the ground. But these are secrets.

Fifteen

'I saw you yesterday at the talk,' Tamer says. I had been pushing Mai on the swing and he appeared with his rucksack as if it is natural for him on his way home to look in on us in Regent's Park.

'Yes it was a good talk,' I say. 'A lot of people turned up so the organizers must have been pleased.'

'I'll push the swing.' He drops his bag and takes my place. The playground is quiet today. The sky is cloudy and I wait for the first drops of rain. Above the treetops I can see the dome of the mosque with the chandelier bright through the glass.

He says, 'I liked the bit in the talk about the signs preceding the Day of Judgement and how people centuries past used to feel that these signs were already coming true. They believed the end of the world was imminent and yet here we are.'

'Maybe imminent can mean many years away.' It had been a good lecture, worth going to. Both Shahinaz and I enjoyed it – it shook us in a way. I say to Tamer, 'Some of these signs were spooky.'

'Yes, the sun rising from the west and the animal that talks – that's pretty spooky.'

'He said it could be allegorical.'

107

'I believe in it literally.' He catches hold of the swing, lifts it high up. Mai squeals when he lets it go.

'It could be, why not? The coming of Jesus is literal. Even the exact place where he will next appear is known.'

'I would love to be alive at that time,' he says.

I smile at his enthusiasm, his faith in himself. 'What would you do?'

'I would rush to Damascus to see him.'

'Leave your university?' I am teasing him but he doesn't notice.

'Oh yes, I wouldn't think twice. Wouldn't you?'

I smile and say nothing. It is not appropriate to mention money and the cost of airline tickets to Syria.

'I would be in the Mahdi's army,' he continues, 'fighting the Antichrist.' He holds an imaginary sword in his hand, swings it.

'I would like to be there when Jesus prays with the Mahdi. I would like to pray with them, but I wouldn't like the war. I am afraid of wars even when they are only on television.' Mai wants to get off the swing. He lifts her out. His fingers are long and thin with the nails bitten.

Mai runs to the slide. She is not afraid to climb the steps, abandon herself to the falling down. Only last week, she was wary of that large slide.

'You know,' he says, sitting sideways on the swing, his legs on either side, 'I read in a book that a Sudanese sheikh in the sixteenth century said that a day will come when people will travel by movable houses and communicate through slender threads – isn't that amazing?'

'It is amazing.' He makes me smile. It's the way he talks or maybe it's just the fresh company. 'The sheikh must have seen that in a dream.'

'That's right. I didn't think of that. He must have seen the future in a dream.'

'Have you been to Sudan?'

'Yes. We used to go every summer when we were in Oman. You're Sudanese, aren't you?'

I am usually wary of such questions, where they can lead, but from him the query sounds harmless.

'Yes, but I've been in London now nearly twenty years.' When I came with Mama and Omar, when Baba was executed, Tamer must have been a baby. I start to talk quickly. 'Do you think you might one day go back and live in Sudan?'

'I might yes. I liked it there. There is so much to do – Khartoum is fun.'

Mai walks over to the sandpit. I help her take off her shoes and she starts playing with a little boy. His Sri Lankan nanny sits on the edge of the sandpit holding a Tupperware box of rice in one hand, a spoon in the other. She feeds him while he scoops sand with a spade. I sit next to her. Tamer moves away from the swing and sits on a nearby bench.

'Do you go back to Sudan for holidays?' he asks me.

'No, I don't have anyone there to visit.'

'Your family are here?'

I nod. It is true. Omar is here. Omar is my family.

'Tell me,' I say, 'what did you used to do in your holidays in Khartoum?' It's been a long time since I was nostalgic for Khartoum.

'Well, with my cousins, we went fishing and we played football. Everyone kept inviting us for lunch. The food is great there.'

I laugh. 'I could cook you Sudanese food if you want.'

'Really?'

109

'Yes. Where else did you go in Khartoum?'

'We went swimming in the American Club.'

'You did! I used to go there all the time when I was young. We were members.' I remember the smell of hamburgers grilling, my friend Randa and I in the bathroom putting on lip gloss, disco lights. It seems such a long time ago. Yet the place still exists, it is not only in my head.

'Do you feel you're Sudanese?' I ask him.

He shrugs. 'My mother is Egyptian. I've lived everywhere except Sudan: in Oman, Cairo, here. My education is Western and that makes me feel that I am Western. My English is stronger than my Arabic. So I guess, no, I don't feel very Sudanese though I would like to be. I guess being a Muslim is my identity. What about you?'

I talk slowly. 'I feel that I am Sudanese but things changed for me when I left Khartoum. Then even while living here in London, I've changed. And now, like you, I just think of myself as a Muslim.'

He smiles. I ask him about Lamya. 'Does she consider herself Sudanese?'

His expression changes, becomes more reserved as if he does not feel comfortable talking about his sister. 'I think she considers herself Arab. Her husband is like us. He's Sudanese but he grew up in the Gulf and studied in the States.'

I have not seen Lamya's husband. He does not come to London as much as Doctora Zeinab had led me to believe.

The nanny and the little boy start to pack up. We wave to them as they leave the playground. I wonder if Lamya and Tamer had a Far Eastern nanny while they were growing up in the Gulf. It is very likely.

'Which Sudanese food do you like best?' I ask him.

'The peanut salad.'

110

'That's very easy to make with peanut butter. I'll make it for you. What else do you like?'

His answer is interrupted by a whine from Mai. She is on the see-saw and frustrated that she can't get it to move. I go and sit on the other side and we start to play, with Tamer watching us. For a brief moment I am not sure who I am, the Najwa who danced at the American Club disco in Khartoum or Najwa, the maid Lamya hired by walking into the Central Mosque one afternoon. I move up and down, slowly so that Mai doesn't fall off and get a fright, but not so gently that she will get bored.

It starts to rain, a few drops that look dark on the red safety tiles under the see-saw. Tamer looks up at the sky. He seems more relaxed than the other day when we met in the street. He might not know it but it is safe for us in playgrounds, safe among children. There are other places in London that aren't safe, where our very presence irks people. Maybe his university is such a place and that is why he is lonely.

The rain is the kind that doesn't need an umbrella but I decide it is best to take Mai home. I put up the plastic hood on her pushchair and the three of us leave the park, walk in the direction of Lord's. Tamer pushes Mai and I think, 'We're like a couple, a couple with a baby.' Is this how we look to people? Or will people think I am his mother? Surely I don't look that old.

Sixteen

With his key, Tamer opens the door of the flat. I help Mai out of her pushchair and kneel to take off her jacket. There are lights in the corridor – Lamya is already home. She comes out of her room. I know she is animated in the evenings, but today her eyes are flashing and she is almost breathless when she speaks to me. 'Where's my pearl necklace? I left it in the morning with the rest of my jewellery, where is it?'

I stand up. She is not asking, she is accusing. 'I don't know.' My voice is flat because things have suddenly darkened, because I can lose this job in a stroke, just like that. 'I didn't take it.' Even to my own ears I don't sound convincing enough.

'Did I accuse you of taking it?' Her voice is harsh, but she is nervous, lacking confidence. 'Why are saying you didn't take it?'

It is a trick question and I will fail. I stand still with my hands in my pockets. Mai struggles with her shoes. I bend down and help her take them off. She runs and hugs her mother's legs but, not finding a response, wanders off to the sitting room. Tamer is next to me. He says, 'Lamya, have you looked for it? Are you sure you've looked for it?' His voice is loud as if to match hers but he sounds calm, as if this is an everyday event. He takes off his coat, bends down to untie his trainers.

'Yes of course I've looked for it.' She is exasperated with him, regards his presence as a nuisance. She turns back to me. 'Well speak, where is it?'

'Lamya,' Tamer says. He is reproaching her. 'We will look for it again. I'm sure you mislaid it somewhere.'

She glares at me, her arms folded. She is wearing the beige trousers I ironed yesterday, a top and a sweater in the same reddish shade of orange. She looks as if she wants to pounce on me and do a body search for her necklace. Perhaps she would have done that, if Tamer wasn't here. She would have rummaged in my pockets, slapped me if I resisted, made me take off my bra . . . I start to pray; the words tumble in my head. Allah, please get me out of this mess. Stop this from happening. I know You are punishing me because I tried this necklace on in the morning, in front of the mirror. I put it round my neck and I will never do that again, ever. I will never try on her scarves; I will never weigh myself on her bathroom scales. But I didn't take the necklace. I would never dream of taking her things. I just tried the necklace on and put it back. I'm sure I put it back because I heard Mai calling me and I immediately unclasped it . . .

'Najwa . . .' Tamer is talking to me. He is saying that we should look for the necklace. 'I'm sure we'll find it,' he says. He looks down at my feet. I look down and see that I am still wearing my shoes. I should take my shoes off and move from the hall to the bedroom to start searching.

Mai comes out of the sitting room. She is holding the pearl necklace in her hand. Tamer laughs. 'There's your missing necklace, Lamya!'

113

She takes one look at her daughter and slaps her hard. The poor child staggers back, the necklace flies from her hand. Tamer is on the floor, he takes her in his arms. She is screaming from the shock as much as from the pain, her face almost purple; saliva dripping from her wide-open mouth. 'This is mean of you, Lamya,' he says. 'Why did you do that?'

Unable to bear it any longer, I turn around, open the door of the flat and run down the stairs.

It is raining and all the cars have their headlights on. I pause in front of the corner of the building waiting for the downpour to ease. I want to get away; I want to forget the past few moments. It had been nice in the park and then to come back . . . What if Mai hadn't appeared with the necklace? I must have left it on the dressing table instead of hanging it on the tree where Lamya hangs all her necklaces. Mai must have picked it up and taken it into the sitting room, perhaps hidden it in one of her toys. This is the kind of miracle that makes me queasy. I know about stealing. Years ago, Omar stealing my own pearl necklace, Omar shouting at Mama to give him more money, shaking her shoulders. He went as far as shaking her shoulders, trying to frighten her. What if Mai hadn't appeared with the necklace? My stomach heaves. I can lose this job easily. Rely on Allah, I tell myself. He is looking after you in this job or in another job. Why are you becoming attached to this family anyway? There is vague talk in the mosque that they want to set up a crèche. That would be a better place, a steadier income. I start to walk to the bus stop, the zebra crossing, turn the corner.

I hear footsteps behind me, someone running, Tamer saying my name. I stop and turn round. 'You're coming tomorrow aren't you, you haven't taken offence?' He is a little out of breath. He's not wearing his coat.

'No, I haven't taken offence.' We move to the side of the pavement. Looking down there is a footpath and a canal running under the street. It runs north to the zoo, south until close to Edgware Road.

'Good,' he says. 'I . . . we were a bit worried after you left.'

'I'm sorry. I should have excused myself first.' The rain eases a little but still the windscreen wipers on the cars flick, people hold up their umbrellas.

'Look, Lamya is wrong. She shouldn't have . . .'

I try to interrupt him. I don't want him to apologize for his sister but he continues, 'I don't approve of her. She hardly prays. She doesn't wear hijab. It's wrong. She has such bad friends. They go and see rude films together. They smoke and even drink wine – it's disgusting. I tell her but she doesn't listen to me. Her husband should tell her but he's just as bad. It's all to do with pride, the way she talked to you just now. She shouldn't . . .'

'Don't worry,' I manage to interrupt him. I try and smile. 'It was just something bad that happened and we should forget about it.'

'Right.' His hair is damp from the rain. He looks tired and I must look worse. He looks down at the pavement. 'I'm relieved that, insha' Allah, you're coming tomorrow.'

'I'll make you that peanut salad I promised you.'

He smiles, more like his usual self. 'Thank you.'

'I should thank you for . . .' My voice trails off. For standing up for me, for standing next to me.

'I knew you'd never take anything. I knew.' He is confident. Like Mai, he trusts me in a childish way. As if I need reminding that he is so young.

'You don't know me well,' I say, 'there's a lot about me you don't know.'

He looks straight at me with neither curiosity nor disinterest. As if he is saying, 'If you tell me or if you don't tell me, I won't change towards you.'

The next day is different. When I ring the bell, it is Tamer not Lamya who opens the door for me. He is in his pyjamas, looks like he had just got out of bed. 'I have a cold.' He clears his throat. 'I didn't go to university.' Lamya had gone out earlier, Mai is still asleep. He goes back to bed and I start to tackle the kitchen. I try not to clatter so as not to disturb him. It is my fault that he is ill – he ran after me in the rain without his coat.

I am relieved that Lamya is already out and I do not have to face her after yesterday. It strikes me that even now, knowing I am innocent, she will never treat me as her equal. I had hoped to come close to her or at least get her to chat with me like her mother did. Now I know that she will never do that. She will always see my hijab, my dependence on the salary she gives me, my skin colour, which is a shade darker than hers. She will see these things and these things only; she will never look beyond them. It disappoints me because, in spite of what Tamer said, I admire her for the PhD she is doing, her dedication to her studies, her grooming and taste in clothes.

When Mai wakes up, I change her and give her breakfast. While she watches TV, I cook. I make lentil soup and the peanut salad I promised Tamer. He wakes up at noon, looking better and says he's hungry. I set the kitchen table for him, heat up pitta bread. He slurps the soup while I iron, blows his nose into a tissue. 'Maybe I have SARS,' he jokes. The day is different.

He starts to talk about his high school in Oman. 'It was an international school,' he says, 'following an American system.' The students chose their subjects. They didn't have to wear uniforms. 'My teachers were nice,' he says, 'nicer than the ones I have now.' He eats with a good appetite, tearing large pieces of bread, scooping out the peanut sauce that is chunky with onions and green peppers. It amuses me that he can eat well even when he is ill.

'My history teacher in school,' he says, 'she was disappointed that I didn't go on to study Middle East History or Islamic Studies. She knew I liked them. But the policy of the school is to respect the family's decision. In my case that meant studying Business.' He stands up, rummages in one of the top cupboards for a fizzy Vitamin C tablet and plonks it in a glass of water. 'Here there're all these anti-American feelings. It bugs me. My American teachers were really nice.'

I fold Lamya's nightdress and start ironing her purple skirt. 'You have to trust your instincts when people are talking. People say things they don't mean.'

'What bugs me,' he says, 'is that unless you're political, people think you're not a strong Muslim.' He gulps down the rest of his Vitamin C. 'Are you interested in politics?'

I shake my head and tell him why I am afraid of politics, why I am afraid of coups and revolutions. I start to speak about my father, things I have never said to anyone else. They surprise me by coming out fresh, measured – maybe because it all happened many years ago.

'You know a lot,' he says, offering admiration instead of pity.

There was a time when I had craved pity, needed it but never got it. And there are nights when I want nothing else but someone to stroke my hair and feel sorry for me.

117

Looking at him now, his nose swollen with flu, I think he could pity me, one day, at the right time, in the right place, he could give me the pity I've always wanted. And because I am struck by this thought, because it suspends me, I say, 'One of the Muslim scholars or maybe even the Khalifa Omar, I'm not sure, said that the Rum, the Europeans, are better than us in that when they fall down in battle they quickly get up, dust themselves and fight again. I try to forget the past, to move on but I'm not good at it. I'm not European.' We smile at each other. I've finished the ironing but the iron is too hot to put away. I fold the board back into the drawer and slide it shut.

He says, 'I have to go pray, I haven't prayed yet,' and he leaves the kitchen, blowing his nose. I wash the dishes and think of what he said to me. 'You know a lot.' If someone else had said that, I would have contradicted them saying, 'Oh no, I am neither educated nor well read. Look at me in a dead-end job.' But I had accepted the compliment from him, perhaps because he is younger than me.

Once, a few years back, Shahinaz had unsuccessfully introduced me to one of her uncles, a man in his early fifties, divorced, looking for a wife. I remember how constrained I had felt with him, his probing questions, the way he looked at me, wanting to figure me out, to determine my type, to 'suss me out' as Tamer would put it. If Shahinaz's uncle had said to me, 'You know a lot,' I would have suspected him of sarcasm, checked his eyes for a sneering look. I am glad he went away. I am glad he did not pursue me and instead married someone else.

Throughout the afternoon, Tamer hogs the television and annoys Mai who wants to watch her cartoons. He sets up his PlayStation and sits on the floor playing one football game after the other. I take her to the park and we do the usual things, feed the ducks, while away time in the playground. A little boy pinches her in the sandpit and she screams and screams. I get her as far away from him as possible, wipe her face, soothe her with a bag of crisps. I push her along by the pond and she calls out to the swans and the dogs out for a walk. I enjoy knowing that Tamer will be there when we get back. On the way, I walk past the flat to the bakery in the High Street and buy him a piece of cheesecake.

We drink tea together and watch *The Powerpuff Girls* with Mai. The room is at its best, with the long windows bringing in the fading light. Tamer eats the cheesecake without offering to share it, without asking if I had paid for it with my own money or the housekeeping money Lamya leaves me. It pleases me that he is informal. It makes me feel relaxed.

He says, 'When I was at school, I hated missing a single day. I hated being ill. Now I don't care.'

I say it would be wrong for him not to take his studies seriously. His parents are paying a lot of money to get him educated in London. He avoids my eyes and concentrates on the cartoon. After finishing his tea, he says, 'I enjoyed being at home today. It was nice.'

I savour the moment before the sound of the key in the door, before Lamya comes home and I have to stand up. A maid should not be sitting on the sofa drinking tea; she should sit on the floor or bustle about in the kitchen. She should not take such delight in her employer's brother. I wish I were younger, even just a few years younger.

Part Three

London, 1989–90

Seventeen

We did things we would never have done in Khartoum. Three weeks after Mama's funeral, Uncle Saleh and I had lunch in the Spaghetti House off Bond Street. If we had been in Khartoum, mourners would still be visiting, the television switched off as a mark of respect. Uncle Saleh sipped his tomato soup; I pushed my fork through smooth, buttery avocado. I had put on weight since we came from Khartoum; most of my clothes didn't fit me anymore.

Uncle Saleh smiled at me across the table. I was his responsibility now. It made me feel sorry for him.

'Have you changed your mind about coming with me to Canada?'

I shook my head.

'So what are you going to do?'

After the focus of Mama's illness, after not even wanting to leave her for an hour, it felt strange to be free. I was wobbly, as if I was not used to being out in public. I said, 'Maybe I should go to Khartoum for a few weeks.'

He put his spoon down. 'It's still not a good idea for you to go back. And besides, when everyone asks you about Omar, what will you say?'

He won the argument that way. It was something Mama would have wanted – not to tell anyone back home about

Omar. I finished my avocado, sucked the remaining dressing off my spoon. 'How can you just leave Sudan and go to Canada?'

'It's called immigrating. I've had it up to here with incompetence and instability.' He was bitter. What happened to my father had made him insecure and my mother's death had triggered anxieties about his own health.

'What about Samir?' My question wasn't loaded but Uncle Saleh looked defensive.

'He said that when he graduates from Cardiff, he'll follow me. Personally, I think he should transfer to a Canadian university. It would be sensible to have a Canadian degree if he's going to work there.'

We both knew why Samir wanted to stay in Cardiff. It was because of his English girlfriend. Whatever hopes Mama and Uncle Saleh had of Samir and I getting married had come to nothing. I would have liked to get married, not specifically to Samir (though if he had asked me I would have accepted) but I wanted to have children, a household to run. 'You didn't finish your education,' Mama used to complain, but deep down she was happy that I was with her every day, keeping her company through all the doctor visits and treatments, the time spent waiting for test results. Uncle Saleh said I was 'nursing her' but really the nurses did everything, especially at the end. Most of the time I just sat and watched TV. The room in the Humana Wellington Hospital had a nice bathroom and a menu for every meal – it was like staying in a good hotel.

The waiter took away our empty plates. 'I keep thinking,' Uncle Saleh said, 'that if you and Omar were younger, still at school, it might have been easier . . .' He paused. I tried to understand what he meant, screwed my eyes in concentration. 'Yes, you're almost adults now but . . .'

'We're twenty-four.' I took a sip of my Coke.

'It's a vulnerable stage, a crossroads in terms of careers and so on.'

'Why don't you think if we were older, in our thirties, settled, then it would have been easier?'

'Yes, I think that too.' He looked somewhat slumped. 'It's pointless really thinking these things.'

The waiter brought cannelloni for me, a dish of garlic chicken for Uncle Saleh. We perked up at the sight of the food. Steam rose from the dishes and the white sauce on my cannelloni was bubbling.

'I think you need to know that staying in London is the expensive option.' Uncle Saleh picked up his knife and fork.

'What do you mean?' I spoke with my mouth full, swallowed.

'Well, life here isn't cheap – not what you're used to anyway. And what your father and mother left you isn't enough.'

'How come?'

'Rotten luck, that's how come. And this new government freezing your father's assets.'

'I see.' My stomach pushed against the waistband of my skirt. I reached back and undid the button, took a deep breath and felt the zipper slide open. I needed to buy new clothes or go on a diet. But even if I did lose weight, the clothes I had were already out of fashion. 'I can get a job,' I said, smiling.

'As what? You're not qualified, Najwa. Do you want to study and get a qualification?'

'No.'

'It might be a good idea. You'd meet people, make friends.'

Something in his tone made me feel that I was a useless lump. Tears blurred the cannelloni on my plate. I wiped them away with the napkin. He didn't notice. 'You have a friend, don't you, studying in Scotland?'

'Randa.' I blinked and my voice was normal. 'She's studying medicine in Edinburgh.'

'Why don't you go study with her?'

'Oh Uncle Saleh, I don't even have A levels. Don't you remember? I went to Atlantic College and came back after two weeks.'

'I remember. You refused to milk a cow.' He laughed.

I smiled, remembering Randa, Samir and Omar – how ashamed they were of me. 'Who do you think you are? You're such a snob! It's part of the course – we have to do community work.' But I had never milked Sudanese cows, why should I milk British ones?

'Have you ever milked a cow?' I asked Uncle Saleh.

'No, I can't say I have. We're spoilt in Khartoum; everything's done for us. The closest I ever got to animals was when I went fishing.' He laughed.

I laughed with him. 'And the zoo.'

'But you should have persevered with your studies, Najwa, cows or no cows.'

'I probably wouldn't have made the IB anyway.' Omar hadn't. He was the only Sudanese who failed his exams; he never got over that. Randa, Samir and the others went on to university and he couldn't.

'Your mother was too soft with you.' Uncle Saleh pointed his fork at me.

'Yes, I suppose she was.' Mama came by train to fetch me. She pretended she was cross but she was relieved that I was with her, near her when the doctor said that the result of her tests was positive.

126

'The right thing is for you to come with me to Canada,' said Uncle Saleh.

'I can't. I need to be near Omar. Besides, I know people here. Uncle Nabeel said he would give me some training in his travel agency.' Uncle Nabeel's wife, Aunty Eva, had been a close friend of my mother, someone who, unlike many others, didn't withdraw from us after what happened.

Uncle Saleh smiled with approval. 'That's a good start. You'll be all right if you live off the interest in your bank account. Don't touch the capital.'

I nodded.

'You must always get in touch with me if you need anything, if you have any problems . . .' His voice became gruff; he disliked these paternal speeches. 'I'll come to London once in a while and you must visit us in Toronto.' He had his own children to worry about; he would not insist that I join them. Already his patience was strained from looking after Mama and from Omar's trial.

I ate the last spoonful of cannelloni. Uncle Saleh finished his chicken, pushed aside the mushrooms and said, 'I have a bit of bad news for you.'

'What is it?' It would be about Omar or our 'not so much as we thought it would be' sources of money.

He lowered his voice. 'We lost the appeal. He's going to have to serve the whole sentence.'

I didn't say anything. Everything about Omar – the mention of what he had done, the memory of his voice – made me feel numb. The word 'drugs' said by anyone, anywhere, made me cringe, even when I read it, even when I read a word like 'drugstore'.

'It'll be fifteen years,' he continued.

Fifteen years sounded like for ever. He would be old then, forty. How could he let them do this to him? A part of my brain still thought, it's all a mistake, a nightmare. It wasn't Omar; it couldn't have been Omar.

'He will be eligible for parole in maybe half that time but to tell you the truth, Najwa,' Uncle Saleh was saying, 'I feel safer about you being in London on your own, rather than with him around.'

I winced. To hear it from Uncle Saleh was uncomfortable. Omar was not Omar anymore. Omar wouldn't shake Mama's shoulders. He wouldn't shout, 'Where's my money? It's MY money.'

Uncle Saleh paid the bill and left me to finish my profiteroles. He had an appointment with his bank manager in Piccadilly Circus. The immigration to Canada was costing him plenty. I felt silly sitting all by myself, self-conscious. It wouldn't be done in Khartoum for a woman to be alone in a restaurant. 'I'm in London,' I told myself, 'I can do what I like, no one can see me.' Fascinating. I could order a glass of wine. Who would stop me or even look surprised? There was a curiosity in me but not enough to spin me into action.

I walked out of the restaurant. There was the fuzzy feeling again, as if I was still not used to being outdoors. For a second I was confused, missed my step – shouldn't I be hurrying back to the hospital? The sound of the traffic was loud, the smell from the French bakery deliberately delicious. People walked fast, knowing where they were going. If I wasn't too lazy, I would have crossed the street and gone into Selfridges, tried some of the new summer fashions.

I decided to save money by taking the underground instead of a taxi. At Bond Street station, I looked at the magazines in the newsagent. I could buy one of those rude magazines, the ones always kept on the top shelf. No one would stop me or look surprised. I would carry it home and I wouldn't even need to hide it. I could plonk it on my bedside table and no on would see it. I hesitated, then I bought a copy of *Slimming* from the newsagent and a packet of Fox's Glacier Mints. The change I got was heavy and I dropped some of it on the ground. It was a struggle to bend down and pick up the coins. In Khartoum I would never wear such a short skirt in public. I might wear it at the club or when visiting friends by car, but not for walking in the street. My stomach was too full. I burped garlic.

Eighteen

Our new flat was not near an underground station. I got off at Edgware Road and walked the rest of the way. 'Our' new flat. I still thought of us as a family. I would buy an Arabic magazine before realizing that it was Mama who had read it, I would put on *Top Of The Pops* on Thursday evening and realize halfway through that it was Omar who cared which song was number one.

I walked past an ice-cream van, a building covered in scaffolding, workmen sitting out in the sun. A whistle and a laugh as one of them shouted out something I didn't catch, though I understood the tone. I flushed, aware that all the weight I had gained had settled on my hips. But still it was a compliment, and my hair was long on my shoulders like Diana Ross's. I looked up to see a face so much like Anwar's that I stopped and stared. The same complexion, a different grin. Anwar laughing when I told him about the President telling me off for answering the phone in English, Anwar lighting a cigarette saying, 'Our country is beautiful. Why do you go to Europe and not want to see your own country instead?' The builder stood up on the scaffolding. Would he come down to talk to me? Would we become friends just because he looked like Anwar and thought I was pretty? I would have a builder for a boyfriend – how could I imagine such a comedown? But I could. I could imagine it because something inside me was luxurious and lazy, something inside me, confronted with a certain voice, a certain smile, could easily soften and give in. I forced myself to look away from him and walk on. It was awkward to walk fast, not only because of my skirt but also because of the high heels of my sandals.

The flat held no memories. By the time we moved here, Omar's whereabouts were so erratic that he rarely spent a night in it. Several times he got confused and headed towards our old flat in Lancaster Gate. I looked into his room. It was impersonal, like a storeroom. His things, the few things he hadn't sold – posters, clothes. He had sold his ghetto blaster, Walkman, Swiss watch and best shoes. That was the beginning, how it started, then he turned to our things and bullying Mama. She didn't live here long, though she was the one who bought the flat. I remember going around with her, looking at flats, deciding which one to buy. We were together like sisters.

I checked my post. Bills. A thick envelope from the Humana Wellington, pages and pages of the itemized bill. Every meal Mama and I had eaten, every long-distance call, every urine sample, a haircut, dry-cleaning, laundry and the total was a staggering amount. Uncle Saleh could not have been thinking of such a bill when he was telling me to only live off the interest in my bank account.

I put on the only Sudanese tape I had, one by Hanan Al-Neel. *I saw you sitting in the middle of greenery, the moon straight up above you . . .* Anwar made me get that tape. 'Why do you only listen to Western music?' he had said. It had earned me his approval and Omar's contempt. For my brother, anything Western was unmistakably and unquestionably better than anything Sudanese. *I saw you sitting* . . . My class at the University of Khartoum would have graduated by now. They would be looking for jobs, the girls marrying one by one, getting pregnant, and looking different. I could imagine myself with them; picture an alternative life to the one I was living in London. I could picture our house, busy and tingling because I was getting married. My mother and father were arguing over whom to invite to the wedding. 'If we don't invite her,' Mama was saying, 'she'll be offended and we'll never hear the end of it.' My skin glowed from the scrubbing and *dilka* it was getting every day. My muscles ached from the new dance routines I was learning. The telephone didn't stop ringing, my friends came over, we giggled nonstop. The bridegroom looked like Anwar but he wasn't Anwar, he couldn't be. He was someone my parents approved of, someone who wasn't a communist, someone whose father didn't work as a technician on the railways. The tape came to an end. I didn't turn it over.

I lay in bed reading *Slimming*. No, I didn't know that a spoonful of ketchup was twenty-two calories. Which diet would suit me? The one where you had a big breakfast and light evening meal or the other way round? I fell asleep and dreamt I was young and ill, lying in my parents' room in Khartoum. Mama was looking after me. I could feel the cool crisp sheets around me, the privilege of being in their bed. She gave me a spoonful of medicine. Delicious syrup that burned my throat. Omar was jealous because he wasn't given any. Omar was sulking. He looked down at me, 'Nana,' he said, 'can I borrow your colours?' 'Leave her alone,' Mama said, 'can't you see she's ill?' She put a cool hand on my forehead. I smiled and closed my eyes. I could hear my father, upset because I was ill. He was

annoyed with my mother, 'Put her on a course of antibiotics,' he said, 'don't leave her like this!' and Mama's
reply defensive, explaining. I rolled over, sure that they
loved me. I mattered enough for them to quarrel over me.
'Put her on a course of antibiotics.' I woke up with my
father's voice and for one tiny stupid second, I couldn't
remember why he wasn't with me . . . It was like looking
at a gash on my arm and not remembering how I got it.
The telephone rang. I made my way to it. The flat was
dark with sunset.

It was Randa, phoning from Edinburgh, saying, 'At last
I managed to call you. You're the one who always seems
to be phoning me.' She sounded like she was carrying out
a duty.

I hardly had any news to tell her. I could not tell her
about Omar. I led her to believe that he was here with me,
that he was thinking of doing his A levels again.

'Is he still taking drugs?' she asked. She had known
about the hashish in Khartoum and suspected harder stuff
when they were in Atlantic College together. She got along
well with him. I remember them dancing together at the
club.

'No, I don't think he is.' Unless they had drugs in prison.

'That's good then.'

'Yes, that's good.' I changed the subject. 'Did I tell you
that Uncle Nabeel said I could start training at his office?'

We talked about work. She started to tell me her news
– the long hours she had to spend in hospital, the exams
coming up soon. I had to keep my mind from wandering,
to sound interested when I asked, 'What do you want to
specialize in?'

'Skin,' she said.

I knew there was a medical term for 'skin' but she hadn't

used it because she thought I wouldn't understand it. 'Why don't you become a gynaecologist? It would be nice to deliver all these cute babies.'

'It's nothing like that, Najwa. Gyna is one of the toughest specializations.' She had never talked down to me back in Khartoum but now she was in a prestigious university and I had a disgraced father.

We talked about her social life. Yes, there were some Sudanese in Edinburgh University – quite a number of families – bored wives, she said, with screaming children. They invited her for dinner; she always declined. 'Why?' I asked.

'So many of them are Islamists. You know the type, the wife in hijab having one baby after the other.'

'Aren't there women students too?'

'Yes, unfortunately. The sight of them wearing hijab on campus irritates me.'

I remembered the girls in Khartoum University wearing hijab and those who covered their hair with white tobes. They never irritated me, did they? I tried to think back and I saw the rows of students praying, the boys in front and the girls at the back. At sunset I would sit and watch them praying. They held me still with their slow movements, the recitation of the Qur'an. I envied them something I didn't have but I didn't know what it was. I didn't have a name for it. Whenever I heard the azan in Khartoum, whenever I heard the Qur'an recited I would feel a bleakness in me and a depth and space would open up, hollow and numb. I usually didn't notice it, wasn't aware that it existed. Then the Qur'an heard by chance on the radio of a taxi would tap at this inner sluggishness, nudge it like when my feet went to sleep and I touched them. They felt fat and for them to get back to normal, for me to be able to move my toes again, they would have to first crunch with pins and needles.

It was like that at the funeral parlour when the four women came from the mosque to wash my mother. They all wore hijab and long dark coats, their faces plain without make-up. 'Do you want to attend the washing?' they asked. I shook my head and waited outside the door, heard the splash of water. 'Which shampoo do you want us to use?' One of them poked her head out of the door, releasing the strong smell of antiseptic. Her name was Wafaa; she was Egyptian. 'Which was your mother's regular shampoo?' Her hands, which held the bottles of shampoo, were covered in light, clear gloves, she wore a thin plastic apron. Afterwards, when she told me that I should pray for my mother, I felt that same bleakness in me. I became aware of that hollow place. Perhaps that was where the longing for God was supposed to come from and I didn't really have it. Wafaa taught me a specific prayer – asking Allah to wash my mother's sins with water and ice. I forgot the exact wording but the image of ice remained and the feeling she imparted that my mother needed me still. Everyone else seemed to think that my mother didn't need me anymore, that I was free.

When they put on their coats and were about to leave, Wafaa gave me her phone number. 'We have classes at the mosque. We get together once a week.' The others nodded. Wafaa smiled and said, 'We enjoy ourselves, come and join us.' Another lady said shyly, 'We would like to see you again.' She was the youngest of them, she had henna on her fingernails, sparkling eyes. I liked her yet felt she was remote, different from me. I took Wafaa's phone number and dropped it in my bag. Couldn't they see that I was not the religious type?

*   *   *

On the telephone, Randa asked if I had any news of Khartoum. 'Do you remember Amir?' I said, starting to tease her. She had liked him at one time. I could never understand why – he never spoke. Perhaps she thought his silence enigmatic while I assumed he had nothing to say.

She laughed. 'Of course I remember Amir – what's his news?'

'Uncle Saleh told me that he graduated from Khartoum University and got a job in Saudi Arabia.'

'Saudi Arabia! Well, he'll make good money there.'

'Yes.' The words were easy in my mouth, like I was going through a familiar routine. 'He'll become the perfect bridegroom.'

She laughed. 'Oh no, don't start. I'd forgotten that old crush.'

I smiled, pleased that we were talking naturally. 'Do you have any news of the guys from the club?'

'Yes. Remember Sundari?' There was still a smile in her voice. 'I heard she's back in Khartoum with her daughter.'

Of course I remembered Sundari, the fuss of the scandal. She and her American marine got married and went to live in the States.

'How old is her daughter now?' I asked Randa.

'She must be four now. Apparently, she's gorgeous and everyone in Khartoum loves her.'

I smiled, imagining the little girl pretty like her mother, chunky like her father. A memory of him doing push-ups in the garden of the club, while Sundari watched, her silky hair touching the grass. I said, 'I'm sorry I missed seeing them.'

'Well, her husband wasn't with them – I forget his name. And that got people asking questions. It turned out that they're divorced and she's come back to live with her parents.'

Tears sprang to my eyes, 'Oh no, how sad, that's really sad!'

'Najwa, you hardly knew her. You needn't get so upset.'

'It is upsetting!'

'Stop it. You're overreacting.'

But I was sobbing now, spasms as if I were vomiting. I couldn't stop.

Nineteen

The letter had been forwarded from our old address in Lancaster Gate. It was addressed to me. I looked at the signature first: Anwar. Yet it was posted from London. *My deepest condolences for the passing away of your mother.* Automatic tears filled my eyes. I brushed them away. *I heard the sad news from the Sudanese community here in London and they tell me you and your brother Omar are keeping to yourselves, not mixing much. Will you make an exception for me – I would like very much to meet you?* I could hear him say this, the teasing in his voice. *What is your news? Are you studying or working? I'm sure you're wondering how I got your address. I got it from the Embassy. Or rather, I had a friend get it for me. I'm not on good terms with the Embassy for obvious reasons. You have surely heard . . .*

Yes I had heard about the coup. Uncle Saleh from Toronto advising me to stay put, not to go back to the Sudan. No, it did not mean that things were normal, he had said, of course the President is not coming back. Who are these people? I asked. My uncle said that he had no idea where they came from.

This military junta, Anwar wrote, *has brought to an end five years of democracy and free press.* Two coups in four years, Uncle Nabeel had said, is not at all good for business. *I was writing for an English language paper, among other things, and they closed it down. Things deteriorated to such an extent that I had to leave. So here I am, a political refugee, and it is reassuring to see that a healthy and vital opposition is gathering in London. Please phone me, Najwa. Here is my number.*

I looked at the number. I would dial it and hear his voice. We would laugh like we did in the university. His letter was so friendly. It meant that our quarrel was forgotten or was too old to matter. He didn't think I would still be holding a grudge against him. He had believed that my father was corrupt. But now he was against this new government, and had probably forgotten all about my father. What was the point of it all? Coup after coup – one set of people after another – like musical chairs.

I am sharing a flat with two other Sudanese. Kamal is a PhD student. He's doing English Literature – what a luxury! He's living up the part – thinks he's a gentleman. The word 'gentleman' was written in English. *The other, Ameen, is a bum but he can afford it, he's loaded. Sleeps all day, cards and cigarettes all night. He's the one who helped me get your address from the Embassy. (Against all odds he somehow managed to rouse himself and get there before they closed!) There are certain people, that merchant stock from which Ameen comes, who support each and every government the Sudan has ever known and I don't exclude the British. For such people, appeasement is the only politics they know.* I smiled.

He would be less talkative face to face, more reserved. He always came across as more relaxed and open in his writing. I knew that about him. He could look at me for a long time without talking. I folded the letter and sat in

139

a daze. The kettle had boiled but I didn't get up to make tea. I looked at my watch: five to nine. I could phone him now (disturb the sleeping Ameen) but I would be even later getting to Aunty Eva. I abandoned breakfast, grabbed my shoulder bag and jacket and ran to the underground station.

I read his letter again in the train. *My dearest Najwa.* But that didn't mean anything; that was just an expression. *Please phone me.* I will. I counted the years on my fingers. Nearly five years. *I have so much to chat to you about.* Me too.

I arrived at Aunty Eva's late. I went to her at home every day now instead of going to Uncle Nabeel at his office. I hadn't liked it at that office. It was off Park Lane, narrow and claustrophobic, even though it was two storeys and painted in calm, pale colours. There was nothing glamorous about the work – shipping freight rather than people across the world. I had imagined myself working in a travel agency that resembled the British Airways office in Khartoum – glass windows, a prime corner spot in the centre of town. All day important people would visit and I would know the details of their travel arrangements. The teaboy would ask me what I wanted to drink and make me feel important.

Instead, I made the tea for Uncle Nabeel and his clients. I didn't like the way some of them looked at me. Greasy men with bleary expressions who spent their evenings in the nightclubs off Edgware Road. It was a relief to walk out in the middle of the day, cross Oxford Street and buy Uncle Nabeel's lunch from Marks and Spencer. He always gave me money to buy a sandwich for myself too, which was kind. Sometimes he would go for a restaurant lunch with his clients. On these days he wouldn't give me lunch money and I would walk to Hyde Park if it wasn't raining and eat crisps and chocolates sitting on a bench. I wasn't really needed in the office: my typing was slow and, though I was good at answering the phone, not that many people phoned.

One day Aunty Eva called. Uncle Nabeel was out and so we chatted for a while. 'I'm struggling,' she said. 'We have a dinner party tomorrow night and all the work is on me. This is the hardship of this country.' She missed her Ethiopian maids in Khartoum. She hadn't brought them with her because of all the stories about maids escaping once they arrived in the West.

'I'll come and help you, Aunty,' I said. 'I'll ask Uncle Nabeel and I'll come to you first thing in the morning.'

Uncle Nabeel welcomed the idea. He gave me money and another phone call with Aunty Eva yielded a shopping list. I arrived the next morning at their house in Pimlico laden with bags of groceries and enthusiasm for the dinner party. To be with a family again, to be with one of mother's friends. Something opened up inside me. The need to be useful, the pleasure in being in her kitchen, in finding out where everything was kept, opening her fridge, putting the groceries away. She taught me that day how to stuff vine leaves, how to set a table, twist and fold a napkin just so. And when she went to shower and change, I put on Radio 1 loud, and enjoyed cleaning the kitchen. I mopped the floor and took the garbage out. That was three months before and I never went back to Uncle Nabeel's office.

Today, Aunty Eva opened the door for me in her pink dressing gown. Her hair was smooth on her shoulders. Even without make-up she looked good, stamped by beauty. She was petite and plump with creamy skin and hazel eyes.

141

There was a warmth about her, in the ease with which her eyes watered and her skin broke in perspiration. When she worked hard in the kitchen she complained of the heat, even in mid-winter. As if reflecting her personality, the house was unusually warm. It was the first week of March and they had already switched off their central heating.

'Come, Najwa,' she said and I followed her into her bedroom. Her accent was typical of the Syrian Christians of Khartoum, familiar to me but still quaint. In the bedroom the bed was covered with photographs, black and white, coloured, in different sizes. 'Today,' she said lighting a cigarette and sitting on the edge of the bed, 'there's no kitchen for us. Your uncle's invited out. I've decided we'll sort out these photographs once and for all.'

I sat on the floor, my elbows on the bed. In sepia, there was Eva the young beauty, in a low-cut dress of the fifties; Eva in the first mini-skirt of the sixties; her two little boys in baby-walkers, in a paddling pool, their Ethiopian nanny in the background. Aunty Eva put on her glasses to take a closer look. Her fingers were covered in liver spots, the nails painted as brightly as the jewels in her rings. 'Labib is older than Murad and he's always been the smaller. Look, Murad had pushed him off his bike. That's why he was sulking.' Her sons were now both married and living outside London. I liked it when they came over with their wives and young children. I learnt how to change a nappy, heat up bottles, pulverize normal food and spoon it into a baby's mouth.

Aunty Eva finished her cigarette and said, 'Make me a coffee, Najwa.'

In the kitchen I put on Radio 1 and tidied away the breakfast things. It was my favourite programme, *The Golden Hour*. When they played the songs of the early eighties, I would remember discos at the American Club, New Year parties at the Syrian Club, songs Omar and I had memorized, arguing about the correct lyrics. I only listened to pop music when I was alone in the kitchen. Aunty Eva preferred the tapes of Feirouz or simply fiddled with the radio dial until she found classical music. She enjoyed cooking but needed me to chop garlic, squeeze lemons and do the basic things like boiling spaghetti. More important than that, she needed me to load the dishwasher, wipe the table and the floor. And of course tackle the horror of the bathrooms. On the line from Toronto, Uncle Saleh had been furious that I wasn't going to Uncle Nabeel's office any more. 'What do you mean you're helping her?' Help. Waiting upon. Servant's work. He didn't understand that I needed her company, needed to hear her gossip about Khartoum, needed to sit within range of her nostalgia.

I carried the coffee back into the bedroom. Aunty Eva was sitting on the bed, one of her legs underneath her, the other sticking out straight: a plump calf, tiny feet. She held up a photograph and smiled. 'Look Najwa what I found. This was a fancy-dress party at the club. I'm dressed as a belly dancer. How could I?' She chuckled and I looked down to see her young and voluptuous in a glittering costume, her eyes merry, her cheeky smile. Next to her a woman was dressed as a Red Indian in a wig of stark black hair in two long braids, with a feather stuck to the band around her forehead. In another photo from that same party, a man with blue eyes was dressed in white Arabian clothes. 'Lawrence of Arabia.' Aunty Eva smiled and stuck the photo in the album.

She picked up another photo and sighed. My mother and father, not in fancy dress but in national costume. My mother in a shining tobe, transparent enough to see her

143

bare arms. Her smile was a little held back, the way she was in company. My father looked almost official, wanting to please. He would have been the one keen on this party – the right connections, the movers and shakers. He thought of my mother as being too laid back, too complacent. Old money, he would say, turning up her nose at the *nouveau riche* and the social climbers but yet unable to do without them. How healthy my mother looked. How sturdy my father looked. They didn't want to die. It happened against their will. Did they know that I was flattened and small without them?

Aunty Eva put her finger on the face of the woman dressed as a Red Indian. 'A close friend of mine. One day she walked into her bedroom and found her husband in bed with this woman.' Her finger jabbed the chest of a woman dressed in a tight black Bedouin outfit, covered in embroidery, with a striking necklace around her throat. Her eyes were large and staring under pencil-thin eyebrows. 'Imagine,' Aunty Eva said, 'in her own bedroom!' It seemed that the location bothered her more than anything else.

'Which one was the husband?'

Aunty Eva flicked through the photographs looking for the errant husband. 'In her own bed,' she murmured, 'would you believe it? There he is – dressed as a cowboy.' He was a jovial, respectable-looking man wearing glasses. The cowboy hat was pushed back to reveal a balding forehead. 'A High Court judge,' Aunty Eva said. He was a man who could have been one of my father's friends, probably was one of my father's friends. He could have come to our home, joked with me. I would have called him 'Uncle' and, as a child, run into his arms. If my father's friend could cheat on his wife, then why wouldn't my father cheat on the Treasury?

Wash my sins with ice. Where did these words come from? A memory of the smell of antiseptic, the splash of water, the funeral parlour. The prayer Wafaa taught me to say for my mother. She had refused to take any money for doing the washing. I should have phoned her afterwards to thank her again.

I asked Aunty Eva, 'Did my father really do all things he was accused of doing?'

The defensive way she tucked in her chin showed she disapproved of the question. She said slowly, 'It's not so black and white. There are grey areas in business and one day being in the grey area is safe and the next day it's taken against you.' She made a spitting sound of disgust. 'The world is treacherous. He had a military trial; they passed a harsh sentence. It needn't have been like that.'

'But did he or didn't he embezzle?' I struggled with the word, almost whimpering.

Her eyes said I was being disloyal. 'Your father didn't harm anyone. He didn't ruin anyone, he didn't kill anyone.'

My tears made her soften. 'Do you know what your mother said to me about him? She said, "He gave me back my dignity. He made me able to hold my head up high in front of people." She was a divorcee when he married her . . .'

'What! I didn't know.'

'She didn't want you to know. She was ashamed of it. Her first husband had walked out on her and disappeared. He went to Australia, he went to America – no one knew. She had to get a divorce through the courts. In those days it was a scandal and she was sensitive, it hurt her. No suitors wanted her after that; she was in her twenties and getting no proposals. People said your father proposed because he was ambitious. They said he was after her money

145

and her family name. Is it true, is it not true?' She shrugged. 'The important thing is that he made your mother happy. Remember that.'

Twenty

We shook hands. I thought we would laugh but we didn't, not like yesterday on the phone. He had answered, not one of his flatmates, and I had teased him saying, 'Do you recognize my voice?' When he immediately said my name, we laughed. But now, meeting face to face, we were awkward, self-conscious. To avoid arriving too early, I had showed up too late and that annoyed him. Also 'in front of Marble Arch tube station' wasn't specific enough. I had gone from Speaker's Corner and walked up and down in front of McDonald's. Anwar stood in the same spot, looking at his watch, waiting.

He looked different, broader, maybe because he was wearing a thick blue jacket. I had never seen him wearing a jacket before. It looked cheap as if he had bought it from C&A. I said, 'Let's go for a walk in the park.' He said, 'It's too cold, let's sit somewhere and have coffee.' His left leg was stiff when he walked; he limped a little. 'Did you injure it?' I asked but he just looked away as if he hadn't heard me. We wandered around, looking for somewhere suitable. This place was too crowded, that looked like a restaurant and we didn't want to eat. Things were much simpler in Khartoum University. I said that and he smiled.

Finally, we found a coffee shop, an empty table. I took

off my coat. He looked at my sweater and jeans, took out his cigarettes. 'You're not allowed to smoke in here.' I pointed towards the sign. He flushed and shook his head, put the packet back in his pocket. Had he always been that touchy?

'When did you come from Khartoum?' I asked him.

'December.'

'You've been here all this time and you didn't get in touch?'

He smiled and looked a bit more relaxed. 'I went to Manchester when I first came – I have a cousin there. Then I came here and it took some time to settle. I thought I would meet you in the street one day. I used to look out for you. I thought I would be in the underground station going down the escalator and then I would see you on the other side, on the escalator going up.'

I laughed. 'We wouldn't have met then. You would have gone to catch your train and I would have walked out of the station.'

'I thought about that. I would have called out to you and told you to wait for me at the top . . .'

'Shouting in the middle of the station – what a scandal!'

He laughed. 'People would just think, "Look at the stupid foreigner."' He looked away. 'I'm realizing I can make my way here pretending I'm stupid – they kind of expect it – but anyway,' he looked back at me, 'I did hope we would meet by chance.'

'London isn't that small.'

'It isn't. It's a big city.'

'What do you think of it?'

He made a face as if to say, 'Wow.'

I tried to see London as he would see it, not like my second home.

'The West is very impressive.' He sounded reluctant or as if he was thinking out loud, working something out. 'Everything is organized. Everyone has a part to play. There's a system in place. A very structured system. I like the underground. If you want to go anywhere, you just ask what is the nearest underground station and then you can get there.'

'I do too, I always have. I like the map, how all the lines have different colours.'

He took out an underground map from the pocket of his jacket. As if suddenly remembering, he took off his jacket and hung it at the back of his chair. He was wearing a cotton, short-sleeved shirt. No wonder he was too cold to walk in the park. He folded out the map in front of me. There were marks on it in pencil. The paper looked worn out, smudged. Something moved in me, an awareness of him. I shifted my chair closer to the table, held one end of the map in my hand.

'See,' he said, 'that's my station, Gloucester Road. It's on the blue line; it's called Piccadilly. It's also on the green line – called the District Line. The Piccadilly Line is deep under the ground, the District Line is higher, like an ordinary train.'

Because he was telling me things I already knew, I felt soothed, comfortable.

'I got lost one day,' he was saying, 'and I was under there coming and going, riding this train and that train. Then when I got out at the right station, I didn't have to pay extra, not a pence! And I had been up and down that line for hours . . .'

Our coffees came, each saucer with two packets of sugar. Anwar put away the map, tore open his packets of sugar. 'They don't put sugar in anything,' he complained, 'they give you everything tasteless.' In Khartoum University we used to buy the tea sweet from the canteen. I gave him my packets of sugar. He refused at first but I insisted and we argued. At last he accepted that I no longer put sugar in my coffee.

'How come?'

'I'm on a diet.'

'Why?'

'For the usual reason most people go on diets.'

'But you don't need it.'

I smiled. 'How do you know?'

He laughed because I was flirting, 'You haven't changed. I thought you would have changed.'

But I had changed. My whole life had changed. There was just me now. No Mama, no Baba, no Omar – just me, fumbling about in London.

I told him about Uncle Nabeel and Aunty Eva. 'Well, I'm impressed,' he said, 'you're not such a snob after all. How much does she pay you?'

I told him and he said, 'That's not too bad. Convert it into Sudanese currency and it sounds pretty good.'

His reaction was totally different from Randa's. 'They're cheating you,' she had hissed down the line from Edinburgh. 'Students get paid more in a weekend waitressing than you're getting working a whole week.'

Encouraged by Anwar's reaction I said, 'They're generous in other ways too. If I go out shopping with Aunty Eva to help her carry her bags, she treats me for lunch in nice restaurants.'

He took a sip of his coffee and smiled. I continued, 'At Christmas, Uncle Nabeel gave me a twenty-pound note.'

He laughed. 'So you're now celebrating Christmas. You've become a true citizen of London.'

I laughed with him. 'I don't know what I'm becoming.'

'How come you're avoiding the Sudanese?'

'Who told you that?'

'I've been asking everyone about you. What's Omar doing?'

I had prepared for this. I focused my mind on Randa, looked Anwar straight in the eyes and said, 'He's studying in Edinburgh.'

'What's he studying?'

'Business. Like he was doing in Khartoum.'

'I've got friends in Edinburgh University . . .'

'He's not in the university,' I said quickly, 'he's in a poly-technic. He didn't get good grades when he sat for his IB.'

'I see.'

It was a relief that he believed me. Aunty Eva was the difficult one. When she asked me about Omar, which she did every now and then, her questions were nosy, her insis-tence to know almost cruel. She would look at me, her eyes sharp as if saying, 'Don't try to fool me, young lady, I'm too wordly to swallow these lies you're peddling.'

'What about you?' Anwar said. 'Why didn't you con-tinue your studies?'

'I guess I'm not really the studying type. I used to mem-orize, memorize without understanding. That's how I man-aged to get into Khartoum University.'

He raised his eyebrows. 'Didn't your Baba pull a few strings?'

'Of course not. The Admissions Office is so strict. They only take students who have the proper grades.'

'You don't say . . .' He was sarcastic like when he had said 'your Baba'. There was no need.

'Why are you being disloyal to your university?'

'I'm just being realistic.'

'They only take qualified students. There's no cheating.'

'I find this hard to believe.'

'But I'm sure. Why don't you believe me?'

'Because I know better.' He was irritated but it was too late to stop.

'You don't. In this case you don't. I'm sure of what I'm saying because my father did try his best to get my cousin Samir into Khartoum University. Samir didn't have good grades and they just wouldn't take him.'

'Well, at least you're honestly admitting that bribery and pulling strings was second nature to your father.'

He sighed as if he regretted going too far. It crossed my mind that I should get up and leave. But I kept sitting, just staring at my coffee, not knowing what to say. He had won the argument even though I was right, even though I was saying the truth.

He touched my hand. 'I'm sorry, Najwa.'

I didn't reply. 'Look at me,' he said.

I liked him holding my hand. I didn't want him to let go. We should not talk about my father, ever.

'Najwa . . .'

I should make an effort so that things would be nice between us again. 'Tell me your news.' My voice sounded bright, sensible. 'You didn't tell me your news.'

He let go of my hand. 'When I graduated, I sat for the examination at the Foreign Office and I got selected.'

'That's great!'

'It was, yes. But then when this new government took over, I got kicked out. Everyone who was left wing was fired.'

I wanted to say something sympathetic. But worse had happened to my father when Anwar's government came to power. Musical chairs. I took a sip of my coffee. It was strict and bitter without sugar.

'You said in your letter you were writing for an English newspaper?'

'Yes, I did that in my free time. They shut it down – no free press. I enjoyed writing. My English is mediocre . . .'

'Oh no, it's very good. I remember reading your final year project.'

He looked pleased, flattered. 'But I'm trying to improve my English. I read the papers here. If there is a word I don't understand, I look it up in the dictionary.' I could imagine him doing that. He would learn fast because he was clever and focused.

He went on. 'I plan to write an article about the current situation in Sudan and submit it to a British newspaper. I'll let you look at it once I've written it.'

'I'd like that.'

He smiled. 'You can correct my English.' He wasn't being sarcastic. He wasn't teasing me about the private schools I had gone to.

Twenty-one

I had not known there was an Ethiopian restaurant in Notting Hill Gate. I sat on a small stool, eating spicy chicken off a table that was only a few feet high. I ate with a fork while Anwar ate with his hands. He made fun of me, brought up in a house where only the servants ate with their hands, but there was a fondness in his voice, he did not mean to hurt me. The food was delicious. I said to him, 'We had an Ethiopian maid who used to make *zighni* as hot as this, but she put boiled eggs in it. Her name was Donna Summer.' His smiled his 'I'm not interested but tell me anyway' smile and I launched into an explanation of why our maid was called Donna Summer. I wondered if sitting on these low stools hurt his leg but he seemed relaxed, at ease. I liked to see him like that.

There were many Africans in the restaurant. The music, the rugs on the wall, the dark solid furniture and the fact that Anwar was not the only one eating with his hands meant he could feel at home. I tried to imagine Omar's reaction to this place and me in it. He would look down on it because he despised the 'ethnic' scene. He would say that I had come down in the world.

When we finished eating, we had tea and Anwar lit a

cigarette. I started to look at his article like I promised I would. 'The light is dim.'

'Leave it then,' he said.

'No, I really want to read it. The light isn't that bad.' I had to tread carefully. He wanted me to correct his English but at the same time he was sensitive to criticism. I flinched when I saw 'the corrupt post-colonial government'. He would have had my father in mind, but thankfully his name, my surname, was not in there.

'Your handwriting is clear, easy to read.'

'I should type it up. But I don't have a typewriter.'

I thought to myself, 'I will buy him an electric typewriter or, better still, a word-processor, something fancy to surprise him.' I had a bank account and I was free to do with it what I wanted. Uncle Saleh was far away so I needn't worry about him saying, 'Just live off the interest, try not to touch the savings.' I would buy Anwar a computer.

'Najwa, stop daydreaming. Read.'

I made some comments. The use of 'the' instead of 'a', minor spelling. 'I don't think you can say, "that was the reason for the failure for which".'

'Why not?' He was becoming tense.

'I don't know. It just doesn't sound right.' I hardly sounded convincing. 'Also "showed interest to", should be "interest in".'

'Anything else?' His hand reached out for his papers as if he was possessive about them.

'Nothing else. The rest is fine.' I was lying.

He breathed a sigh of relief, took the article and folded it away.

I wanted to change the mood. 'Is it wise to let a silly girl who didn't finish university comment on your work?'

He laughed and I relaxed again. 'I have no choice.' He was teasing me.

'So that is why you invite me and phone me – because you have no choice?'

'My feelings for you leave me no choice.'

'Clever answer.' But I said it softly. I was touched by the way he looked at me. He gave me hope that I would not be in limbo for long, that I would not be without a family for long. But there were prickly areas between us, things I couldn't say to him. His opinions were so clear-cut, there was no room for my murky thoughts, the questions that I asked myself: what am I doing here, what happened to Omar, will I ever go back to Sudan and what will it be like without my parents? Would Anwar ever change his mind about my father? I hoped he would. He was changing in other ways. There was the awe with which he turned over the pages of the *Guardian* and his addiction to watching *Question Time*. He used English words more and more, was less sharp in his criticism of the West. And this was the same Anwar who had led student demonstrations against the IMF and burnt the American flag. I did not dare ask him if he felt his anti-imperialist convictions contradicted seeking political asylum in London. Perhaps because the Berlin Wall had fallen, he was softening too.

I made a mistake last week and told him about Omar – how he had been caught dealing drugs. But I didn't give him all the details and led him to believe that Omar was serving a short sentence and would be out soon. Anwar's response was, 'What do you expect from a spoilt playboy?' I made him promise not to tell any of the other Sudanese, but even after he promised I felt he might break his promise one day, to prove a point, to make an argument stronger. Since then I had been wary of saying certain things to him.

This holding back disappointed me. I wanted us to be true friends, transparent and unashamed.

I looked at him across the table – at his intelligent eyes and moustache. He was speaking about human rights in the Sudan, the new junta government. He said this had to be stopped and that had to be stopped. He said Sudan had the highest internally displaced population in the world.

'And you and I are displaced,' I said.

'We're not in the same boat. You're very lucky, Najwa. What do you know of imprisonment or torture or just plain poverty? You can't compare yourself with other ordinary people.'

'Of course I didn't mean to compare myself.' I would always be inferior to his 'masses', my problems trivial and less worthy. But sometimes I craved his pity more than love. 'Why do you always put me down?'

'I don't mean to. You're the nicest thing that happened to me in London. It would be unbearable without you.'

'I'm afraid,' I blurted out, 'that what happened in Khartoum will always affect us.' But it was not really what happened, but who I was, whose daughter I was. I searched for the right words. I did not want to mention my father and risk becoming teary.

'Look,' he was smiling, 'here no one knows our background, no one knows whose daughter you are, no one knows my politics. We are both niggers, equals.'

I laughed at his new use of that English word. I wanted to sit close to him, the way we sometimes sat on the bus. Every time he touched me, I forgot that prickly space between us, forgot that if my parents had been alive, they would never have approved of him.

'I wanted you to come with me yesterday.' I had gone to visit my mother's grave.

'I don't like going to cemeteries.' He moved back, took his elbows off the table. 'What's the point?'

'I don't know. I just wanted to do something because it was her anniversary.'

'Did it take you a long time to get there?' He was trying to sound interested.

'Yes, it's at the end of the tube line. It was nice – the weather was better than today.' The cemetery was colourful with grass and flowers. I had to walk quite a bit to get there, down a lane, past open fields. There were families who had parked in the cemetery car park. The children played around the graves, innocent and happy. I sat on a bench and watched them. They made me wish I were a child again. One man stood at the side of a grave, talking or praying, moving his lips. He had so much to say. I wondered what he was saying. He was wearing a cap, which made me think he was religious. I wondered if religious people were comfortable in cemeteries. He seemed religious, raising his hands up to pray. There was no way of knowing if his deceased relative was a man or a woman. All through life there were distinctions – toilets for men, toilets for women; clothes for men, clothes for women – then, at the end, the graves were identical.

I wanted to speak to my mother but I didn't feel she was there. I couldn't imagine her under the ground though I was sure that she was. It was like I knew for sure that one day I too would die but I couldn't imagine it. All my life I had been living. How to imagine any other state? What was my mother feeling now? Did she know I was here? I could ask that religious man. He might know but you couldn't just go up to people and ask them such questions. My mother was vivid and alive in my dreams. She was always in Khartoum, wearing a pretty tobe, on her way out, Musa opening the car door for her, or she was in her room and I was sitting on her bed – how I loved my parents' bed – and she was in front of the mirror combing her hair, dabbing perfume on her neck, chatting with my father, raising her eyebrows, glancing at me in the mirror, and we would laugh, sharing a joke about my father: laughing at his fuss over his clothes, how he liked his moustache just so, at his pride in the brand new suit he had brought on his last trip – Pierre Cardin he would say, not just anything, Pierre Cardin.

There were prayers engraved on the bench. They were blurred but I blinked and made an effort, read them out carefully. I searched for the words, the reason I had phoned Wafaa, and they were there: *Wash my sins with ice.* I need not have phoned her after all.

Before going to the cemetery, I had dialled Wafaa's number. I had kept the piece of paper; I hadn't lost it or thrown it away. A child answered the phone, babbling. He dropped the receiver, picked it up. I couldn't understand what he was saying. 'Call your mother – where's your mother?' I kept saying but it was no use. I nearly gave up when a man picked up the phone. He said '*Salaamu alleikum*' but spoke with a London accent. Was she married to a convert then? I was curious. He said Wafaa was out and asked me if I would like to leave a message.

I said to Anwar, 'It's interesting about converts isn't it? What would make a Westerner become a Muslim?'

He made a face.

'I think they're brave.'

'You say that because as Muslims our self-esteem is so low that we're desperate for approval. And what greater stamp of approval can there be than a white man's?'

He had fixed ideas about religion. The Islamist

159

government in Khartoum was his enemy. He liked to point out its faults and contradictions. I was surprised when he asked, 'Did she phone you back?'

'Yes, she did.'

'What did she want?'

'I was the one who phoned her. Wafaa was just returning my call.'

'I'm sure she invited you to accompany her to a religious lesson or offered to lend you books – they're all the same that type.'

Because he had guessed right, I kept quiet. I did not want him to make fun of her. She had once washed and shrouded my mother; I would always feel a connection to her, a kind of gratitude. She had said, 'My husband and I can pick you up on our way to the mosque. There's a ladies' class tomorrow evening. You don't live far from the mosque, aren't you lucky! Phone me if you want us to pick you up – don't be shy.'

I didn't feel enthusiastic about her suggestion, just faintly sad.

'Do you pray, Najwa?' she asked.

'No . . . no I don't.' I had learnt to pray as a child. I had prayed during Ramadan, during which I fasted mostly in order to lose weight and because it was fun. I prayed during school exams to boost my grades. I liked wearing my mother's white tobe, feeling the material around me. I liked feeling covered, cosy. But I had often bobbed up and down, not understanding what I was saying, impatient to get the whole thing over with.

'But you should pray, Najwa,' Wafaa said, 'so that Allah will bless you. It's the first thing we're going to be asked about on Judgement Day. We're going to be asked about our prayers.' I didn't like her mentioning Judgement Day.

It made me feel nervous and gloomy. But her voice was cajoling and soft as if she were talking to a child, or someone who was ill. She made praying sound easy and possible, she made getting Allah's blessing sound like something within reach, accessible. I wished I could believe that everyone was able to reach out to Allah, that it was possible to be innocent and clear. It would be difficult for me to pray, to remember the times of the prayer, to wash, to find clean cloth to cover myself. It would be an uphill climb. I felt a stab of guilt at my laziness but I pushed it away. Anyway, Anwar would laugh at me if I started to pray, he would really laugh.

Twenty-two

He told me what happened to his leg. They had put it in a pail of ice for a whole day to hurt him, just to hurt him. They had asked him to spy on the activities of the Communist Party, offered him money and a car and, when he refused, took him away and put his leg in a pail of ice. 'That's the tool of torture in the poorest country in the world.' He laughed in a sarcastic way. 'Nothing elaborate, no specially-built torture chambers and no expensive equipment, just a pail of ice.' I started to cry and he said, 'Don't cry. There are others worse than me.' One had to have his leg amputated, others got shot, and others didn't have, like him, a sister in the police to help him escape. But I didn't know the others; I only cared about him. He said he would not be surprised if by now his sister had lost her job or worse. He said he had not said goodbye to his mother. 'I don't want to get depressed,' he said. 'Chat to me, Najwa, about something else.'

I bought him a jacket. I wanted him to look cool; we were in London after all. He liked it. I knew he did by the way he took it out of the bag; by the way he tried it on, slowly as if he was not eager for it, as if he was unconcerned. I was almost breathless to see him look so handsome. He said, 'Thank you,' in an offhand way, became

162

distant for a while. Maybe it hurt his pride to accept a gift from me. He wasn't working. He was not allowed to work until after six months, and then he had to find casual work. What does 'casual' mean? he asked me. He was smoking too much, because he was idle, he said. He had always been active; he had always been involved. 'But you are doing something,' I would tell him, 'you're writing.' He wrote articles for the Arab newspapers based in London. Sometimes, though, he found himself writing about himself, about his childhood, his father. 'I never used to write personal things,' he said, 'but now I wake up in the morning with such vivid memories of Khartoum. I just start jotting them down.' He wrote smoothly and effortlessly in Arabic. It was writing in English that made him struggle, that made him need me. He said, 'I want to write reports for Amnesty International.' He suggested we talk in English all the time, so that his pronunciation would improve. He liked certain words: frustrated, inevitable, sexy. It made us laugh, mixing the two languages, Arabic nouns with English verbs, making up new words that were a compound of both. It made him happy to discover that he could read all the papers for free in the public library. It was warm there too; he didn't like the cold.

But he would sneer at me sometimes, out of the blue. I could never feel entirely safe with him. We would be happy and chatting and then suddenly the conversation would twist. 'You and your family must be the Home Office's ideal asylum seekers – a flat in London, bank accounts filled with the money your father swindled.' Yes, we had the flat but the bank accounts were not full. He said, 'Don't try to kid me, I'm not stupid.' We quarrelled. I hated quarrelling with him, hated that I would explain and explain yet he never believed me. And he had a knack of

163

winning arguments even when I was in the right, even when I was telling the truth. 'Your father must have had another account then, offshore, somewhere else – Switzerland. It's ironic that you can't get hold of the money but believe me it's there.'

I wanted him to meet me halfway but he would argue his point. He would not give in. I learnt that there were reasons behind his moods – bad news about his colleagues and family in Khartoum, the humiliation of having to prove he was a genuine asylum seeker. 'You're too sensitive,' I would tell him, 'they're just asking you routine questions, you'll get it in the end.' He would smile and squeeze my hand, loosen and start to talk. 'I tell them "If the government fell today I would go back tomorrow. I don't want to live here", but they don't believe me.' The number of times he said, 'The bitter reality of Sudan,' until the words floated in my head and I wanted to know how to live with that, how to be happy with that. Change, he would say, revolution. But I had been hurt by change, and the revolution, which killed my father, did not even do him the honour of lasting more than five years.

Anwar liked me to talk about working for Aunty Eva. I told him how she needed me all weekend when her sons and their children came. She needed me on Monday to tidy up after they left and from Thursday to start preparing for their visit. That was why Tuesday and Wednesday were my days off. He said, 'When my six months is up, I'll apply for a security position – many Sudanese have found work in Arab embassies.' He said, 'We're now like the Eritrean refugees in Sudan' and I remembered the lifeguard at the American Club who used to stare at me when I came out of the pool. Maybe he had been educated too and did not want to work as a lifeguard. I had not thought of that before. There were a number of Eritrean bouncers who sat round a table at the entrance of the club and made sure that only members were allowed in. I remember them reading. My eyes would flicker over their books and I'd be surprised – 'Since when did servants read!' – and then I would forget all about them.

'What's wrong with us Africans?' I asked Anwar and he knew. He knew facts and history but nothing he said gave me comfort or hope. The more he talked, the more confused I felt, groping for something simple, but he said nothing was simple, everything was complicated, everything was connected to history and economics. In Queensway, in High Street Kensington, we would watch the English, the Gulf Arabs, the Spanish, Japanese, Malaysians, Americans and wonder how it would feel to have, like them, a stable country. A place where we could make future plans and it wouldn't matter who the government was – they wouldn't mess up our day-to-day life. A country that was a familiar, reassuring background, a static landscape on which to paint dreams. A country we could leave at any time, return to at any time and it would be there for us, solid, waiting. I said to him, 'Thank God my parents didn't divorce. At least I had a stable family – a fractured country but not a broken home.' He said, 'Silly girl,' and laughed as if I had made him forget his worries. 'What does divorce have to do with it?'

He put his arm around me because we were not in Khartoum, because we were in Hyde Park and the few people who walked past didn't stare. They didn't care what we were doing and would not have been surprised. We were free. I could not yet get over that. Freedom enthralled me when I was with him and when I was alone. Like an experiment, it made me hold my breath and wait.

'I missed you.'

'Let's go home. It's cold here; it's uncomfortable. Come with me home. We'll be more private at home.'

'Your flatmates would see me.' But I could ask him to come over to my place. There was no one there. I dared myself to speak. My heart started to beat.

He said, 'Ameen and Kamal are out this time of day.'

'They might come back. What would they think of me?'

'They're very liberal minded. Don't worry about them.'

'They're Sudanese.'

'So am I.'

'Why do you always win arguments?'

He kissed me instead of answering.

'Do you love me?'

'Yes.'

'Why?'

He looked into my eyes. 'Because of the tight skirts you used to wear in university. You don't know what you did to me.'

I laughed. If I went home with him, would he introduce me to his flatmates as his fiancée? I couldn't ask him. But I could go; I could go with him and find out. I would see his room, sit in it, breathe in it. The awe of knowing that it could be easily done, that no one could stop me, was like standing on the brink, daring myself to move further. I stood up and said, 'OK, let's go'. I made my voice calm, my eyes casual so he wouldn't guess I was joking. He was delighted, couldn't believe his luck.

We walked out of the park. 'This way to the station.' He held my elbow.

I smiled. 'No, this way.'

166

He said, suspiciously, 'Where do you want to go?'

'Selfridges.' I laughed at the expression on his face, the realization that I had tricked him. He laughed too; he was in a good mood today. It was fun to try to guess his mood, to gauge how much teasing he could take.

We passed a couple of Arab women dressed in black from head to foot; their faces were veiled. Anwar made a face and, when they were out of earshot, he said, 'It's disgusting, what a depressing sight!'

His expression made me laugh. 'Aren't you curious about all the beauty they're hiding?'

'I'm only curious about this,' he said. He put his arm around me and squeezed my waist. The pressure of his fingers made me giggle.

We went into Selfridges through the door that led into the men's department. My father had liked to buy his clothes from here. Christian Dior shirts, a Burberry jacket that he would only wear in London, red boxer shorts. If I mentioned my father now, Anwar would sneer, make a comment about bourgeois spending and the good feeling between us would go away.

'Do you want to try anything on?' I asked him, 'You don't have to buy it.'

'So what's the point?' He seemed uneasy, taken aback by the largeness of the shop.

I shrugged. 'Just for the fun of it.'

In the perfume hall, I tried on a new perfume, spoke to my mother about it in my head, heard her saying, 'Don't buy it from here, we can get it cheaper at the Duty Free shop.' I lifted my hand for Anwar to smell. He would never believe that my mother had cared about saving money. He thought the rich spent without thinking. His nose brushed against my wrist. He was self-conscious in front of the sales girl; he always became uncomfortable under the gaze of anyone white.

I persuaded him to try on perfume too. 'Enough,' he said when we reached Calvin Klein after Chanel and Paco Rabanne. He still didn't believe me that it was OK not to buy anything, the sales girls didn't care.

Upstairs in the ladies' section, I tried on an evening dress. It fitted perfectly, was low cut, sleeveless. With satin against my skin and my eyes shining I was not in London but going to a wedding at the Khartoum Hilton, my mother complaining that the dress was too revealing but my father indulgent, having the final say, 'Leave her, let her wear what she likes.' I walked out of the changing room and some shoppers turned to look. The elderly sales lady put on her glasses and said, 'It's lovely on you.' Her voice was low as if she knew from long experience that I would not buy it. I laughed when I saw Anwar's face, the way he forgot to be nervous of the sales lady and was ogling. For a minute I was completely happy, fulfilled. His admiration was like a prize.

On our way out, I bought a box of Millie's cookies. We ate them in the bus going to the Victoria and Albert Museum, which Anwar wanted to visit. We sat on the top deck because he wanted to smoke even though the stairs bothered his leg. 'We could be happy in London,' I said. 'We could forget all about the problems in Sudan.' He didn't reply. For him, more than for me, London was temporary, exotic. His life was on hold, he was constantly waiting to go back and take up his rightful place. When the government fell (he did not allow me to say 'if' – it had to fall, he said, it must fall) we would go back to Khartoum and get married.

'How did you describe me to your flatmates?' I wanted him to say, 'As my fiancée.'

168

'I told them we were together in university. I told them you were pretty.'

'Pretty? Every other girl in university was pretty.'

He smiled. 'When they meet you they'll know you're stunning.'

'And what else did you say?' I bit into my chocolate chip cookie. It was how I liked it best, melting.

'That your English is excellent.'

'What else?'

'Nothing.'

I raised my eyebrows. 'Really. Nothing,' he said and with his thumb wiped a chocolate smudge from the corner of my mouth.

I didn't believe him. He would have spoken about my father for sure.

Twenty-three

I bought him the best, most up-to-date computer and the day it was delivered was the first day I went to his flat. We set it up in his room, which was small and smelled of cigarettes. I opened the window for fresh air, something he apparently never did because he did not like the cold. Beside the open-plan kitchen and sitting room, there were two other bedrooms in the flat. The largest one belonged to Ameen, whose father owned the flat. I liked him straight away. He was flabby and smiling, his manners gentle and diplomatic. He was a doing a PhD in Chemistry down the road at Imperial College but always seemed laid back about his studies. I imagined that Anwar expected me to be like Ameen, upper class but committed to the communist cause, lavishing on it bourgeois money. Kamal was different, studying on a scholarship, aspiring. I didn't like the way he studied me, as if I were a puzzle to be figured out. He never looked at me directly. He was always shifting his eyes, but not from shyness. It was something else. A rivalry sprang up between us. It was silly but he took it seriously. Anwar would go on about how good my English was, better than Kamal's who was specializing in it. He would joke about it but I think Kamal took offence and took every opportunity to put me in my place. Ameen and

Kamal kept different hours to Anwar. They would be arriving or leaving while I was there, would stroll into Anwar's room for a chat. They never knocked – they never had to with the door wide open – and this informality pleased me. They acted as if I were a cousin or a sister, as if Anwar and I could not possibly be doing anything wrong. This lulled me.

The summer was not sunny, not fresh but clammy, close. I knew Anwar's moods now. Rage when he couldn't get a security job (they turned him down because of his leg) and afterwards the quiet bitterness. He worked nights in a restaurant instead, the same Ethiopian restaurant he had taken me to. Often he brought back food and, unless the other had got to it first, I would heat it when I came during my days off. We would eat together with his papers and the computer between us. He did not know how to touch-type but I did. We sat with the computer manual and learnt Word Perfect together. Sometimes he gave me things he had written by hand and I typed them in. Or he would have started a file and I would go over it, checking the grammar. He insisted that I learn to type Arabic too. He dictated to me and I typed. It made us both feel important.

One day he said he had written a poem about me.

'Show it to me.'

'No, you might not like it.' He smiled, holding the paper out of my reach.

'Please.'

He shook his head but I managed to snatch it and ended up laughing on his lap. The poem was direct, simply erotic.

'Are you angry?' He was smiling, not caring if I was.

'Of course not.' I wanted him to think me daring.

Ameen poked his head into the room and I put the poem

171

away. 'Come, let's play cards,' he said. It was twelve o'clock and he had just got up, looking puffy. 'I'll wait for you in the sitting room. We can drink a glass of tea, have a bite to eat.' He was hinting that he would like us to make tea, crack some eggs for breakfast. Because this was his flat, he expected the others to wait on him. Poor Ameen. Like Aunty Eva and so many of us, he felt deprived without his Khartoum servants. It was as if he was waiting for them to magically reappear, to clear up after him, to make the flat neat. We heard him putting on the TV, the blare of the news. Anwar closed the door and kissed me. He was different and I was different because I hadn't been angry about his poem.

It was inevitable that one day I would sit on his bed, that he would put his arms around me and ask, 'Haven't you teased me enough?' We had circled each other for months, flirted for months, all the time aware that we were in London, conscious that we were free. And I had known in the back of my mind, that I would hold out and then give in to that side of me that was luxurious and lazy, that needed to be stroked and pampered and through him never be the same again. Afterwards, after the playing and the seriousness, such silence. I could hear the hum of the computer. The grating sound of the key opening the door of the flat, Ameen's excited voice, 'Anwar, did you hear the news, come and hear the news.'

We leapt up, scurrying, guilty. Yes, guilty. And it was a relief that Ameen headed straight to the sitting room, the familiar on and off blare of the TV as he searched the channels for the news. Anwar and I thought the same thing: 'A coup in Sudan, the government has fallen.' Another coup. Musical chairs, the carpet pulled out from underneath

172

someone else's feet. Anwar dashed out of the room. We could go back now, I thought, and pick up our lives again. I could go back to the university, be a student again, Anwar would get his job back. We would get married.

I walked to the bathroom, conscious of every step, a little dazed, like I had been feverish for a long time and now was cool. I walked slowly as if I were fragile. My right hand was too weak to flush the toilet or turn the tap – I needed both hands. My face in the mirror looked as if nothing had happened. My hair was dishevelled as if I had been asleep. I smoothed it down with water, cleared my throat. Would my voice sound normal? 'Yellow suits me,' I thought and a memory came of another bathroom mirror, of me admiring myself while Baba packed and Mama fussed over him. Admiring myself in my yellow pyjamas, while Baba left the house for the last time. I should have been with him instead. When I vomited into the basin, there were bits of tomato like flecks of blood.

The room looked wrong, messy, student-like and smelled of Anwar's cigarettes. It should not be like this. It should be a room in the best hotel in Khartoum, my wedding dress hanging in the cupboard, the sheets white and crisp. A view of the Nile and henna on my hands. I would slip my arms through the sleeves of a new dressing gown that matched my nightdress. Mama had bought me that set from Selfridges, peach-coloured, expensive. And she would have told the sales girl that her daughter was getting married and they would have smiled the smile they save for foreigners with money. I should not be wearing my ordinary jeans and yellow T-shirt. My mother should be a phone call away, anxious, waiting to ask, 'Are you all right?'

Anwar came into the room, smiling, shaking his head, and tapping his finger to his forehead. 'Ameen is mad. He's excited and the news has nothing to do with Sudan.'

'What happened?'

'Saddam Hussein invaded Kuwait.'

So the Khartoum government hadn't fallen and we were not going back.

'Why are you so glum? Are you all right?' He was trying to be kind but he was thinking of the news. I said, 'I have to go home, I'm not in the mood for Ameen.' He understood and did not urge me to stay. I walked down Gloucester Road and thought that whatever happened to me, whatever happens in the world, London remained the same, constant; continuous underground trains, the newsagents selling Cadbury's chocolates, the hurried footsteps of people leaving work. That was why we were here: governments fell and coups were staged and that was why we were here. For the first time in my life, I disliked London and envied the English, so unperturbed and grounded, never displaced, never confused. For the first time, I was conscious of my shitty-coloured skin next to their placid paleness. What was wrong with me today? I had a warm bath when I got home. I heated up a tin of soup. My dislike of London went away and left me feeling ill.

He said, 'I love you more than before.' I wasn't sure whether I loved him more or less or just the same. I belonged to him more now, he knew me now more that anyone else and more than my family even knew me. It was strange that someone could come close to me like that. His voice became distant as I worked out when my next period was due. Who would care if I became pregnant, who would be scandalized? Aunty Eva, Anwar's flatmates. Omar would never know unless I wrote to him. Uncle Saleh was across

174

the world. A few years back, getting pregnant would have shocked Khartoum society, given my father a heart attack, dealt a blow to my mother's marriage, and mild, modern Omar, instead of beating me, would have called me a slut. And now nothing, no one. This empty space was called freedom.

'Talk to me, Najwa, don't daydream.' Imagine telling Anwar about a peach satin nightdress, clothes bought specially for a honeymoon. He said the soreness would go away. He said the guilt would go away. 'Like every other Arab girl,' he said, 'you've been brainwashed about the importance of virginity.'

He was right about the soreness but the guilt didn't go away. His stories of prospective Sudanese brides paying for operations to restore their virginity depressed me. He had a friend, a doctor, he said, who was doing quite well performing illegal abortions on unmarried girls. 'You would think them demure,' he said, 'covering their hair and acting coy, but all that is hypocrisy, social pressure. Do you remember the girls who went missing whose photos were shown on TV? They weren't lost, these girls, they weren't missing – they were killed by their brothers or fathers then thrown in the Nile.'

He went on as if I were a child who needed to be taught the facts of life, as if I lived in a happy, innocent world and needed shaking up. 'Arab society is hypocritical,' he would say, 'with double standards for men and women.' I remembered how Omar was allowed to smoke and drink beer and I was not. The seedy parties he went to without taking me. I had taken these things for granted, not questioned them. Anwar told me that most of the guys in university used to visit brothels. Then they would beat up their sister if they so much as saw her talking to a boy.

'Did you go to a brothel?' I asked him and knew he would say yes.

'There was a girl there who became attached to me.' He laughed a little. She was an Ethiopian refugee as so many of them were. He seemed surprised that a young prostitute would have feelings for him. It annoyed me that he was talking about her as if she were a pet.

'Why shouldn't she love you? You were probably nice to her.'

He laughed and said, 'Are you jealous, Najwa?' I threw a pillow at him and he ducked.

He tried a different line of argument. He talked about the West, about the magazines I read – *Cosmo* and *Marie Claire*. 'Tell me,' he said, 'how many twenty-five-year-old girls in London are virgins?' That was when I laughed and felt a little better. It became a game for us, every time we were out, looking at girls. 'Is she? Isn't she?' He was right, I was in the majority now, I was a true Londoner now. I could take a quiz in a magazine: 'How Hot is Your Love life?' or 'Rate Him as a Lover!' I could circle the answers based on experience not on imagination. 'I know you're Westernized, I know you're modern,' he said, 'that's what I like about you – your independence.'

But I would have preferred the breathlessness of a wedding, its glow of approval, not his room smelling of cigarettes, the sheets he rarely changed, not his flatmates' laughter, the knowing way they now looked at me. At times there would be a moment of clarity, a moment with no sound, no touch and I would wonder, staring at a strand of my hair clinging to his pillow, what I was doing, how had I gone that far? Did Omar wake up to see prison walls and prison sheets and did he wonder for a second what he was doing?

Anwar said, 'You can't still be feeling guilty, you're enjoying yourself too much.' He laughed and said, 'If your conscience was troubling you, you wouldn't be so eager now.' So I kept my thoughts to myself. They churned in my head, my active, uneducated mind; my kind of loneliness. 'You have become quiet,' he said, 'you have become dreamy.' I dreamed of nothing, no happy dreams and no sad dreams. I lay in my bed awake, listening to the sounds of the street; the windows wide open because of the heat. I remembered things I had left behind in Khartoum: a pair of beige sandals, a poster of Boney M, my schoolbooks and photos. Where were these things now – in whose hands had they fallen? Our house was looted. It was looted for the television sets, the video recorders, the silver, freezers, cars, hi-fi system and cameras. Even the air conditioners were stripped from the walls, the fans unhooked from the ceilings. It was looted because my father was a symbol, even more than the President had been, of an order that was being usurped. His letter opener made of ivory; my mother's china and crystal glasses – did they smash in the chaos or were they delicately taken away? I would never know. I should forget, let go. Yet I could still feel a tattered Enid Blyton book in my hand, smell the chlorine clinging to my swimsuit, a copy of *Cosmopolitan* borrowed from Randa and never returned.

I phoned her up in Edinburgh to apologize for the magazine. She laughed. 'I can't believe it! It's been five years – how can you remember it?'

'There's a novel too – I never got round to returning it,' I said. 'One by Danielle Steele.'

'Ach, I don't read her any more. I've moved on.' There was a laugh in her voice. It made me feel like I was old and pedantic.

177

I could lie in bed all day. A phone call to Aunty Eva to say I was not feeling well, then back to bed to stare at the ceiling, and I would look at my watch and, strangely enough, an hour had passed just like that, two hours, three. I liked it when I had my period and Anwar kept away from me. The guilt lost its edge then. I liked it that he was not too keen on us meeting in my flat. The aura of my parents weighed on me. Aunty Eva did a clear out and gave me piles of magazines. I cut out the pictures of princesses in exile: daughters of the Shah, daughters of the late King of Egypt, the descendants of the Ottoman Sultan. They were all floating in Europe knowing they were royal, but it didn't matter, it didn't matter any more. Muslim countries had rejected the grandeur of kings and wanted revolutions instead. After his fall, the daughter of the Emperor Haile Selassie was imprisoned for years in a small room. 'Well, I know for sure whose side I'm on,' Anwar would say, 'the side of the people.' He would be happy if Britain became a republic and I would be sad. Uncle Nabeel bought the new biography of Prince Charles and when he finished with it, I read it from cover to cover. 'You waste your time,' Anwar said but the books he gave me to read always disturbed me.

Out of the blue, Wafaa phoned me. But it was not really out of the blue. She had been phoning once every two or three months, saying the usual things, come with me to the mosque, come to a Ladies' Eid Party, so have you started to pray like you promised you would? This time her voice seemed to come from another planet. 'So, Najwa, have you started to pray?' I nearly laughed out loud. I was further away than she thought; I was out of it now. She had no idea. If my heart had been soft, I would have burst into tears and asked her how to repent. But my heart was not soft. I saw Wafaa through Anwar's eyes; a backward fundamentalist, someone to look down on. My voice was cold when I answered her questions, yes, no, sorry I'm busy, got to go. Unless she was completely thick skinned, she would never phone me again. Yes, I wanted to pray in the same way that I wanted to sprout wings and fly. There was no point in yearning, was there? No point in stretching out. In my own way, in my own style, I was sliding. First my brother, and now it was my turn to come down in the world.

Part Four

2003–4

Twenty-four

I am shy when speaking in front of a large gathering. There must be more than a hundred ladies at this Eid party. They chat and laugh and their children squeal and run about. Presumably, when I start reading the prayer, they will quieten down. Mai tugs at my dress. Her mother had refused to let me take the day off and now she refuses to let any of my friends hold her. She stays close by my side, suspicious, unused to being in a crowded place. Around us the mood is silky, tousled, non-linear; there is tinkling laughter, colours, that mixture of sensitivity and waywardness which the absence of men highlights. My voice sounds strange in the microphone. Still the children run around, a baby is wailing. I only agreed to do this because Um Waleed nagged me. She said it was only right that different sisters should get a chance to participate. 'It's only a short prayer,' she insisted. 'You're so well liked, everyone will enjoy seeing you as part of the programme.' I remind myself that I must not mumble. It gets easier as I go along. 'My Lord, we have believed in Your Messenger Muhammad without seeing him, please don't deprive us of seeing him in the Hereafter.' Everyone murmurs, 'Peace be upon him.' I hold up the paper closer to my face, my sight is not what it used to be and I am too vain to wear glasses. 'My Lord, You are the One who created us, You are the One who guides us, You are the One who feeds us and when we fall ill You are the One who cures us. My Lord forgive us our sins . . .' My voice breaks, the words blur. Yet I am not sad, this is a happy occasion and I am happy that I belong here, that I am no longer outside, no longer defiant. One more line to go. 'My Lord give us from your Mercy and blessing so that we can love what You love and so that we can love all those actions and words that bring us closer to You.'

I put the microphone down on the table and scoop Mai up in my arms. On the way to my seat I greet those of my friends I hadn't seen earlier, the few I hadn't met yesterday at the Eid prayer. We are pleased to see each other without our hijabs and all dressed up for the party, delighted by the rare sight of each other's hair, the skin on our necks, the way make-up brightens a face. We look at each and smile in surprise. It is not only the party clothes; some of us are transformed without our hijabs. For a split second I cannot connect the tight trouser suit, the geometrically cut blonde hair, the perfectly applied make-up with the young woman who is usually covered in sombre black, pushing her hyperactive toddler in a pushchair. Today she is as glamorous as a guest on a television talk show. She smiles at me and now I know another side of her, that she is chic and sharp. Even her nails are painted today. It is time for Um Waleed to talk. She talks about how Ramadan was special and now it is over. Throughout Ramadan, Allah had been decorating Paradise for those who were fasting. 'Imagine,' she says, moving her hands, 'it's just as if you are expecting guests and you get everything nice and ready for them.' Without her hijab, in a tight crimson party dress, her hair tinted, her face brimming with make-up,

184

she looks so Arab, so unsubtle that I think this is how she is, her secret self. She is not by nature a puritan, not by nature reserved or austere. It is only faith that makes her a Qur'an teacher with hardly any pay, pleading with us to learn, to change. It is not her personality that makes her cover her soft ample body in a huge *abaya*. The alarmed look in her eyes is not really alarm – it is her own excitement over life.

She speaks about Eid and how the angels are handing out gifts to us. Then she tells us to try and keep up all the high standards of Ramadan, not to slack off like we usually do. The extra prayers, the extra charity, the daily reading of the Qur'an, not back-biting, not gossiping, not envying, not lying – we should make the intention of keeping them up throughout the year. 'And don't forget the voluntary fast of six days of Shawaal. If you can't do six, do five, four. Even fasting one day is better than nothing.' Her words will stay with me – they always do. Strange that she is not my friend, I can't confide in her and when we are alone the conversation hardly flows. Our natures are not harmonious; we orbit different paths. One day she will move on and forget me yet, when she speaks about Allah, when she says, 'He is talking to us, aren't we lucky? We can open the Qur'an and He is talking directly to us,' there is a breakthrough in my understanding, a learning fresh as lightning. When she says, '*Ya habibi, ya Rasul Allah*', I feel I love the Prophet as much as she does.

In the lull between Um Waleed's talk and the next item on the programme, there are more hellos, memories of sisters who were with us in past Eid parties but who have now moved away. There are more children in new clothes to kiss and admire, the surprise – I almost squeal – of seeing a friend for the first time without her hijab. This one is all peaches and cream, this one is like a model, this one is mumsy with or without her hijab, this one in her smart jacket looks like she wants to chair a board meeting. This one with the glasses and unruly hair looks like a student and she is one, but this one looks like a belly dancer and she is definitely not. She is the staid wife of a lucky doctor with four daughters kept well under control. This one looks like a tomboy. I can imagine her, when she was young, playing football with her brothers; now she's a nursery teacher. This one looks Indian, as if the hijab had made me forget she was Indian and now she is reminding me – in the sari with her flowing hair and jewellery, she is relaxed, traditional. And the one who looks like a model confesses to me in a whisper, don't tell anyone else, Najwa, please, but she was actually Miss Djibouti long ago, before coming to Britain, before having children and covering her hair with a scarf.

I am told: 'You look like a gypsy,' and I laugh. It must be my earrings and curly hair, the skirt of my dress. Or perhaps I look intriguing, with secrets I don't want to share. This is not a fancy-dress party. But it is as if the hijab is a uniform, the official, outdoor version of us. Without it, our nature is exposed.

Children sing as part of the programme. There is a short play, awkward and badly produced but it still pulls a few laughs. Then Shahinaz dances. She has been practising for weeks – she wanted to get it right, to make it perfect. I hold Mai up so that she can see better. 'Look at Aunty, doesn't she look like a princess?' A drumbeat and I watch her feet, her ankle bracelet, the way she moves her hands. None of us can take our eyes off her. Only baby Ahmed is oblivious, chubby and gorgeous in a new sailor suit complete with a hat. When his grandmother brings him over and they sit next to me, I take him from her and hug him. I kiss his smooth cheeks and dimpled hands. Not all babies inspire in me the feelings he does. I whisper in his ears, 'Are you going to be as good at dancing as your mummy, are you?' He laughs and I look up at Shahinaz, delicate and skilled – it is as if we are watching a proper performance, a film. I catch her eldest daughter watching her, fascinated, as if she is finding it hard to believe that this moving vision is her mum.

In comparison, when we Arabs dance it is all laughter and chaos, nothing ordered, nothing practised. But even Shahinaz finds it hard to copy us, though I know that she has often practised at home. I am warm from the dancing. It makes me laugh but it distresses Mai to see me different. I hold her in my lap until it is time to eat.

While we balance paper plates and children, Shahinaz tells me that she has applied as a mature student to do a degree in social work. I congratulate her and she talks about next year, how her mother-in-law will look after the children, how busy she'll be. 'You haven't been to my house this Eid,' she says and invites me to go home with her for the rest of the day.

'I wish I could but I have to take Mai home.'

She stands up to kiss me goodbye. 'We used to see each other every night at Taraweeh prayers and now everyone will get busy again.'

I know what she means. Ramadan had brought us close together. For a month the mosque had been full of people. We were making an effort, sloughing off our faults, quietened down with hunger. In the last ten nights, it was even more crowded, the recitation more powerful, all of us listening to the same verses, enjoying the same mood. Once, a women next to me remarked, 'Today I almost felt like I was in Mecca. It's the same feeling, all the people gathering and the spiritual pleasure.'

Now that Ramadan is over I wonder where I got my energy from – fasting all day while working, then, instead of going home, going straight to the mosque. There I would break my fast, wedged in the crowd, sometimes there was hardly a place to sit and then we would all stand up to pray, and suddenly there was more space and the imam would start to recite.

In Ramadan I was chauffeur-driven home every night. This miracle took the shape of the wife of the Senegalese Ambassador, one of the many women who come to the mosque only in Ramadan. She prayed next me, shoulder to shoulder, every evening just because we happened to like the same spot, away from the radiator, close to the window with the night air coming in from the street. I didn't tell her that, once upon a time, diplomats like her husband and even the President of the Sudan were regular visitors in my father's house. I didn't tell her more than my name and what I did. There was no need – we had come together to worship and it was enough. Our movements matched; she didn't fidget while standing and that pleased me; she stood close to me and didn't irritate me by leaving a gap. Evening after evening, every day for three weeks, we stood and knelt together. Then our periods swung and arrived at the same time. One day I was praying and she was not there. The next day I was absent too.

On the drive home, we hardly talked and she instructed her chauffeur to drop her off first. I liked that about her. She was kind without being condescending. In her smooth luxurious car, I used to doze to the sound of the car's indicator and her voice speaking on a mobile phone in Senegalese. I would dive in dreams to become small again, pampered by my parents. They loved me and I was safe with them, special. I made them laugh. The rest of the year I have hope but in Ramadan I have confidence, the certainty that, if I keep plodding this path, Allah will give me back that happiness again, will replace the past with something grander, more potent and enhanced.

Tamer is in the flat when we get back. I see his shoes in the hall but he is in his room with the door closed. I give Mai her dinner. She is hungry because she had refused to eat anything at the Eid party. Even the party bag each child was given, full of sweets, balloons and crayons, stayed clutched in her fist, unopened. She relaxes now that she is back in familiar surroundings. The kitchen is as we left it this morning, with her highchair and the dinner I had quickly cooked knowing I wouldn't have enough time in the evening. She sings and babbles away, banging her spoon on the table. 'You'll wake your uncle,' I say. 'Maybe he's asleep.'

He had spent the last ten days of Ramadan in seclusion at the mosque. Lamya disapproved. She told me so in a rare moment of friendliness. 'He's missing days of classes, how will he ever catch up! It's so unnecessary. I don't know why he does these weird things.' He came back home the last evening of Ramadan with a large bag of laundry and a scraggly beard. He looked right through me, his eyes clear and shining, as if he really could see other things, as if he had been through a cleansing, humbling experience. I long to hear him talk about it, what it is like to spend days away from it all, fasting and praying and reading Qur'an.

He walks into the kitchen carrying in both hands what looks like a box inside a plastic bag. He says it is for me;

189

it is for the Eid. He smiles and, though we had not spoken for days, it is as if our friendship is taking off from where we left it. I wipe my hands on my apron and open the box. It is fine buttery biscuits submerged in castor sugar: Eid *ka'ak*. I thank him and he ignores me, ruffles Mai's hair, lifts her from her highchair. She shows him her bag of goodies and I explain about the party.

He stops smiling and says, 'Lamya should have given you the day off.'

'It's no problem. Mai was no trouble there at all.'

'But still, Lamya made a mistake. If I had known, I would have spoken to her about it.'

'She probably has important classes she can't miss.'

'She doesn't have classes. She's doing a PhD.'

I shrug. 'Well, it's over and done with. You needn't be concerned about it.'

He looks straight at me, his bright eyes even more intense since he'd done the retreat. 'It's nice for Mai that she went with you. What has her mother done for her? Nothing. No new dress, no toys, no outings.'

I automatically defend her. 'She's busy with her studies . . .'

He interrupts. 'Studying, studying, it's an obsession with this family! It's actually a religious obligation to celebrate. We should be happy, we should give it time.'

I offer him one of the *ka'ak*, as a way of changing the subject. He shakes his head, 'No, they're for you.'

'Please. We can have them with tea.'

He sits down and I fetch plates from the cupboard, put the kettle on.

He says, 'Instead of complaining that Lamya hasn't done anything for Mai, I should do something.' I smile and he goes on. 'If you would like, we could take her tomorrow to the zoo, if you like . . .' He sounds vague, it's shyness.

'Tomorrow is my day off.' I am going to see Omar.

'After tomorrow then.'

I nod and in the pause that follows say, 'Tell me about your seclusion at the mosque. What was it like?'

'I found the first two days hard but at the end I didn't want to leave. It felt strange at the beginning not to watch TV, not to go to lectures. Time went slowly. I missed having my own bathroom, sleeping on a bed. There were quite a lot of us there and while I was asleep they'd be talking in a loud voice or reciting Qur'an. I couldn't sleep well. Then, after the second day, I got used to it, like I settled into it and I didn't mind any more about the bathroom or the curry they gave us at three o'clock in the morning for *suhur*. Imagine!'

I laugh. 'I can only eat cereal or toast at that time in the morning. I can never eat a proper meal.'

'I'm the same, but cereal was in short supply.'

'Next year, next Ramadan you must remember to be well stocked.'

'Yeah,' he says as if next year is too far to think about. I used to have that feeling too when I was young, that time was slow and heavy. Now it skips along; these moments watching him relax, hanging on to his smile.

'You looked changed the day you came out of seclusion. Like there was a light coming from your face.'

'Have I lost it now?' The almost girlish interest in himself.

I pause. 'No.'

He makes a face; he doesn't believe me.

'You won't lose it that fast.'

He had not said this to anyone else, I can tell from his voice, the slow words. 'I did feel spiritually strong. I did reach a kind of detachment, like things didn't matter, not in a careless, angry sort of way but more like I could take them in my stride. So what if I didn't like what I was studying, it would just be three years and they'll pass fast. But the feeling didn't last long. I couldn't get it to last. While it did though, while I was there, I was happy.'

I take my first bite of *ka'ak*, savour the sweetness, the way it sticks to my teeth. Looking at him across the table, I become conscious that I am celebrating; I am not fasting any more. I have danced in the afternoon and now this gift in the evening. Happiness makes me bold enough to say, 'Can I ask you something but promise you will answer with the truth?'

'Yes.' He's serious, both hands around his mug of tea.

'Did Lamya tell you to get me these biscuits?'

He shakes his head, 'No, she didn't.'

'She didn't say to you, "Tamer do me a favour, get something for the maid for Eid"?'

He smiles, 'No, she didn't.'

'So why are you smiling?'

'I am just smiling.'

'It sounds like you're not telling the truth.'

He smiles. 'I am. Really. Do you want me to swear?'

Twenty-five

I try and take the feeling of Eid to Omar but the prison puts me in my place. It shrinks me like it shrinks him. I wish it would purify him, wring him and bring him back to me restored. Instead, it contains, habilitates. He had been put through courses designed to make him 'address his crime', 'acknowledge his guilt'. But there is no catharsis, no purge. There are things that can't be said, thoughts that never see the light of day. I wish that he had been punished the very first time he took drugs. Punished according to the Shariah – one hundred lashes. I do wish it in a bitter, useless way because it would have put him off, protected him from himself.

'Did you know,' he says, 'that when I first came in I was put in the hospital wing? They do that to everyone who is sentenced for more than four years. They want to make sure we don't try and kill ourselves.'

'How horrible.'

'What's horrible? That we would want to commit suicide or that they would stop us?'

'It's all horrible.'

His voice is soft. 'You shouldn't visit me, Najwa. It upsets you. All these years you've been coming.'

'Don't be silly. I have to . . .'

'You feel it's some kind of duty, don't you?' When he speaks like this, he is not Sudanese any more. He has forgotten the fusion of duty, love and need. It is impossible for me not to visit him. As long as he is in prison, I am punished too.

I say, 'I phoned Uncle Saleh to say Eid Mubarak. He sends you his regards and asked why you've stopped writing.'

Omar shrugs. 'It's not easy to write. I haven't seen him for years.' He takes off his glasses and cleans them with the edge of his shirt.

'Well, I asked him if he was going to come here or go to Sudan. He said he doesn't like travelling any more, especially such long distances. It tires him.'

Omar puts his glasses back on. 'How's your work?'

I tell him about Tamer's seclusion at the mosque. It amuses him. He laughs and calls Tamer a fanatic. I feel disloyal but I am pleased that he is laughing, listening to me. But I can't sustain his interest for long. We withdraw, I to my thoughts of Tamer, and Omar to I don't know what. I don't know what goes on in his mind.

'I'll be coming out soon,' he says, shifting in his seat. 'Within a year, maybe after six months.'

He could have been out seven years ago. But he was discovered with drugs just before he was due for parole and lost his chance. Now I force myself to sound positive, to sound like I believe in him. 'That's wonderful! What will you do?'

'Go to Burger King.' He laughs a little and looks away from me.

'I mean what will you do about work. Will you look for a job, will you train?'

He folds his arms. 'Yeah, I'll be assigned to a probation

194

officer. They'll give me advice.' He wipes his forehead and I realize he is wary, maybe even afraid of coming out. Perhaps it will hurt, the way light hurts after being too long in the dark.

I blurt out, 'If I had the money, you could go back to Sudan. There you can start all fresh. No one there knows what you've done or where you've been the past fifteen years.'

He shakes his head. 'I would only go back there for a visit,' he says, 'to prove that Baba was innocent. They never had any hard evidence against him and I can prove it.'

I remember how Omar and my father used to argue. Yet now Omar is his staunchest defender. 'I want to clear his name,' he says.

And what do I want for my father? Every day I pray that Allah will forgive him; every day I ask mercy for his soul. But I am not motivated to clear his name. A sentence was passed and we have to live with the consequences.

I ask Omar, 'What good will it do him to clear his name?'

'It will do us good. We might get back some of our inheritance that the government took – the house or the farm.'

'Maybe.' I imagine a long bitter fight and little gain.

Omar insists. 'Just to prove that it was all lies against him, all motivated by malice and politics.'

'But for him, where he is now, it is better if we pray, if we give money to the poor. That's what matters when you're dead.'

'When you're dead, you're dead, Najwa, and nothing else matters.' He sits back in his chair and a world separates us in spite of genes and love.

'You're wrong; things are not what they appear. Why are you here?'

'What are you talking about? You know why I'm here.' He's annoyed now. I must not make him annoyed because he might stop sending me VOs and I will not see him again. But I feel different today and so I say, 'You are here because you broke Mama's heart. A son shouldn't hurt his mother. She cursed you with bad luck and Allah listens to a mother's prayer.'

He looks down at the ground. 'I didn't hurt her.'

'You pushed her. She was ill and you pushed her.'

'I didn't mean to. She wouldn't give me her purse. It was my money. She made me so angry!'

When Tamer asks me, 'Why is your brother in prison?' I say, 'Because he stabbed someone and almost got them killed.'

We are walking home from the zoo. The caged foreign animals weighed me down and only Tamer's company and Mai's joy made the outing pleasant.

I say, 'It was one of the policemen who was arresting him. They were arresting him for selling drugs.'

'How, how did he do it?' He is excited by this violence; there is a ring in his voice. He is especially handsome today, the cold brightening his skin. It hurts to look at him.

'With a knife.'

'A penknife?'

'A Stanley knife.'

He breathes out as if to say 'Wow', but reason takes over and he sobers down. 'That's terrible.'

'Omar didn't know the man was police. He wasn't dressed like a policeman.'

'Plain-clothed,' he says, 'that's what they call them.'

196

'Yes, there were two of them. They followed him to arrest him and he fought them.' Years of secrecy and now I am spilling all this out to a kid. I realize that I have never been able to visualize the violence I am describing. I am saying words without pictures coming to my head. It's denial. Denial of the harm my own flesh and blood can do. We leave the road and go down to the path along the canal. It is easier to talk away from the traffic, more gentle. Mai turns to gaze at the water.

'Can I come with you next time you visit him in prison?'

I laugh. 'Why would you want to do that?'

He shrugs. 'To see what it's like.'

I explain why he can't. He is clean and should not be fascinated by sin. I explain about visiting orders and his eyes don't leave my face. 'I feel sorry for you,' he says. I need this from him. It feels right, nourishing. Then he asks me if Omar has ever tried to escape, like prisoners do in films. He flickers between soulful depth and immaturity. This flickering is attractive; it absorbs my attention.

Twenty-six

'How come you're not married?' He is self-conscious now, avoiding my eyes like he knows he's stepping into new territory.

'I don't know.'

He raises his eyebrows.

'OK I'll try again. Fate.'

'That doesn't tell me anything.'

I shrug. 'When I was your age, I imagined I would get married, have children, the usual things. I didn't imagine anything different. I had friends who wanted to be doctors, diplomats but I never had these ambitions.'

He looks at me and says nothing. Mai turns around from the television and asks for crisps. I get her a packet from the kitchen and when I sit down it is an opportunity to change the subject. 'While you were out, Hisham, Lamya's husband, phoned.'

'He's probably confused about the time difference.'

'I asked him if he wanted to speak to Mai but he said no need.'

Tamer makes a face. 'Typical.'

Hisham's voice had not inspired sympathy. I didn't think, 'Poor man, abandoned by his wife while she does her PhD.' He seemed well in control, hardy.

'He's not at all like you.'

'Of course not.' The words come out of him stiff. 'I told Lamya not to marry him because he drinks. But she doesn't mind. And neither my mum nor my dad listened to me. They thought I was just a kid.'

I imagine him young, twelve or thirteen, voicing an opinion that seemed to his listeners irrelevant. He is not happy today; he is not himself. I ask him why.

He says, 'At dawn I didn't get up to pray. I just couldn't. When the alarm went, I put it off and went back to sleep. Now I feel the whole day's gone out of balance.'

'Well, you did set the alarm last night. You can't blame yourself for not trying.'

'I know. It's just that I feel I've missed out.' He pauses and says, 'If I were married, my wife would have made sure I got up to pray.'

I smile. 'It depends on what type of girl you marry.'

'Oh, I would only marry someone who was devout. And she would have to wear hijab.' There is an upbeat youthfulness in his confidence.

I change the subject. 'How are your studies?' It is the wrong thing to ask because he becomes gloomy again.

'I don't care any more. Maybe the world will end and it won't matter what I study.'

'Maybe it won't.'

'Maybe,' he says without interest. He stretches out on the sofa. It crosses my mind that Lamya would disapprove of this. She would say that the sofa is for guests to sit on. He stares straight up at the ceiling; his face is tired, a little drawn. He lost weight in Ramadan and has not yet regained it. He is carrying a burden, studying a subject that does not interest him, insisting that strong faith would make it lighter. I overheard him yesterday pleading with his father on the phone to allow him to transfer his studies to another university, where he could study Islamic History instead of Business. Afterwards he locked himself up in his room. When I knocked, carrying coffee and cake, he said, 'Leave me alone, I don't want anything.' He didn't want me to know that he was crying.

'I spoke to my dad yesterday,' he says as if he can read my mind. 'He said it was still early days and I will get used to the course soon and start to enjoy it.'

'Maybe he is right.' I wish the television didn't have to be on but it is the only way to keep Mai quiet.

'I don't think he was listening to me. He will never change his point of view.' He mimics his father's voice, the accent. 'If you study Business you will get a good job. Studying Islamic History is for losers. Where will it get you?'

'You could teach.' I close my eyes and imagine him older, teaching.

'There isn't much money in that – that's what he says.'

'Maybe you can study both.'

'No.' He pauses and then says, 'My mum is coming soon – just for a few days on her way to a conference in the States.'

'That's nice,' I say and I mean it. 'It will be nice for you to see your mother.'

'It won't make a difference, she's on his side.'

'But they've already paid the fees. How can you just drop out? Then you'll have to pay fees in another university too. The sensible thing would be to finish your first year here and then transfer.'

'And suppose I fail this year?'

'Why should you fail?'

He is irritated. 'Because it's difficult stuff we're taking.'

'You should ask for help, talk to someone about this.'

'Tell my adviser I was in seclusion in the mosque and missed days of classes. Fat chance she'll be sympathetic!' He laughs. I see him being sarcastic for the first time. It doesn't suit him.

'But she should know that you are having difficulties.'

'I can't talk to anyone. I can only talk to you.' There is resentment in his voice as if talking to me happens against his will.

'I am not in a position to advise you. What do I know of universities or careers?'

He swings his legs and sits up. 'It annoys me when you put yourself down like this. You're better than a lot of people; you've just had bad luck. I bet so many men wanted to marry you!' It is like there is a jolt in the room, the sting of that last sentence. He persists. 'I'm right aren't I?'

I stare at him and he repeats, 'Aren't I?'

To think that Anwar is still here, a couple of underground stations away, still waiting for the Khartoum government to fall. He married his cousin after all; he brought her over when his career took off.

'There was someone, yes.' My voice sounds thick. 'He was an atheist so I didn't marry him.' I look down at the carpet so as not to see Tamer's reaction. I don't know why I put it like that – it's true but not a hundred per cent true. There are many other ways I could have put it. Anwar didn't want my genes; he didn't want my father's blood flowing in his children's veins.

Tamer's voice is harsh, and so is the way he looks at me. 'How could you?'

'I loved other things about him, not that he was an atheist.'

He winces at the word love, punishes me for it. 'Well, that wasn't very clever of you, was it? Can't you spot an unbeliever the first time they open their mouths?'

I shrug and look down at the floor. 'I regret the whole thing. I often wish I could go back in time and erase what I've done. But it doesn't matter whether I forgive myself or not. I only want Allah to forgive me.'

'I'm sorry,' he says.

'It's OK.'

'No, I upset you. I'm sorry. I mean it.' His large eyes are all worried and looking at me. He says, 'You're not upset are you?' as if he's coaxing me.

No, I am not upset, not upset at all because I see a gleam of jealousy in his eyes, sense possessiveness.

Twenty-seven

I pass by the closed door of Lamya's bedroom and hear her say, 'He can't now – three months into the semester – say it's not working.' I strain to hear Doctora Zeinab's reply but I can only make out the tone, soothing, diplomatic. Then Lamya again. 'He promised he would come for visits – he never did. He even phones at the wrong times.' They are not talking about Tamer. I lose interest and continue on my way to the kitchen, Lamya's voice in my ear. 'Hisham agreed that I would come here to do my PhD, he can't grumble about it now . . .' I miss Tamer. He was out before I arrived. Perhaps his mother's arrival yesterday urged him to be more serious about his studies.

The kitchen is not the usual battlefield. The table has been cleared, the dishes washed, a casserole sits in the sink, full of soapy water. Only the breakfast mugs and dishes need washing. Doctora Zeinab's presence is tangible. She had brought trays of *baqlawa* and *basboosa*, jars of green olives, tins of *foul*, even frozen stuffed vine leaves and *moulokhia*. All these things are available in London but they are probably cheaper in Cairo. For Mai there is a doll and a stuffed rabbit. She toddles in now clutching them in both hands. I give her breakfast and try not to get cereal on the new toys. The slam of the door means that Lamya has gone out, forgetting to kiss her daughter goodbye.

Doctora Zeinab smiles as she walks into the kitchen. I like her – her thick auburn hair, the way she beams at Mai, the way she stands waiting for the kettle to boil, her hands on her hips, not caring that her stomach is bulging. I have always been vain and careful. Even when I am completely alone, I watch my posture, check that my eyebrows are smooth, that no food is stuck between my teeth. Whenever I come into contact with women like Doctora Zeinab, large and unselfconscious, I admire them.

She speaks and I warm to her accent. 'I'm glad Lamya and Tamer are well. *Alhamdullilah*, this set-up is successful. I thought it would be when I planned it all out for them. It's nice that they're together, nice that they're in a proper home, not in student halls. I could have kept Mai with me in Cairo – maybe Lamya would have even preferred that but it's better that they're not separated. And Hisham will be coming here for visits. His wife in London, his daughter in Cairo – that wouldn't be sensible.'

I nod and hide my surprise, remember to swing back into my role as maid, play the part. I have been lax because of Tamer. I am surprised that she is saying all this when Lamya is having problems with her husband and Tamer hates his course. Perhaps she does not consider these complaints to be serious, which is reassuring for me. If they abandon their studies and leave London, what will become of me?

She chats. 'I wish I could stay longer but I have to travel to New York the day after tomorrow. And I can't pass by on the way back either – my ticket is New York to Cairo direct.'

'It must be tiring to spend so much time on the

aeroplane.' I stuff laundry into the washing machine, his shirt and underwear.

'Oh, I just take a sleeping pill and I don't know anything till the stewardess wakes me up and says we've arrived.' She laughs.

I've always been wary of sleeping pills as if I can't trust myself with them. What would life be if I were like her; professional, capable and mobile, not bogged down? 'Envy devours your good actions like fire devours fuel,' the Prophet, peace be upon him, said. I know it but I still do it, I still yearn for what others have.

In the afternoon I offer to go grocery shopping in Church Street. The Tesco there is cheaper than the nearby Europa store. This comment earns me an approving smile and Doctora Zeinab says that she and Mai will accompany me. I carry Mai and her pushchair down the steep steps that lead to the canal. I feel a twinge in my back – sometimes these twinges disappear, sometimes the ache sets in and lasts for days. It is pleasant to walk along the canal, marvel at the houseboats and how some people live on them. Another flight of steps and we are in the bustle of Church Street, a world removed from St John's Wood. We enjoy the street market, the sights and sounds. 'They've got everything,' says Doctora Zeinab, 'even fresh okra.' The supermarket is not big but we pile up a trolley and this abundance pleases her, this stocking up. In the cab going home, she says, 'Until Lamya and Tamer go home for the Christmas holidays, they won't need to do any more shopping.' Lamya is going to her husband in Oman, Tamer is going with his father to Khartoum.

After I put the shopping away I tidy his room. It is changed because of his mother's presence – both beds unmade instead of only his, the smell of her perfume, her suitcases on the floor. There is no sign of his book *A Treatise on the Art and Practice of Arab Love*. He had hidden it from her. The door opens and she is taken aback to see me smoothing his pillow, 'Why didn't you do this room in the morning when you did all the cleaning?' I flush and have no adequate reply, only an apologetic mumble. She sighs at my stupidity, 'Come and start the cooking.'

I am taking the chicken out of the fridge when he walks into the kitchen. He comes close to me and whispers, 'You weren't in the park today.'

I am flattered. I swell with it and say, 'I went shopping with your mum.' I remove the chicken from the Tesco packaging.

He looks at my hand and the surprise makes him raise his voice. 'What are you doing? Why did you get this chicken? You only ever get halal ones.'

'Your mother bought it.' I throw the cling film in the bin.

'Why didn't you stop her?'

Does he imagine that his mother and I are on equal terms? 'She said the butcher in Finchley Road is too far away.'

'This is exactly what I was telling you about the other day,' he hisses. 'She can be so lax at time, it bugs me.'

'Shush, she'll hear you.' I wash the chicken under the running tap. Inside it is a small plastic packet full of the innards – something the chickens from the halal butcher never have. It is pleasing to have him standing next to me.

'Well, I'm not going to eat it.' He must have looked like that when he was little and annoyed, with the frown and flashing eyes. He moves away from me and jerks open the cupboard. He takes out a giant pack of tortillas and tears it open.

I want to tease him, to soften his mood. 'I thought you said you weren't going to eat standing up any more?'

He pulls out a chair. I pass him a jar of salsa dip and he takes it without a word, twists the lid open and dunks a crisp into the chunky mixture. I love giving him food, watching him eat. He munches and says, 'I can't believe you're going to cook this chicken.'

'I am.' I pick up a knife and start cutting the wings.

'I'm not going to eat it.'

'Neither will I.'

'So I'm supposed to just starve today?' His mouth is full and it makes me laugh.

He swallows. 'What's so funny?'

I look at him, knowing he is hungry, knowing he is spoilt. 'You won't starve. You can have rice and salad.'

'This is not your fault.' He puts his tortillas down and walks out, calling his mother. I hear them talking in the next room. He sounds childish and nagging. She brushes his arguments aside, saying he is silly, saying he is making a big fuss over nothing. It is a mistake; he becomes aggressive and raises his voice. I freeze, the kitchen knife poised in my hand, as echoes of other quarrels and other mothers ring in my ears. But Omar and Tamer are miles apart, miles apart. I try and reach him. I whisper, 'Control yourself, control yourself, it's not worth it. You will regret your rudeness afterwards; your sensitive nature will be troubled.'

Twenty-eight

He asks me what I did over the Christmas and New Year. He smiles, fresh and relaxed after having been away. 'Did you watch lots of TV?'

I tell him why I don't have a set. He doesn't know what a TV licence is or how much it costs. His mother pays for all these things he takes for granted.

He tells me about his holiday in Khartoum. He watched hours of satellite TV, was invited out to lunches and dinners. He chats about the food he ate, his new digital camera, playing football with his cousins, how it sucks to be back studying again. 'I can't understand the lectures sometimes, actually a lot of the time I don't understand.' The world of business is meaningless to him, unreal.

He says, 'I've missed you.' I missed him too; I missed the delight and sweetness. We make up for the lost time. We walk in Queen Mary's Rose Garden when the weather holds, sit in the cafeteria when it rains. Every day is longer; the light is different. We discover playgrounds for Mai deep in the park, larger, more adventurous. We never get lost because we can see the minaret of the mosque and head home towards it. He says, 'You actually listen to me. You talk – most people don't talk – as if they have no time.' He misses Oman, he says. He misses his schoolfriends and teachers. He had a friend, Carlos, from Bolivia whose father worked for an oil company. Carlos was a devout Catholic. He loved football and he spoke Spanish. When Carlos was ten he wanted to become a priest but he changed his mind and is now studying Environmental Science at John Hopkins University. They email each other sometimes. Tamer says, 'I can't make friends here. I don't know why.'

It is my turn to say, 'You listen to me when I speak.' I speak about Omar, about a disappointment that can't go away. 'Please pray for him,' I say, 'they can keep him locked up and they can let him go but unless Allah forgives him, nothing will change for him.' I want to cry about Omar, to let go and wail like the Palestinian women do on TV when one of their men is killed, but I can't because he is not innocent and there is a bitterness towards him that I hide and try to drown but it doesn't go away.

'More than anything else,' I say, 'I would like to go on Hajj. If my Hajj is accepted, I will come back without any sins and start my life again, fresh.'

He says, 'I want to ride a camel from Medina to Mecca like the Prophet, peace be upon him, did.'

We talk of Hajj because it is the season. In the mosque there are classes starting for the lucky pilgrims who are due to leave. They seem so ordinary now and when they come back they will be transformed, privileged. I see this every year, the genuine joy and adventures they speak about. The crowds, the hardship of sleeping in tents, long bus rides, the way they were squeezed and wrung.

He says, 'I am ashamed that my parents haven't yet gone to Hajj. Even though they have the money, they keep putting it off.'

'One day, insha'Allah, they will go.'

209

He makes a face. It disturbs me when he is harsh about his parents. It is the only fault I find in him. And over the months I have looked for faults.

Crossing the bridge in the park, we meet Shahinaz, her children and mother-in-law. Tamer stands aside with Mai while I chat with them. I sit on my heels to talk to Ahmed. He is grand in his pushchair, all hidden away in a new spring coat much too big for him. It takes some time for his eyes to focus on me. '*Habibi ya* Ahmed, have you forgotten me, have you?' He smiles, a lop-sided, grudging smile, as if he would rather fall asleep. I stand up and Shahinaz asks, 'How come *he's* with you?' She keeps her voice low. I look towards Tamer. How boyish he looks, how young! His height doesn't add to his age, it only makes him gangly. He holds the handles of Mai's pushchair, leans down to peel away a leaf that is stuck to one of the wheels, wipes his fingers on his jeans. I ignore Shahinaz's question, bend down to kiss Ahmed's head. But she goes on, laughing, 'Why is he tagging along after you? Does he need a baby-sitter too?'

I feel myself blushing. I mumble, 'He's free to do what he likes.' I am unnecessarily defensive when all she is expecting is a witty reply, a shared laugh.

She looks at Tamer and then at me. A long look.

'I'm in an awkward position,' I say.

She puts her hand on my arm, 'I understand.'

'No, I don't think you do – really.' Her mother-in-law turns to look at me, curious.

'Come to my house and we'll talk.' It's an automatic response from Shahinaz. 'Come to my house tonight.'

When I join him, we walk and then he asks, 'What's

wrong? You're in a funny mood after talking to your friend.'

I take a deep breath, 'She said something about us . . . about us coming to the park together.'

'What do you mean?'

I shrug.

He goes on. 'She didn't think it was proper?' People pass us; a man walking his dog, a woman jogging. Perhaps it is not a good idea to start this conversation. I decide to play things down. 'She was just a bit surprised that's all.'

He says, 'I've been thinking along the same lines myself.'

I make my voice light, casual. 'What have you been thinking?'

'It's not very Islamic for a man and woman to be friends.' He is calm, almost as if he had rehearsed this line. His calmness makes my bones feel stiff and cool. I am suddenly afraid of losing him.

He says, 'I heard a sheik once say that it's like putting gunpowder and fire next to each other.'

I stop walking and he is forced to turn and look at me, 'Which one am I then – the gunpowder or the fire?'

He flushes. 'Don't joke about this – I'm not a little kid!'

'I wasn't joking.' I pause. 'I could leave this job.'

'No, you can't.'

I know I can't.

He says, 'I miss my classes to be with you.'

'I come to work every day because of you.'

He blurts out, 'We should get married.'

The shock of it makes me laugh. He is hurt; it shows in his face. He folds his arms against his chest, walks off, away from us.

I push Mai faster and catch up with him. I try to cajole

him out of his mood. I tell him about an Egyptian film I once saw. A widow in her late fifties is getting married and she's all excited about it. She goes to a beauty salon and then she dies with her hair all in rollers, sitting under the hairdryer. The hairdresser says, 'Her heart was weak, it couldn't bear the happiness.'

'The hairdresser is my favourite actor,' I say. 'Ahmed Zaki. Do you like him?'

'Yes I do. He's good.'

'He looks like you.'

'No he doesn't.'

'The same type. Lovely eyes, the boyish scruffy look.'

'I don't want you to talk like that . . . to talk about other men.'

I smile. 'Why not?'

'I get jealous.'

I warm to this. It is so gratifying.

He says in a different tone, 'I meant what I said before. I can do what I like here in London. My parents aren't here.' There is a sluggish rebellion in him, a discontent. 'These exams coming up, I don't need to study for them if I don't want to, it's up to me.' When I was young like him, I also thought no one could see me in London, I was free. But you can't be free of yourself.

I listen to our footsteps, the wheels of Mai's pushchair, the sounds of the park. 'When you said we should get married, did you imagine it?'

'Yes.' He blushes and lifts his hand to touch the handle of Mai's pushchair, lets it drop.

'I meant, how did you picture the ceremony itself?'

'Oh I don't know. I don't know how people go about getting married. You could have found out, asked around.'

'Sure,' I say, 'I can find out.'

212

'You're teasing me again, aren't you?' He is hostile now, like I have gone too far.

We can't talk any more. We go through the motions of taking Mai to the playground. In the cafeteria, he sulks and refuses to eat cake or drink tea.

Twenty-nine

'Doesn't his sister suspect anything?' She hugs the cushion on her lap. It is amber and round, worn out by the children and overnight guests who use it as a pillow.

'No, I don't think so. Maybe there is nothing to suspect. Maybe you're overreacting.'

'I'm not. He has a crush on you.' Shahinaz has a soft voice when she's at home. She changes when she closes the front door behind her, when she takes off her coat and pulls off her headscarf. She relaxes and becomes gentle, off-guard. It makes her more beautiful now at home than at the Eid party with the make-up and shimmering clothes. Maybe this is how it should be.

'It will wear out,' I say. 'It'll pass.' This is what I'm doing; waiting for the day he will outgrow me, heading towards it like death.

'And between now and then?'

'I'll be careful. Nothing will go wrong.' But I am standing back and watching, watching how his attachment to me will play itself out.

She sighs and takes a sip of her tea. Her children are asleep, her husband is upstairs, her mother-in-law is moving about in the kitchen. I like being with a family, even these fleeting visits, these temporary sounds and smells. 'I wish we were living centuries ago and, instead of just working for Tamer's family, I would be their slave.'

She makes a face. 'You mean concubine.'

'There would be advantages in that.'

She shakes her head. 'I can't believe you're saying this. No one in their right mind wants to be a slave.'

So I don't tell her of my fantasies. My involvement in his wedding to a young suitable girl who knows him less than I do. She will mother children who spend more time with me . . .

'Look,' she says, 'I know you regard him as a kid brother but does he know that? Maybe you should tell him.'

'I can't because it's not true.'

I watch the realization settle on her face. She blushes and I feel ashamed. She says, 'When I think of a man I admire, he would have to know more than me, be older than me. Otherwise I wouldn't be able to look up to him. And you can't marry a man you don't look up to. Otherwise how can you listen to him or let him guide you?'

I don't have anything to say. I stare down at my hands, my warped self and distorted desires. I would like to be his family's concubine, like something out of *The Arabian Nights*, with life-long security and a sense of belonging. But I must settle for freedom in this modern time. Shahinaz envies me sometimes, when her husband, children and mother-in-law weigh her down, when she has no room to herself, no time to herself, she envies the empty spaces around me.

She puts away the cushion she has been cradling. 'So many times I've introduced you to prospective bridegrooms and every time you said, "I can't feel anything towards him." Now suddenly you've changed!'

The impatience in her voice makes me clam up, the way

she mimicked me. I feel myself slowly shutting down. She says, 'It's not going to work out, Najwa. His parents will never agree.'

I take a deep breath. It is as if the room is too small, too warm. It is time to change the subject, to talk about her, to ask about the course she has applied to. It is the right tactic because she beams and says, 'Yes, I heard from them. They've accepted me.' She stands up and moves to the mantelpiece, opens a drawer and comes back with the letter of acceptance. She shows it to me proudly. It is from the same university Tamer attends. I think of him with the burden of studying a subject he doesn't like, and her with her enthusiasm. She is going to be a mature student. Every day she will go to class and after three years she will get a degree. It is an old wish, a hankering she had had ever since she got married, and then one baby after another dampened her hopes, kept her at home. 'Sohayl is supportive,' she says. 'He wants me to study. He filled the application form for me.'

I am touched by her life, how it moves forward, pulses and springs. There is no fragmentation, nothing stunted or wedged. I circle back, I regress; the past doesn't let go. It might as well be a malfunction, a scene repeating itself, a scratched vinyl record, a stutter.

Thirty

The next day stretches out long and crackling, after a night of disjointed sleep. Lamya is having a party. Perhaps it is her birthday. She doesn't tell me. Instead she says she is going to the hairdresser and lists all the things I have to do, from filling little dishes with nuts and crisps to borrowing extra chairs from the neighbours. Tamer disapproves of the party and grumbles when I ask him to help with the chairs. 'I can't bear her friends,' he says, giving me an injured look. I apologize for the way I teased him yesterday at the park. I speak as we heave the sofa from one side of the room to the other. My apology sounds careless as if I am desperate to get it out of the way. 'It's OK,' he says, but he doesn't look at me. He is still cross. He pushes the armchair against the wall. It has little wheels and we need not have carried it. I nearly stumble over Mai who is excited by all the changes. She screams, 'Juice, juice.' Her day must go on as normal, her needs must be met.

Tamer spends the morning shut up in his room, studying for his exams. I would have liked him to come out more often, to help me look after Mai. At noon I take him coffee and sandwiches. He is softer then and says, 'I'm sorry I'm in a bad mood – it's this silly party!' I suggest that he goes out to avoid it. 'Yeah, maybe I should,' he says but I know that he won't, partly because he is lazy and partly because he is enjoying his disapproval of his sister and her friends.

In the afternoon Lamya returns with fluffy hair and a carrier bag with Knightsbridge and a designer's name written on it. She lifts a dress out of the bag, shaking away the white tissues clinging to it. The dress is lovely, a crisp red taffeta. She is excited and rushes to Tamer's room to show him. I pick up the sheets of tissue from the floor, come across the receipt and gasp when I see the price. It stays with me, that breathing in, that sharpness in my gut. The catering arrives from a Lebanese restaurant; large oblong trays covered with aluminium foil. In the kitchen I peel the foil back and my mouth waters when I see the *kubeibah*, when I smell the stuffed vine leaves, samosas, puff pastry filled with feta cheese. Tamer starts to help himself with Lamya saying, 'Keep away from the food,' and he insisting that he is making his picks discreetly, not to mess up the arrangement. 'Those friends of yours won't eat, believe me,' he says with his mouth full.

'It's none of your business.' She is kneeling on the ground, searching for something at the back of the cupboard, 'It's not right. No one offers guests food that's been touched.'

'Who cares!' He reaches out for the ketchup. Our eyes meet and he smiles. He has forgotten about yesterday, we are friends again.

She says, 'You've always been a slob. Bet you haven't had a shower today.' He is still in the pyjama trousers and T-shirt he sleeps in.

He makes a face. 'Actually I haven't.'

She fetches out a silver tray. 'Then go have one now. I don't want you in the shower when they're here. I want both bathrooms clean and dry before they arrive.' She looks at me and I nod. Mai toddles into the kitchen, puts her arms around her mother. I finish wiping the glasses. They are talking as if I am not here. All their lives they've had servants, and my presence does not make them uncomfortable. I know what it feels like to have silent figures moving in the background, reassuring, always getting the work done.

He says, 'It's bad enough I have to be locked up in my room all evening, now you're saying I can't use the bathroom.' She frowns back and untangles Mai's arms from around her neck. The child is clingy today, disturbed by all the changes. There is no time to take her to the park. I polish the tray and start arranging the set of glasses. The tray reflects my white headscarf, my dark sullen eyes, wide because he is in the same room as me.

'Where did the thermos go?' She turns from the cupboard to look at me and I stiffen. I don't like her voice when she asks me such questions, as if she is accusing me. Perhaps I am paranoid. Before I reply, she turns to Tamer. 'You took it with you back in Ramadan when you did the seclusion at the mosque.'

'Yes,' he says. 'I left it there.'

'What do you mean you left it there?' She bangs the cupboard shut.

He is evasive, turns his eyes to rest on me. 'I just did.'

'You gave it away to someone, didn't you?'

I can tell from his face that she has guessed right. She is shrewd.

He shrugs. 'It's just a thermos. We can get another one.'

'It's too late now, look at the time! I wanted to use it

instead of the teapot. I don't know how you can do that, just hand things over. They probably took advantage of you in that mosque – an idiot with money, that's what you are!'

'Lamya . . .' His face is red and I slip out of the room, because he would not want me to see him stammering. From the sitting room, I can hear them quarrelling. Their voices aren't loud but I can hear her desire to hurt and his to rebel. This rebellion is half-formed, half-baked; it lacks a focus and a goal.

The curtains are drawn, the doorbell rings and it all starts. The guests are Sudanese and Arab girls in their twenties, wearing the same type of clothes as Lamya, the same make-up. I guess that Tamer is right and they will only peck at the food. They manage to look both slim and satiated at the same time. But it is quite unfair of him not to like these girls. They look like they come from decent homes. They're all studying so they must be clever and some of them, beyond the designer clothes and hairdos, are genuinely pretty. I pass around a tray with glasses of cola and orange. One of the girls, her hair in a short bob, makes a comment about the boycott, asks me about the brand of the drink. She leans forward to listen to my answer because my voice is low and around us there is much chatter, the occasional shriek of laughter. She gives me a tight smile, takes the orange and leans back. I like the way she is hogging the best armchair, sitting back relaxed while others are sitting up straight in dining chairs. Now why can't Tamer fall in love with a girl like that? I must tell him about her. On my way to answer the doorbell I catch her name; Bushra. Yes, he will do well with a girl named Bushra. Into the room flow more sparkling guests, an older bunch this time, a young mother who kisses Mai and admires her dress, tells her she has a daughter exactly the same age.

A blast of music, hectic drumming; modern Arab songs are loud and irritatingly monotonous, the beat nags and tantalizes. Jerky rhythms clash with lyrics of reproach and loss. The message is one of futility; we are to sing our failures loud and clear and still clap and jerk our hips. I must make sure that every guest is served at least one drink. I must pick up the empty glasses and return them unharmed to the kitchen. If one of them smashes, Lamya will be furious, not because of the loss but because of the inconvenient scattering of glass, the disruption. She is dancing now, striking in her new dress, her hair done up. There is something geometric and simple about her figure, the bland way she moves her hips. A quality is missing from her movements but I can't pinpoint it. She smiles and bends down to say something to the two English girls, sitting side by side. They wear dark mini-skirts and hold their glasses tight in their hands. They look slightly bewildered, ruffled by culture shock, yet they do not exchange whispers and comments but remain separate as if they must experience this evening alone. One of them has straight red hair – she reminds me of the Duchess of York.

The lady who has a daughter Mai's age asks me to make her a cup of tea. She addresses me in English and I suspect that she has a Filipina maid and has become used to speaking to maids in English. It's bothersome to make her tea. The thermos would have been useful as Lamya said. Now I have to scramble to find the best teapot, fill the sugar bowl. In the kitchen, I can still make out the songs. They excite me; it's a bubbling shallow excitement. Lamya strides in. 'We need more chairs!' She grabs two of the kitchen chairs and carries them out saying, 'Bring the other

221

two and if later we need more we can use the one in Tamer's room.' He won't like it; he won't like us taking the chair he is sitting on. I wonder if he can hear the music, the attractive laughter. I follow her with the remaining kitchen chairs and return to fetch the tea tray.

I must keep an eye on Mai. She has lost interest in the dancing and is getting bored. She sidles up to a dish of pistachios and knocks it down. It falls unharmed on the carpet. She sits on the floor in the middle of the scatter of nuts. I rush to sort things out, scold her but she is unperturbed and walks off. When Bushra reaches out for her hand, she is responsive and smiling. They look nice together, curled up in the armchair, Mai playing with the straps of Bushra's handbag, their heads close together. Their hair is the same colour but one's is curly and the other one's straight. Bushra looks up when the latest Amr Diab song starts to play. She joins in the clapping, mouthing the lyrics. Tamer should see her like this.

The doorbell rings and it is Lamya who opens the door for the latecomer, I am too far away. I hear her shriek with laughter, followed by the others in the room. I look up and see a girl in hijab, wearing exactly what I wear when I go out, a beige headscarf, a floor-length skirt and a short coat that doesn't reach the knees. I don't understand why everyone is laughing. The girl looks familiar, like one of my friends at the mosque. She starts to take off her coat, removes her headscarf, loosens her curly hair. When she throws her headscarf across the room and everyone shrieks I am sure something is wrong. Her smile and her gestures are theatrical; everyone is looking at her. She starts to dance and the music is just right for her cheeky smile, her glittering eyes. The centre of the room is all hers now and she is moving slowly as if doing a striptease, unbuttoning her blouse to peals of laughter, untwisting her wrap-around skirt. I laugh too as if laughter is contagious. They clap for her in time with the music. She is now in a black sleeveless dress, silky like a negligee. A red sash is tossed towards her; she ties it round her hips and dances across the room, triumphant. The party will be remembered for this. Lamya is all delight and laughter. She leans towards the Duchess of York. 'We don't make fun of our religion, but just today, just once today.'

I have to tell him. I have to be with him. The lady has finished her tea and gestures for me to take her cup away but I ignore her. The doorbell rings and I ignore it. To walk down the corridor to his room is to move from yellow gaiety to mellowness, calm and cool like the first moments of sleep. I push open the door and he is at his desk, twiddling his hair. He turns round and smiles and I am laughing and telling him how they all knew it was a joke from the beginning, from when she walked in wearing hijab and I was the silly one crouched on the floor picking up pistachio nuts, looking up and seeing a familiar figure, thinking it is like one of my friends at the mosque. I laugh and say, 'Would you believe it, for them the hijab is a fancy dress!'

He doesn't laugh with me. He gets up from his desk and says, 'This is terrible. This is wrong; they shouldn't do that. I'm sorry, Najwa. You must be upset, you must be offended.'

'Oh no,' I say, 'they are just young girls. Just young girls playing, they don't mean anything, I can even dance better than them. It's nothing personal against me. I am nothing to them, nothing. I don't matter . . .'

'Stop it.' He puts his hands on my shoulders and he shakes me a little. His eyes are solemn, clear and I see

223

goodness in them. I have always wanted goodness, I have always believed in it and here it is. He says gently, 'Stop it, stop putting yourself down.' He should not come close to me but he does and I cling to him, I cling to him because I am sour and he is sweet. He kisses me and he doesn't know how. I should push him away, not let him learn, but his smell holds me still. Suddenly Lamya is at the door, half in, half out. The very presence of her dress, her face rigid with dislike strikes me as an aberration. I should move away from him but I am stunned.

'What's this!' She's swollen with how dare you, how dare you, how dare you. She is more shocked than we are. I move away from him, my hand on his T-shirt and something snaps in her. She takes a step towards me, lifts her arm and strikes me across the face. It stings and I gasp as her rings and bangles grind my skin. There is darkness when I close my eyes. It is Tamer erupting as the blood pounds in my ears. It is Tamer shouting at her not me.

Part Five

1991

Thirty-one

S he said she would call the police if I didn't give her the money. I had a hundred pounds. I was sure I had a lot of money – a hundred pounds – but my purse was full of bank statements on pink paper. I kept flicking through them and there was no money. She wanted ID and I searched frantically but my passport wasn't there and neither was my library card. I didn't know this woman. She spoke Arabic; she was dark and wearing an evening gown. She looked down at me and said that she would call the police. She spoke calmly but at the word police, my blood turned cold . . .

'Najwa!'

I opened my eyes. Silence and calm after the nightmare. 'You were mumbling in your sleep,' Anwar said.

I sat up and breathed. I shouldn't doze off during the day; it brings no rest. 'Why have you stopped coming over? Why do I always have to be the one coming here?'

He looked up from the letter he had been reading. 'Because it's more sensible for us to meet where the computer is.'

He tossed me the letter and turned back to the computer screen. It was from his sister in Khartoum, long and chatty. I read it, searching for my name. Surely by now he would have mentioned me to his family. 'Who's Ibtisam?'

'My cousin.'

'Why does your sister mention her a lot?'

He was typing and he didn't stop. 'They're close.'

'Is that all?'

'Sort of.'

'Is there something between you?'

'Nothing formal.'

Was I supposed to worry or not worry? 'Nothing formal means there is something informal.'

He turned to look at me. 'No it doesn't. Her mother and my mother talk and make speculations. They've been planning things since we were kids, but it's just talk. I don't feel any strong inclination towards her.'

I folded the letter. Now, if he could come over and put his arms around me, say, 'You mustn't feel insecure, you mustn't worry.' But he wouldn't do that, as if there was a law: Anwar must not feel sorry for Najwa.

'Come and check this,' he said. I walked over to the computer, pulled up a chair, started to make a few comments and corrections. I could sense his growing irritation the more errors I found.

'But all in all, it's very good. As if you copied it from a newspaper.'

'What newspaper?'

'I just meant it's sharp, professional.'

'If you're accusing me of plagiarizing, you might as well tell me from where.'

I knew why he was defensive. Hardly any of the English articles he sent out got published, and every other day he was turned down for a job. I knew the comforting words I was expected to say but today I didn't trust myself to speak. I would say the wrong things and start a quarrel.

Quarrels took too long to patch up, they took too much grovelling; hours of coaxing and patience.

It was a relief to hear Ameen call out, 'It's time for the news. Kamal, where are you? Anwar?'

We moved towards the blare of the TV as if it were a magnet. The familiar faces of the presenters, serious and, over the days, endearing. I was becoming attached to them as to characters in a soap. We slumped on the sofa and the chairs. There was a sense of anti-climax now that the war was over, now that the news was not meaty enough.

We had bonded watching the Gulf War on TV. Now that it was finished and the news left us unfulfilled, we played cards instead. Ameen often won, which annoyed Kamal. Neither he nor Anwar liked to lose to Ameen. It threatened their sense of justice that he, the bourgeois owner of this Gloucester Road flat, could also have such innate luck. To give Anwar a chance, I sometimes held back my good cards, stopped myself from winning but it didn't always work. We played *kunkan* and put down very small amounts of money: fifty pence, the last of the one-pound notes. There was an atmosphere to these games, metallic because of the war, stifling because of the cigarette smoke and whisky. The drinking made them crave certain food. I heated tins of *foul*, mashed it with feta cheese and toma-toes. Often I fried eggs, aubergines and *ta'amiyah*, heated endless loaves of bread. I didn't like eating with them but I liked the concentration of the game. The smooth, pretty cards held me in a pleasurable suspense.

None of us yet had put down any cards but we had been going several rounds since lunch. Any time now, one of us was bound to have the necessary fifty-four points. 'It's nearly five o'clock,' said Ameen, 'I'd better be going soon.' He drew a new card from the pile. He laid out three kings and three queens. 'I'm invited for breakfast.'

'Breakfast at five!' I laughed and so did Kamal. I looked at Anwar. He smiled but his eyes were on the cards. Ameen was laying his hand on the table; six of hearts to the Jack with a Joker in the middle.

Ameen tossed his remaining card in the middle, took a draw of his cigarette, collected his winnings. He smiled, 'It's Ramadan breakfast, you heathens!' I caught my breath. 'Oh no!' They laughed at my reaction. Kamal said he knew it had started but had forgotten about it. Why would anyone in his right mind fast in London? 'Or anywhere else?' said Anwar. 'The thirst people endured in the heat of Sudan was not healthy at all.'

Ameen called back from his bedroom, 'These relatives of mine are fasting here normally and every single day at sunset they have the table set out for breakfast.' It jolted me that Ramadan could happen, could come round and I would not know about it. I looked at Anwar and he was calm, normal as if nothing unnatural had happened. 'Why didn't you tell me?'

'Why should I?' said Anwar. For some reason that made Kamal laugh.

'What do you mean why? It's important. It's Ramadan. I should know about it. It shouldn't happen without me knowing. If we were in Khartoum we would have known, our daily routine would have changed.'

'So now you know. Are you going to fast?'

'Yes, I always fast.'

'What kind of fasting?' He was teasing me now as he shuffled the cards, Kamal an appreciative audience. They often joked about how Westernized I was, detached from Sudanese traditions.

'The normal kind of fasting.'

'To lose weight?' Anwar smiled. My attempts at dieting always amused him. Kamal looked at me in that way I didn't like.

'Well, partly,' I said.

'So why don't you fast any other time of the year, why this particular month?'

'Because it's the month of fasting, that's why. Everyone's fasting.'

'But we're in London now,' Kamal said. 'People in London don't fast.'

'We've always fasted.'

'Really, your whole family?' Anwar and Kamal shared a smile.

'Yes,' I said. 'In Khartoum all my family used to fast.'

'I didn't. Did you, Kamal?'

'No. Ameen did though.'

'Well, I don't see why I shouldn't keep it up when I'm here.'

Anwar sat back and looked at the cards in his hands. 'But what's the point if it's a community activity?'

'It's part of our religion.'

He looked at me. 'Shouldn't you question these things, though? Shouldn't you ask yourself if it's suitable for every time and place? When you fast, your productivity is reduced, you can't work to your full potential.'

'But we're not working today. We're just playing cards.'

'When are you going to learn how to have a proper discussion?' He had said this before but I couldn't remember the occasion. A sense of *déjà vu*, 'When are you going to learn?' slips in again.

'I am having a proper discussion.' I felt sick not because he was having a go at me but because I was all alone, alarmed about something he didn't care about. Was it madness to see something, know something all by yourself with everyone else oblivious?

'Go,' he said, suddenly bored, 'go get me more ice.'

I went to the kitchen and opened the fridge. I stared at its contents, smelled the cold food. There was lunch in my stomach and there shouldn't be, the taste of Coke in my mouth. I missed the lightness of fasting, my body clean, my mouth dry and then the special food at sunset, the drinks in jugs with ice, purple for *helomur*, orange for *gamar el-din*, pink for grapefruit, and guests, cars parked in front of our house, my mother's hostess smile, saying, don't drink too much, don't fill your stomachs with water, you won't be able to eat later.

Instead of getting the ice, I locked myself in the bathroom. My mind felt tilted. I almost expected to look in the mirror and see my neck craned to one side. I had always observed Ramadan even when Mama was ill in hospital. The nurses in the Humana knew about Ramadan because many of their patients were Arabs. One of them had worked before in Saudi, made 'a bit of savings', she said. Fasting was the only religious thing I ever did – how many days had I missed? Anwar knocked on the door and I thought, 'He knows I'm upset, he's come looking for me.' But he just needed the toilet.

We talked, standing in the bathroom, the cistern filling. I would never forget this day. How we were wedged in a stinky bathroom instead of being somewhere clean.

'What's wrong with you these days?'

I shrugged.

'Are you depressed?' He smiled. I used to laugh whenever he opened his eyes wide like that.

232

'I have something on my mind.'

'What is it?'

I sat on the edge of the bathtub; it was uncomfortable. I put my head in my hands. I spoke slowly without looking at him. 'Uncle Saleh is going to Khartoum next week. I'm thinking it would be a good idea for your father to speak to him so we can be officially engaged.'

He sounded cautious, like he had thought about it before. 'It's not a good idea.'

'Why not?'

'Because I'm not making plans until this government falls.'

'Getting engaged is not making plans. It's not going to change anything.'

'Exactly. So why bother with it?' He had proved his point.

'So that people would know that we're getting married.' It was not what I had wanted to say. I had wanted to say something else but I couldn't put it into words: it was vague and complicated.

'What people? Do you count Ameen and Kamal as "people"? And who's seeing us in London? Who's got time to criticize our relationship?'

He had won that round but I stood up and lunged again. 'Yesterday you upset me.'

He groaned. 'What did I do?'

'What you said about my father.'

'What about him?' He didn't remember. He genuinely couldn't remember.

'You said you didn't want his blood flowing in your children's veins.'

'I was joking, that's all.'

'Joking.'

233

'Yes, can't we joke? Do we have to be serious all the time?' He looked at me again with the wide eyes.

'I can't go on like this.'

'Oh God.' He unlocked the door. 'A drama now! You're going to make a drama out of this. Grow up.' He walked out of the bathroom.

I picked up my things and went home.

I tried to fast the next day. In the early afternoon black blobs appeared in front of my eyes while I was mopping up Aunty Eva's kitchen. I broke into a sweat and had to sit down. My hands were cold and clammy; I dropped the mop on the floor. Aunty Eva was showing a surveyor around the house. His assistant was taking measurements. I could hear the three of them talking in the next room. I gave up and put the kettle on. I would not be able to make it through the day without a cup of tea, without the lift of sugar.

When the surveyor left, Aunty Eva came into the kitchen. She had tears in her eyes when she said that they were selling the house and moving to Brighton to be nearer their sons. Uncle Nabeel's office wasn't doing well and he was going to retire. The information went into me; I felt its coolness pass my skin. I was about to lose this job, lose Aunty Eva's company but, today of all days, it all seemed unreal, the bad feeling mixed with hunger. 'I will visit you in Brighton,' I said, calm, grown up.

'Of course you will. Of course, any time, I'm like your mother now.' She was always sweet, always and now I would lose her too.

She said, 'Don't worry, Najwa, I will ask round and try to find you work with one of our acquaintances. There is a Syrian lady I know. She's pregnant and has very high blood pressure. The doctor told her to rest but how can anyone rest in this country? She has three mischievous little boys. She'll definitely need help. But are you sure you want to keep on doing this? You don't want to go to university and complete your education? There will be many opportunities for you if you have a degree.'

I shook my head. Anwar was the one who was going to start a PhD. He had got an acceptance from the London School of Economics and I had lent him the money. I did not think I could sit in class and write clever things. I would not be good at it. Anwar always said I was not intellectual.

I tried to fast again. I set the alarm so that I could wake up before dawn and have a snack. Perhaps the alarm didn't go off or I put it off and went back to sleep. Again the black blobs floating in front of me like jellyfish, the faint feeling, giving up. My failure bewildered me, my body's refusal to obey. I began to fear the black blobs, the dizziness – to think that in Khartoum I used to fast and still do my Jane Fonda workout an hour before the sunset meal. I told myself that Ramadan would come to an end and with it the relief that I need not try again.

In the Eid, Randa phoned from Edinburgh. She had done her best to fast in spite of having to sit for her finals. She had celebrated the Eid with the other Sudanese students in Edinburgh: an average Sudanese girl, not too religious and not too unconventional. I was once like her and then things changed along the way. She said she had finished her degree and was going back to Khartoum as a fully qualified doctor. I could urge her to stay with me a couple of days before her flight, lure her with London's shops. But it would be painful to see her successful, fulfilled, with parents and a career waiting back home. I would not be able to keep my envy under control. Besides, we only had the past in common; it was time to move on.

Uncle Saleh phoned from Toronto, also for the Eid. I did not dare tell him that I would be starting work for Aunty Eva's friend – an official maid now, paid by the hour. No more the illusion of helping my mother's friend. He had been right that day in the Spaghetti House. I should have gone with him to Canada; he would have protected me. But he was strained by his immigration, disgusted with Omar, embarrassed that his son didn't want to marry me. I did not want to be another burden. Now if he asked me on the phone to join him, I should say yes. But he chatted and made no mention. Canada was no longer an option for me.

Anwar phoned to say, 'Where are you? Where have you been? I need your help with an article – it's urgent. You're still not sulking are you?'

'No, I'm not,' I said because it was the right thing to say.

'Can you come over tomorrow? I'll be finished with the first draft by then and you can look at it.' I thought of correcting his article, treading gently so as not to hurt his pride. After saying to him, 'You need to change this, you need to change that,' I would have to flatter and soothe him. He needed my constant assurance that he was clever and handsome, that his limp was becoming unnoticeable, that one day he would achieve his dreams. But I needed things from him too.

Now he said, 'Don't be late.'

'I won't be.' It was easier than saying, 'I'm not coming. I can't help you with your English any more.' It was easier to tell a lie – 'See you tomorrow' – than to start a quarrel.

When I put the receiver down, when I walked bare-footed back to the bedroom, I felt a kind of peace. I lay in bed and fell deeply asleep. When I woke up I had a shower, but it was not an ordinary shower, it was like starting afresh, wanting to be clean, crying for it.

The first time I walked into the mosque I saw a girl sitting by herself, an open Qur'an on her lap, reciting Surat Ar-rahman. I sat and listened to the repetition of the verse, to the repetition of the question, 'So which of your Lord's favours do you deny?' There were other ladies in the room, the elderly ones leaning their backs against the wall, a group of lively mothers with babies who looked like they were pleased to be out of the house. There were teenagers in jeans and headscarves; there were neat middle-aged ladies who looked like they had just come in from work. But it was the girl reciting who held my attention, her detachment that was almost angelic. 'So which of your Lord's favours do you deny?' She must have taken lessons to be able to read so well. Or perhaps her mother taught her at home. She must be confident of herself, otherwise she would not be reading out loud. I wished I were like her. That in itself was strange. She was pale and serene, her clothes unremarkable, her face neither lush nor pretty. She did not shine with happiness or success, qualities I usually envied. But still I wished I were like her, good like her. I wanted to be good but I wasn't sure if I was prepared.

I was wearing what I believed to be my most modest dress. It had long sleeves and fell to below my knees. When I bent down to pray, my calves and the backs of my knees were bare. Someone came up from behind me and threw a coat over my back. I guessed it was one of the elderly ladies. I sensed the difficulty, the heave with which she got

237

off the floor and approached me. The coat slipped when I straightened up. There was the shame that I needed it, then the silly inevitability of it slipping off. I heard a sigh behind me, whispers in a language I couldn't understand – Turkish, Urdu? When I finished praying, I could not meet the eyes of whoever owned the coat. It lay in a heap behind me. I sat hunched on the floor, knowing I wasn't good, knowing I was far away and just taking the first step in coming here still wasn't enough.

Thirty-two

It was becoming clear that I had come down in the world. I had skidded and plunged after my father's execution and through my mother's illness, when I dropped out of college, then after Omar's arrest and through my relationship with Anwar. That process took so long, was mixed up and at times gave the illusion of better things. There was a glamour in coming to London, and Omar and I had fun during those first weeks before Baba's trial. We didn't know that we were being exiled, we didn't know we were seeking asylum. There was the comfort of our holiday flat and my mother was generous with pocket money. When I worked with Aunty Eva it was there too, the softness of a familiar voice, the memories of Khartoum all around me. Now she was gone and her Syrian friend knew neither the Sudan nor my parents. She employed me as a maid and I became one. I was a servant like the servants my parents had employed. It didn't feel strange. I almost didn't mind. In the mosque no one knew my past and I didn't speak of it. What they could see of me was not impressive: my lack of religious upbringing, no degree, no husband, no money. Many warmed to me because of that, they would talk about themselves and include me as someone who lived on benefit or came from a disadvantaged home. It didn't feel strange. I almost didn't mind. The skidding and plunging was coming to an end. Slowly, surely I was settling at the bottom. It felt oddly comfortable, painless. It felt like the worst was over. And there, buried below, was the truth.

My guides chose me; I did not choose them. Sometimes I would stop and think what was I doing in this woman's car, what was I doing in her house, who gave me this book to read. The words were clear, as if I had known all this before and somehow, along the way, forgotten it. Refresh my memory. Teach me something old. Shock me. Comfort me. Tell me what will happen in the future, what happened in the past. Explain to me. Explain to me why I am here, what am I doing. Explain to me why I came down in the world. Was it natural, was it curable?

Wafaa materialized. The woman who had shrouded my mother. The woman who had phoned every now and then to speak to me across a gulf, my indifference making her voice faint, her pleas feeble. I called to accept the invitation she had issued two years ago and she was not surprised. 'We'll pick you up at seven o'clock,' she said. As I was waiting for her, I struggled to remember what she looked like.

A blue van drove up in front of my flat. Her husband was driving. He was English and blond. I had never met anyone like him before, a convert. I sat next to their children, one long-haired boy, two skinny girls. Wafaa seemed livelier and younger than I remembered, was wearing trousers and a brown headscarf. Perhaps she was cheerful in the presence of her family. Her husband didn't speak or look at me while she chatted in Arabic all the way to the mosque. She complained about the children's school and the media coverage of the war, but I got the impression that she took all these things in her stride. The van smelt of turpentine and there was a scrap of wallpaper lolling on the floor. Her husband, Ali, worked as a painter/decorator. As for her, she was a dressmaker's assistant in a tailor's shop off Bond Street. 'I can make you some clothes,' she said and I took it to mean that my clothes were unsuitable.

Ali intrigued me. I had got the impression from Anwar that the English were all secular and liberal. Ali was nothing like that, yet he was completely English and had never set foot outside Britain. When I got to know Wafaa better, she told me about his conversion, how he used to be a devout Christian and felt that the Church was not strict enough for him. The more lifts I accepted from them, the more I got to understand him, listening to him complain to Wafaa about the traffic or joke with one of the children. It was not only his accent that I found odd. He was not very bright but I was touched by his patience with the children, the way he took on life. I thought of Anwar and Ali, how they would never meet, how the existence of one somehow undermined the other.

I knew Anwar well enough to guess what his reaction would be to what I was hearing and seeing around me. His views on religion were definite and he hated fundamentalists. He believed it was backward to have faith in anything supernatural; angels, djinns, Heaven, Hell, resurrection. He wanted rationale, reason, and he could not help but despise those who needed God, needed Paradise and the fear of Hell. He regarded it as a weakness and on top of that it was not benign, he would argue, it was not harmless. Look at what happened in Sudan, look at human rights, look at freedom of speech and look at terrorism. But that was exactly where I got lost. I did not want to look at these big things because they overwhelmed me. I wanted me, my feelings and dreams, my fear of illness, old age and ugliness, my guilt when I was with him. It wasn't fundamentalists who killed my father, it wasn't fundamentalists who gave my brother drugs. But I could never stand up to Anwar. I did not have the words, the education or the courage. I had given in to him but he had been wrong, the guilt never ever went away. Now I wanted a wash, a purge, a restoration of innocence. I yearned to go back to being safe with God. I yearned to see my parents again, be with them again like in my dreams. These men Anwar condemned as narrow-minded and bigoted, men like Ali, were tender and protective with their wives. Anwar was clever but he would never be tender and protective. Once I told him that Kamal had come up behind me in the kitchen, pressed against me quickly pretending it was an accident. All he said was, 'You're sophisticated enough to deal with this, Najwa. Don't make a big thing out of it. Be flexible with him, the poor guy has lots of hang-ups.'

Wafaa said, 'I'm so pleased that you're coming with us to the mosque every week. I'm so pleased you like our gatherings.'

I did like them. I liked the informality of sitting on the floor and the absence of men. The absence of the sparks they brought with them, the absence of the frisson and ambiguity. Without them the atmosphere was cool and gentle, girly and innocent with the children all around us, chubby little girls sitting close to their mothers, baby boys who crawled until they reached the wall, pulled themselves up to stand proud and unsteady. I liked the talks at these gatherings because they were serious and simple, vigorous but never clever, never witty. What I was hearing, I would never hear outside, I would never hear on TV or read in a magazine. It found an echo in me; I understood it. *No matter how much you love someone they will die. No matter how much health you have or money, there is no guarantee that one day you will not lose it. We all have an end we can't escape.* I thought such talk would make me gloomy, would bring me down, but I would leave the mosque refreshed, wide awake and calm, almost happy. Maybe I was happy because I was praying again – not like when I was young when it was just to boost my grades or to complement my fast in Ramadan – but with the intention of never giving it up. I reached out for something new. I reached out for spiritual pleasure and realized that this was what I had envied in the students who lined up to pray on the grass of Khartoum University. This was what I had envied in our gardener reciting the Qur'an, our servants who woke up at dawn. Now when I heard the Qur'an recited, there wasn't a bleakness in me or a numbness, instead I listened and I was alert.

One of the Prophet's companions used to stand up in prayer for most of the night. He prayed on his roof and a little boy looking up thought he was a tree. A tree growing on top of a house, how odd! If that man wasn't enjoying himself, how could he have resisted sleep, how could he have continued to pray for so long? And the enjoyment came because he humbled himself . . .

Anwar phoned every now and then. At first he was angry that I hadn't helped him with his article, then he was perplexed. I told him about my new activities and friends. 'It's a phase you're going through,' he said. 'You're not like these people, you're not one of them, you're modern.'

His first impression of me was the one that had endured. The university girl in the tight, short skirt who spoke private-school English, who flirted and laughed, was daring and adventurous.

'I've changed, Anwar.'

'No, you haven't. You're just imagining.'

'In the mosque I feel like I'm in Khartoum again. It's the atmosphere, the way people . . .'

'You're wrong. There's more to Sudan than Islam.'

I didn't want to argue with him. He would win with figures and facts, his arguments well thought out. But I was following my feelings and I didn't know how to defend them.

He said, 'I miss you. Don't you miss me?'

'I do but I can't handle the things you say about my father any more. I can't live a life where I don't even know that Ramadan has started. I can't. I'm tired of having a troubled conscience. I'm bored with feeling guilty.'

If he had proposed marriage there and then, I would have accepted and gone back to him. But fate made him say, 'You don't feel guilty, Najwa. It's these people brainwashing you. What's between us is love. It's nothing to feel guilty about.'

He was talking about something else, as if he was not talking to me. And he knew how to hurt me. 'If everything you hear in the mosque is correct, your beloved Aunty Eva will go to Hell because she's not a Muslim. How can you justify this, after all the good she's done for you?'

I started to stammer, I burst into tears, whimpering into the receiver. He tried but he couldn't stop himself from laughing.

To leave one forbidden thing is better in the sight of

244

Allah than going on Hajj fifty thousand times. When we show restraint, when we respect the boundaries of Allah, He gives us countless rewards. If we didn't make mistakes we wouldn't be human. But we have to repent too and ask for forgiveness. Even the Prophet Muhammad, peace be upon him – who had no sins – used to ask for forgiveness seventy times a day.

Can I ask forgiveness for someone else, someone who's already dead?

Yes, you can. Of course you can. And you can give charity in their name and you can recite the Qur'an for their sake. All these things will reach them, your prayers will ease the hardship and loneliness of their grave or it will reach them as bright, beautiful gifts. Gifts to unwrap and enjoy and they will know that this gift is from you.

I stood in front of the mirror and put the scarf over my hair. My curls resisted; the material squashed them down. They escaped, springing around my forehead, above my ears. I pushed them back, turned my head sideways to look at the back and it was an angular hump, a bush barely covered with cloth. The cotton scarf was almost threadbare. It was an old one that my mother used to wear when she oil-treated her hair. Now it flopped at a defeated angle over my forehead. I didn't look like myself. Something was removed, streamlined, restrained; something was deflated. And was this the real me? Without the curls I looked tidy, tame; I looked dignified and gentle.

Untie the material; observe the transformation. Which made me look younger? Scarf or no scarf? Which made me look more attractive? The answer was clear to that one. I threw it on the bed. I was not ready yet; I was not ready for this step. The smell from the scarf was of the oil my mother used on her hair. I pictured her coming back from the hairdresser in Khartoum, her hair soft and straightened, with a bit of static in it and the deep smell of hairspray. On such days, her tobe would barely cover her hair and she would gladly let the material slip. When I was very young I liked to stroke her straightened hair, enjoy its temporary smoothness. 'Your hands better be clean!' she would say. A drop of water or perspiration would restore a strand of hair to its original curl and on a day like that she would be going out to somewhere special where she would shine and make heads turn. But in sombre times, when her hair was not done, she would hold it back in a bun and not let the material of her tobe slip. Then she came close to looking like she was wearing a full hijab. She would not have believed it but even then she looked beautiful too, squeaky-clean, fragile without make-up and the way the glow in her eyes was revealed.

I took out one of her old tobes – yards of brown, silky material. I tied my hair back with an elastic band, patted the curls down with pins. I wrapped the tobe around me and covered my hair. In the full-length mirror I was another version of myself, regal like my mother, almost mysterious. Perhaps this was attractive in itself, the skill of concealing rather than emphasizing, to restrain rather than to offer.

Wafaa took me shopping for my first headscarves. I ended up buying them from Tie Rack. I chose the colours but followed her guidance in buying squares as well as long rectangles. Back in her house, in her bedroom, with her daughters as audience, she showed me how to tie each one, what folding I needed to do beforehand, where to put the pins. 'You look very nice,' she said, all enthusiasm and encouragement. Where did she come from, this woman? It was her role to shroud my mother for her grave and teach me how to cover my hair for the rest of my life. She was a guide, not a friend. One day she would move away to another pupil and I would graduate to another teacher. Now I sat at her dressing table, took a pin from her hand, looked at her perfumes and creams. When Ali returned home, she refused to let him come into the room. He gave a resigned response from behind the door and we all giggled. When I went home, I walked smiling, self-conscious of the new material around my face. I passed the window of a shop, winced at my reflection, but then thought 'not bad, not so bad'. Around me was a new gentleness. The builders who had leered down at me from scaffoldings couldn't see me any more. I was invisible and they were quiet. All the frissons, all the sparks died away. Everything went soft and I thought, 'Oh, so this is what it was all about; how I looked, just how I looked, nothing else, nothing non-visual.'

The more I learnt, the more I regretted and at the same time, the more hope I had. *When you understand Allah's mercy, when you experience it, you will be too ashamed to do the things He doesn't like. His mercy is in many things, first the womb, the* rahim, *He gave it part of his name, Al-Rahman – the All-Merciful. It is a place we have all experienced. It sheltered us, gave us warmth and food . . . do you remember . . . ?*

Sometimes the tears ran down my face. I sweated and felt a burning along my skin, in my chest. This was the scrub I needed. Exfoliation, clarifying, deep-pore cleanse – words I knew from the beauty pages of magazines and the counters of Selfridges. Now they were for my soul not my skin.

It was inevitable that Anwar would seek me out one last time. He came to my place and rang the bell. Instead

247

of buzzing him in, I said, 'Wait, I'll come down instead.' I put on my new ankle-length skirt, my long-sleeved blouse. I put on my headscarf. It was like the day in Selfridges when I had tried on that skimpy black dress and walked out of the changing room to twirl in front of him. There was still laughter in me, the desire to tease him one last time. I tied my headscarf with a pin. I slowly walked down the stairs to the shock on his face.

Part Six

2004

Thirty-three

I am out of a job now; I am unemployed. It is the first time for me to be fired, to be told don't come back. I don't set the alarm but I still wake up at the usual time. I open the curtains and the sun hurts my eyes. A day for pushing Mai on the swings. Lamya hadn't given me the chance to kiss her goodbye. Instead she picked up the phone and summoned her mother. Doctora Zeinab arrived to look after Mai until another nanny is found, or a place becomes available at the university crèche. She arrived too, to deal with her wayward son. It wasn't only his behaviour on the night of the party that brought her but his exam results as well. He had failed. They were at him all day, mother and sister, nagging and blaming until he packed and flounced out of the flat. For the past few days, he has been bunking down at the mosque. No doubt Lamya blames me. She thinks I have seduced him, manipulated his youth. She thinks I am after their money. I can hear her voice buzzing in my ear, what she is pouring out to her mother, bringing her into the distorted picture. Perhaps they sit around the kitchen table with their coffee mugs while Mai watches TV, the washing machine churning away, the man who collects the garbage clambering up the service stairs. I flush, thinking what Doctora Zeinab will hear, how I can't defend myself. No wonder it is a sin to talk about people behind their back, it is such a power.

I haunt St John's Wood High Street. I pass their flat, the red pillar box in front of it. I pass the newsagent that has just opened. A van is parked on the road; it unloads cartons of milk, juice and eggs. The boutiques are still closed. I stare through the windows at a beige outfit with matching handbag and shoes. There are no price tags; the design is minimal, only a few items are displayed. I need not wonder what it feels like to walk inside, to choose a dress. I know. I know the privileged welcome, the luxurious dressing room, the hush of thick carpet and perfume. I cross the road to Oxfam. It is also closed. The coat in the window looks nice and wearable; I should go in one day and try it on. Perhaps it is high time for me to shed my pride and wear second-hand clothes. I have long found out that, here in London, middle-class women wear second-hand clothes for fun. But I'm not middle class; I do not have a degree. I am upper class without money.

The scent of fresh baked bread draws me to the bakery. I buy croissants and sit in the small park in front of the flat. The park is almost empty this time of morning. An elderly lady is taking her walk; a man sits on a bench reading the *Telegraph*. They know that this is the best time of the day, the freshest. The lady smiles as she passes me and says good morning. People are nice in this area. The elderly are refined. They remind me of my mother. I dream of her a lot these days. She is ill and troubled, worried about Omar. I must read Surat Yasin for her, now that I have free time. I watch Lamya as she leaves for the day. Her clothes are familiar to me from the times I've ironed them, hung them in her cupboard. I've collected that jacket from the dry-cleaner. I watch her walking to her car. She is attractive but slight, lacking in allure. A neighbour passes her and she greets him deferentially, smiling widely. I have not seen her deferential before; this is another side of her. I look up and catch Doctora Zeinab pulling open the curtains, the sun reflects on the window and I can't see the expression on her face. It must be hard work for her – Mai and the flat. Somehow I can't imagine Lamya lifting a finger to help but this is unrealistic, she must be doing her share.

I meet Tamer in the Regent's Park. It feels strange, the two of us without Mai. He looks rumpled, haggard. He is neither eating nor sleeping properly at the mosque. For the first time, he looks unclean but he is soon bored with questions about his well-being. He brushes my concern aside and is not interested in the croissants I got him. He is distracted by thoughts and plans. 'I'm not going to do my re-sits. I don't want to do them. I'm going to transfer to another university outside London.'

I think of the cities outside London. They must be dull and green in comparison. 'Unless your parents approve, how will you manage on your own? They already have the flat here. Will they pay for your accommodation elsewhere?'

He stiffens. 'I'll get a job.'

'As what?'

'I don't know. I'll deliver pizza.'

'It won't be safe for you at night. There are people who might hurt you.'

He doesn't insist that he can look after himself. Instead he kicks an empty carton of juice towards the side of the path. 'I tried asking in the mosque for work but once I start talking everyone wants to know why I have left home, why I quarrelled with my family. I don't like that. I want to be left alone. I don't like people being nosy. We have to get married, then I can come and live with you.' He looks at me, pleading.

'Your parents will never approve.'

'They'll have to accept it. The longer I stay away from home, the more they'll realize that I'm determined.' He is like someone else, a common rebellious teenager.

I try again. 'If you hurt them, you won't be happy and I want you to be happy.'

He still doesn't soften. 'I have to think of doing what will please Allah, not what will please anyone else. I don't want to commit a sin.'

'You won't commit a sin.' How can I be sure? I've seen people slide and fling themselves; I've seen it in myself.

He stops walking and looks at me, 'You never said yes. You never said you would marry me.'

I laugh. 'Didn't I?'

'No you didn't. I just assumed.' He looks handsome now; his eyes brighten.

'Well, to say yes, you must promise me you'll take a second wife.'

'What a stupid thing to say, Najwa!'

'Because I might not be able to have children.' The regret in my voice startles me.

'I don't care about children.'

'You don't mean that.'

'I do.' He wants my full attention; he wants to be my child.

'Maybe now you're not interested but when you're older, you'll want a pretty young wife, a conventional marriage.'

He shrugs and says, 'I don't care about the future. I only care about now.'

But for me the future is close, round the corner, not far

away. 'I wouldn't want you to divorce me. I would rather be in the background of your life, always part of it, always hearing your news.'

He says softly, 'I don't like it when you talk like that. I don't want to think of the future – all the stupid studying I have to do. I don't even want to do my re-sits.'

'If you could do anything, if there were no restrictions, what would you do?'

He smiles and looks his age again, soft and dreamy. 'The two of us would go back in time. A time of horses and tents; swords and raids.'

I smile and he continues. 'There wouldn't be any "Business" and I wouldn't have to go to university.'

We are both too simple for this time and place. Sometimes I want to die; not out of despair or fear but just to step away from life and stand in the shade, watch it roll on without me, changeable and aggressive.

The park is sweet and not crowded. We are the first to buy ice cream from a lonely van and sit on a bench looking at the swans.

'Do you think Mai remembers me?' I ask.

'She is probably bored without you.'

'I dreamt of her last night.'

He smiles. 'I love you. You know that, don't you?'

I nod. Pity gushes through me and brings tears to my eyes. To stop myself from blubbering I lick my ice cream and say, 'Lamya owes me money. I left on the twenty-eighth and she never gave me that month's salary.'

'She's difficult.' He opens his wallet and gives me all the notes he has. Crisp twenty-pound notes, his pocket money. He takes money for granted. It is obvious in the way he touches the notes. He can get more from the till, from the bank account his parents fill for him. He thinks they will always be around, will always give to him unconditionally. I was like that at his age. I put the money away.

'You should go back home, Tamer.' I say it gently but he turns rigid and shakes his head. He stares down at the grass instead of meeting my eyes. I try again. 'It's wrong. You know it's a sin to cut someone off for more than three days, specially your mother and sister.'

'I spoke to my mother on the phone. She knows where I am.' There is guilt in his eyes, buried in the defiance.

'What about Lamya?'

'Did she get in touch with you? Did she apologize?'

I shake my head. I am not expecting her to.

'Well, she should. I told her I'm going to marry you. You will become my wife and, whether she likes it or not, she will have to treat you like a sister.' This is a new hardness. He is all grown up. And that quality I had adored, that glow and scent of Paradise, is nearly gone. Soon he will be like the rest of us.

'And your mother – what was her reaction?' I had not asked him before.

'She said, "I can't believe my son is doing this to me," and she started to cry. It was horrible.'

I blurt out, 'She's used to a high standard! What you've done is nothing compared to what my mother had to put up with from Omar. People think the leukaemia killed her but it was her broken heart.' He moves away from me. He is defensive about his mother; they were always close.

After he reluctantly leaves for his university, I walk towards the mosque. At the corner with Wellington Road, I see Doctora Zeinab and Mai getting into a taxi. It is Mai I recognize first. Doctora Zeinab is altered. Her face is puffy, her hair lank and there are dark shadows under her eyes. Her movements are awkward as she helps Mai into the taxi then heaves herself in. She draws the taxi door shut but she has not pulled hard enough and has to repeat the action. She is not herself. Her confidence has taken a blow; she is walking through a storm.

At the mosque, in the ladies' prayer hall, there is class led by Um Waleed. She looks alarmed to see me during working hours, but alarm is her usual expression. She gestures for me to join in the circle. The class must have been going on for some time because the zuhur azan is due. Um Waleed hands me a Qur'an. This is a tafseer class and they are discussing verses from 'The Heights'. I remember Wafaa, years ago, handing me a copy of the Qur'an, saying, 'This is for you to keep.' She and Ali are in Birmingham now. People move on, sisters leave and new ones take their place. Um Waleed can pull anyone away from their personal problems and make them listen. Perhaps it is the urgency in her voice. 'There are different interpretations of why these men are on the Heights. The Heights are a mountain that stands between Paradise and Hell. These men are stuck in the middle, desiring Paradise and fearing Hell, able to see both. One interpretation is that their good actions and bad actions are equal in scale. The other interpretation is that they are young men who left home to fight the Jihad without the permission of their mothers and fathers. Because they died for the sake of Allah they have been spared Hell, but because they broke their parents' hearts, they are deprived of Paradise.'

Thirty-four

So she sits before me, in an armchair in my flat. It is as if we are suspended in tension. It fills the room and makes my voice and movements slow. I think that when she leaves I will be exhausted; I will have to lie down. Mai is not with her which means that this is a formal visit, one that Lamya knows about. Since Doctora Zeinab phoned, I have been cleaning, tidying, baking a cake and washing my hair. I must make a good impression, not only for Tamer's sake but also for mine because I admire her, sense a goodness in her, not the metaphysical kind that her son has but one that is solid, rooted in pragmatism. I notice today more than ever how much Tamer looks like her, how much he is from her, her masculine side, her only son. She looks better, more controlled than the day I saw her getting into the taxi. There is still the puffy face and the dark-ringed eyes but her hair is set, her make-up well applied and she is elegant in white trousers and a pale green jacket. It is the first time for her to see me without my hijab. Her eyes flickered over me when I opened the door and she saw my transformation. But she did not say anything or hid her surprise well. Perhaps it was something she was expecting. I want to show her that I am attractive, that there is more to me than being a maid. When she speaks, I realize that she knows.

We probe general, safe topics – Mai, the weather, how crowded London becomes in the summer. I offer her fresh orange juice, coffee and banana cake. She does not refuse my hospitality and I am grateful. It is her good manners which makes her drain her glass, compliment me on the cake and even allow herself a second piece. Perhaps we can become friends if I am too old to play the role of daughter-in-law. We can become sisters. I relax and find myself speaking to her about my mother and, with a sense of unreality, show her old photos. She says that Tamer had told her about my father. Her voice is matter-of-fact, like a doctor discussing a serious illness, and I must not forget that she is a doctor. She makes it clear that she will not taunt me with my past but she will not ignore it either. I should not be surprised that Tamer told her. It is a good sign that he is talking to her even if only by phone. But I have become used to secrecy, it has become a part of me. Now I feel vulnerable.

'My husband knows your father,' she says.

'Of him, you mean. Most Sudanese do.' There is an edge to my voice because of the futility of trying to make someone see him as my flesh and blood, not a symbol, not a public figure.

She looks me straight in the eye. 'Yes, of him. Politics is a difficult profession in our countries, all these ups and downs.'

'Yes.' But my father was not strictly a politician. He did not care what policies governed the country as long as his career was successful. It would be unfair to ascribe to him the role of wronged political idealist or fallen hero, comforting though it may be. My comfort is Allah's mercy, Allah's justice.

She says, 'The climate is changing now in Sudan. The future looks good.'

'Perhaps some people will start to go back.' I think of Anwar and his wife, their two little boys, or will it be too late for them to go back?

She raises her voice a little. 'Would you like to go back?'

Her question seems odd, pointed. She drops her eyes, stirs her coffee.

'Yes,' I say slowly, 'it would be lovely to go back, but it is unlikely.'

'But you deserve a better position, better than the kind of work you do here and it's only in our own country that we can really feel respected. May Allah preserve your health but we are all getting older and one day you will need others to care for you.'

I know what she is saying, probing for my deepest insecurity. We talk of it in the mosque, what will happen to us, those of us who don't have children or whose children can't cope? Will we end up in nursing homes where they will spoon-feed us mashed pork and we won't know the difference?

'You can get a decent job in Khartoum just by being who you are and because you know English. You can perhaps run a nursery for little children or work as a supervisor in a girls' hostel.'

Her suggestions require capital and courage. She is leading to something, but I still can't understand her implications.

'You can have your own maid in Khartoum,' she continues. 'Apparently it's Southerners now that people are employing, not Ethiopians like in the past – they're too expensive.'

I say, 'It's always nice to chat about Khartoum and to remember the past.'

She looks taken aback as if she expected a different response. It is odd that she is not talking about Tamer. Surely he is more important than me. She puts her cup on the table and says, 'I really came to apologize for what Lamya did. She can be hot-tempered sometimes. She behaved very badly with you and I'm sorry . . .'

I interrupt her. 'Doctora Zeinab, it is enough that you are visiting me. You don't need to apologize. I regard her as my sister and Mai as my daughter. She lost her temper and I did not take offence.'

She looks at me seriously, almost brooding. 'Lamya's always been a bit stiff. She sees things in black and white, no compromises for her. I often used to wish that she was the boy and Tamer the girl.'

I smile at what I regard as a humorous remark but she does not smile back. Instead she continues. 'I don't know what she's going to do with these problems she's having with her husband. I tell her she has to be diplomatic, she has to give and take. For the sake of Mai, at least.'

I am curious to know of Lamya's problems. She satisfies my curiosity. 'Hisham has been seeing some other woman and, when Lamya confronted him, he said it was all her fault for leaving him and staying in London.'

I absorb this piece of news. I am touched that she is confiding in me. In a sense it brings me closer to her, to Tamer, to being part of a family again.

'Tamer never liked Hisham,' she continues. 'From the beginning he just never took to him. I don't know why.'

'Because he is not fooled by appearances, because he can look deep into people.' I sound fervent, perhaps too fervent. I can tell by how she shifts in her chair that I have made her uncomfortable. We should talk about him now. This is why she is here, isn't it?

261

But she says, 'Lamya has to be diplomatic – please him and please herself. That way she can both keep her husband and get her PhD.'

'Of course,' I murmur.

'My daughter's not easy.' She shakes her head and sighs. 'Problems. Children get older and their problems grow with them.'

'Insha' Allah they will be solved soon.'

She picks up her handbag, opens it and takes out a cheque. 'Lamya owes you money. Here's your month's salary and some compensation for what happened.' She puts the cheque on the table. I glance at the figure. I blink and look again. My voice comes out in a gasp, almost a laugh. 'This is much more than I usually get. There must be some mistake.'

She shifts in her seat, shakes her head with impatience. When she speaks, she speaks as if I am stupid. 'There is no mistake. This is all for you.'

I stare back at her. She picks up the cheque, she moves her hands emphatically. 'This is a compensation for you because you are not going to work for us again and because my son has made you promises he is incapable of keeping. You will have nothing to do with our family again. Do you understand what I am saying?' There is a tremble in her voice. It weakens the impact of her words.

'I'm sorry,' my voice is cool, 'but I don't understand you.'

'You are pretending you don't understand me!' Her face is a deep colour.

'No. I am not.'

It is a turning point. Tears come to her eyes. She shifts to sit at the edge of her seat. 'You will take this money and stay away from my son! Just take it and leave him alone. You're ruining him, ruining him.' She struggles to compose herself, to stop the flow of tears. Her attachment to him is so deep it is like he had never left her and now she is afraid, afraid of losing him.

I move to sit beside her, to put my arm around her shoulder. She feels damp; she is perspiring. I say, 'Don't upset yourself. Everything will work out.'

'*If* you take the money,' she snaps at me, '*if* you leave him alone.'

She can't understand what Tamer sees in me. She doesn't want to understand. I withdraw my arm. I am of no use to her. She does not want me; she is not accepting me. I had been naïve to think she would. She is breathing hard and takes a tissue from her handbag. 'I can't sleep at night for worry.' She sniffs. 'What is going to become of him? He fails his exams and instead of applying himself and working hard, he imagines himself in love. And with who? You're old enough to be his mother even if you don't look it! And he tells me the Prophet, peace be upon him, married Khadijah and she was fifteen years older than him. Is this an argument? We live now, not then. And when I reason with him, he storms out of the house and for one whole day puts his mobile off so I can't reach him!'

Her words pour over me and I remember my mother speaking like that, crying about Omar. That was the good times, when she would let it all out. Most times she couldn't speak.

'Tamer's always been a good boy. Good in his studies, not brilliant enough to go into Medicine or Engineering but hardworking and diligent. He did his best. There was no wildness in him, no nagging us to get him a car, no girlfriends, no staying out late. What do parents worry about? Drugs – he wasn't anywhere near that. What a relief, we thought, that he's sober and religious. Being religious is good; it protects him though sometimes we worried maybe he'll become fanatical . . .'

I wait for her to finish, to spend herself. I sit immobile, my hands in my lap, looking at the cheque on the table. I can go on Hajj with this money, I can get a plane to Mecca, stay in a nice hotel not far from the Ka'ba – I can enjoy myself. I can get a degree with this money, go to university with Shahinaz and become a mature student. I can help Omar next month when he comes out of prison. Maybe he can be persuaded to become a student. The more she talks the more frustrated I become, because she is really talking about herself and not about Tamer.

'Once or twice he did sound fanatical, nagging me and Lamya to wear the hijab, making a fuss because I smoked – but he kept his limits, he was never extreme. We regarded him as a minor irritation. At times I worried that he was spending too much time at the mosque. Maybe, I thought, a terrorist group would mess up his mind and recruit him but thankfully he's not interested in politics, so that's a relief. And now this, out of nowhere, he wants to marry the maid!'

He is better than her and she will not acknowledge it. I see this clearly now. She is an obstacle to his spiritual growth or, more precisely, her disapproval is. She is a test for him and he will have to pass. I will not let him fail. I will not let her curse him, not like my mother cursed Omar. I remember how he shook her shoulders, shouting, 'Give me my money. It's my money!' I saw fear, stark genuine fear in her eyes. And she used to feed him when he was little, scoop him in her arms. When he got what he wanted from her and stormed out of the flat, she said, 'I hope he is never ever successful. I hope he is never ever happy.' She spoke without anger, without bitterness, calmly like a judge passing a sentence. This is how a mother can curse her son.

I pick up the cheque and say, 'This is not enough.' She misunderstands me of course; she thinks I want more money.

'Yes,' she says eagerly, 'this is what I have been trying to tell you. If you stay as far away from him as possible, if you leave London and go back to Khartoum, I will help you even more. In Khartoum I can find you a place to live, set you up in a business. Your own nursery school or . . .'

'Going back is not an option for me. I can't leave my brother . . .'

'But he can join you. Why not? It would be good for him too . . .'

The extent to which she is prepared to go! It shakes me. It makes me fear and pity her. I interrupt her flow of bribes. 'You didn't understand me. When I said it is not enough I meant that it is not enough that I keep away from him. He has to be convinced. And you too have to sacrifice and help him solve his problems.'

'What problems?'

She doesn't know. She doesn't know that he has his own frustrations and view of the world. She doesn't know that he is not an extension of her.

I tell her. And by telling her I give him up. I put the key in her hand. Perhaps she will not do what I say, perhaps she will. She is an intelligent woman. She pulls herself together and listens.

Thirty-five

'I don't believe you,' he says. He looks worse today, fuzzy from lack of proper sleep, almost gaunt. His clothes haven't been washed and his shirt is rumpled. He has run out of clean socks and now his trainers chafe against his bare ankles and irritate him.

I repeat what I've said before. His mother is willing to allow him to change his course of studies. She will talk to his father and persuade him.

'You don't have to do your re-sits, Tamer. You don't have to study Business. You can study what you want, wherever you want.'

He breathes out. It is almost like a laugh. He shakes his head in wonder. 'You convinced her of this. You made her change her mind!'

'Yes,' I say, looking away. The hard bit is yet to come, the painful bit. Now he must feel relief. I must let it seep through him, this breath of relief; the burden of studying what he doesn't want easing away. And the triumph that his exile from home has yielded something. I must let him feel satisfied for the moment.

'Swear,' he says, still smiling, gaping with disbelief, 'swear that my mom has given in.'

'I swear.'

266

'You are so kind, so good to me.'

'No, you are the one who deserves it.'

'You are so gentle, the way you speak.'

Tears come to my eyes. 'We are talking about you, not me. You have to start thinking of your future.'

'I used to be vague about the degree I wanted to study for. I knew it wasn't Business and I knew that it would include Islamic History. Sometimes, out of boredom, I would read prospectuses and stuff in the university library and look up things on the Internet. And now I know the name of the degree I want – it's called Middle East Studies. It's different disciplines: history, economics, geography, language – it's multidisciplinary.'

I smile to see him animated, to see him looking forward. His enthusiasm nourishes me. 'This is the real you,' I say. 'I love seeing you like this. Now you have to research whether you need to transfer to another university, or whether you can stay where you are.'

'But I have to go home first,' he says, moving to sit at the edge of the bench. Already he wants to go to her, to patch up his quarrel and bask once again in her approval. I feel a pang of envy but I can keep it under control, I am not finished with him yet, I am working now, working on him. So I smile. 'You really must beg your mother's forgiveness. You hurt her by leaving the house.'

'I know.' He speaks lightly, already thinking of something else.

'No, you don't know. She has been sick with worry over you.'

Something in my voice makes him look at me. 'Is that all she wants – for me to come home?'

'What do you mean?' I am playing for time. I am reluctant to go on.

'In return for allowing me to study what I want – all I have to do is come back home?' He is beginning to suspect. Even while he asks the question, he is unsure.

'And you have to be realistic about certain things. Sometimes . . .'

'Stop it. What did she say about *you*? What did she say about us getting married?'

I fear his anger, his disapproval of me. But there is no way out now. I take a breath. 'She said it can't be. She asked me to leave you and I said yes.'

He cries. It is instant. The tears, his shoulders shaking. He weeps and I suffer. It is as if my skin is being grated from the inside, frustrating and intent.

'You tricked me,' he says, 'you tricked me. You are so mean, so mean.'

I can't defend myself. He will never cry like this again. It is the end of his childhood. In the future it will be manly tears, manly pains, but not these sobs. He leaves me and half-runs, half-walks in the direction of his home. He will go to her now, he needs her now, her arms around him, the comfort and relief.

I sit, twisted by cruelty. An hour passes but time means nothing. I can still hear his voice, smell him. I can still see the confusion in his eyes, the way he looked at me as if I were a criminal.

I walk across the park towards Baker Street. In the bank I deposit the cheque Doctora Zeinab had written out for me. As I fill in the payment slip, I realize that the amount is exactly the same as the sum I lent Anwar, years ago, to do his PhD. He had never paid me back, not even part of it. Over time I had accepted this loss as a penalty, the fine I had to pay to extract myself. Now, in this strange way, I am getting my money back.

*   *   *

A few days later, I wait to press the buzzer of their flat. She said six o'clock. The High Street is in a mood of careless summer. Sports cars with their tops down drive past, streaming music and long straight hair. The customers of Café Rouge sit out on the pavement. An ice-cream van stands on the corner; its engine running. There is a queue of children and plenty more in the park; I can hear them. This is the last time I will lift my hand and press this buzzer. It had been autumn when I first started to work here. I remember the fresh bare trees, the cleanliness of a cold morning. Now I look up to see the minaret of the mosque above the trees. I might not see it again from this particular angle.

Doctora Zeinab buzzes me in. I have pulled open this door and left it to shut behind me so many times, alone or with Mai. I linger to press my feet on the carpet and to say goodbye to the old-fashioned elevator that made me talk to Tamer. I run my fingers on the luxurious wood of the banister. Mai does not come forward to greet me; she hides behind her grandmother's skirt, peeking at me with shining eyes. She is shy because of the weeks I have been away, because of the anti-Najwa speeches her mother must have delivered. I must wait for her to follow her natural instincts and come into my arms. It might take the whole visit or it might not happen at all.

I notice with satisfaction that the flat is not as clean as it was when I was working here. I glimpse a pile of Tamer's clothes in the kitchen waiting to be ironed, plates stacked in the kitchen sink. Doctora Zeinab leads me to the sitting room, treating me like a guest, welcoming me warmly with Egyptian hospitality. She is subdued but her relief that he has come home is obvious. He is standing in front of the window. I notice the difference in him straight away:

269

clean clothes, a proper shower, a good night's sleep in a bed, not on the floor. But it is not only the comforts of home. He is cleansed now, relieved of guilt and the burden of studying Business. The sweetness is almost back, that aura of freshness.

But he is wary of me, still sore. He folds his arms across his chest. I comment on the white cap he is wearing. 'I have never seen you cover your hair before.'

'Until he gets it cut.' His mother answers for him. 'It's become far too long and untidy.'

He accepts her comments and we sit down. She bustles about with Mai following close behind her. I am offered Ferrero Roche and apple juice followed by tea and cookies from the patisserie down the road. To make polite conversation, I say, 'Did you hear the programme on radio about Sufism?'

'No I didn't.' He doesn't smile and I wish that things were how they were months ago when he used to come back from university and talk to me.

'I do listen to the radio,' says Doctora Zeinab, 'but I didn't catch it. How much sugar shall I put for you?'

When I reply, she says, 'Tamer was listening to a tape by Amr Khalid.' She stirs the tea, warns Mai not to come too close to the teapot.

'What was the lesson about?' I ask him.

He looks down at the carpet. 'Being satisfied with what Allah gives us.'

We are self-conscious because of her pointed presence. It is almost like visiting Omar but here is the appropriate sheepishness, the catharsis and calmness it brings. Mai keeps her distance but can't take her eyes off me. I remind her of shared games and days we spent at the park. She comes closer. I take out the gift I had brought her: *This is the House that Jack Built.* I turn the pages and say, 'Come and sit next to me, so that I can read it with you.'

She shakes her head. I put the book on the table so she can at least look at the pictures.

The phone rings and Doctora Zeinab answers it. While she talks, Tamer and I remain silent; he avoids looking at me. At one point he closes his eyes. He is still tired, still bruised. When she finally says her goodbyes I ask him, 'Was it straightforward to get your transfer from the university?'

'It was easy.' He had given a pledge to his mother not to phone me, not to meet me, not to write to me. It will be easy to keep because he will go back with her to Cairo.

She gestures with her hand towards the dining table, 'Show her, Tamer, the pages you printed out from the Internet.' He stands up with some reluctance. She says, 'All his classes are going to be in English because it's an American university.'

I read the details of the courses: *Studies in the Qur'an, Islamic Architecture in Spain and North Africa, Ibn Khaldun.* He will be fulfilled there, active and interested.

'These topics are inspiring,' I say.

For the first time, he warms towards me, for a moment becomes his normal self. 'Yes, they are inspiring. I am looking forward to them.'

I can sense the beginning of a fire in him; it makes me smile. 'You are lucky.'

Doctora Zeinab sighs. She does not think he is lucky. She does not think that loving me has been a blessing.

We are quiet. What I am doing here, why had I so much wanted to come? Do I expect him to apologize or am I the one who owes the apology?

He hesitates and then asks, 'What will you do now?'

271

'I will go on Hajj, insha'Allah. I am planning for it.' The excitement slips through. I have not told anyone else and I am glad that he is the first to know.

He smiles for the first time, a shy guarded smile. 'Congratulations, Najwa, this is nice.' He says my name with ease.

Doctora Zeinab looks at her watch. I should leave. But Mai carries her book and sits next to me. She wants me to read it for her. I start to read *This is the House that Jack Built* and I forget Doctora Zeinab's presence. There is only Mai's attention and Tamer looking at us. For as long as the book lasts, we are poised, no future, no past.

Mai wants me to read again but I must not overstay my welcome. I look Doctora Zeinab straight in the eye and her gratitude for me is buried under layers of practicality. She does not want me to weaken, to pull out of the deal at the last minute. This visit has been a risk and she knows it. She looks at my face as a doctor examines a patient and I feel dizzy with fatigue. I feel as if I had worked all day, stood cooking for hours, ironing for hours, fetched and carried. I want to crawl into bed and sleep. It is time to leave. I bend down and kiss Mai goodbye.

Thirty-six

Shahinaz stands in my doorway. When she speaks, her voice comes from far away. 'You sounded odd on the phone. I thought I should come and see you.' She is clutching a lot of things: Ahmed, his pushchair, what looks like a sleeping bag. She follows me inside. 'Sohayl said I might as well stay the night as it's so late.'

It's late, she's saying and I don't know what time it is. If it is dark outside, it must be late.

She asks, 'Did they leave?'

It takes time for the question to reach and hurt me. I sense her waiting, her concern. 'Yes, they left this afternoon.' Doctora Zeinab acted fast, no dithering. She didn't want to risk me weakening; she didn't want to risk him changing his mind.

Shahinaz reaches for my hand. 'You're finding it hard, aren't you – but you did the right thing.'

'Last night I couldn't sleep and all day today I tried but I couldn't.'

She settles herself and I lie down again on the couch. I close my eyes and listen to her talking to Ahmed. 'Aunty's not well today.' Not well today. Not well today means that tomorrow I will be better. It is a realistic prediction, a reassuring one. I just have to wait. Tomorrow I can go to the travel agent, ask about Hajj packages, what prices they offer and how far is the hotel from the Prophet's Mosque. Ahmed is babbling away: words that don't make sense, strung together with inflections and exclamations of surprise, as if he is talking in a foreign language. His voice is lovely. I close my eyes. There is nothing to work out, just memories, impressions. Their plane would have landed in Cairo by now. I want to sleep; this is what I need more than anything else.

She says, 'I'll make you some chamomile tea. It always makes me sleepy.'

I make myself sit up and smile at her. 'Come, Ahmed, come and sit on my lap.' Instead, he crawls away from me fast, across the room. He pulls himself up to stand, leaning against a chair. He is playing a game with me, pausing, looking straight at me, smiling as if to tease me.

'Come,' I say, 'come.'

He does at last and I lift him to sit on my lap. 'Aren't you the cutest baby ever, or aren't you a baby any more? You're a big boy!'

'He's everywhere,' she says bringing the tea. 'I have to keep the bathroom door closed otherwise he's in there throwing his toys in the loo.'

I tickle him. 'Is this what you do, Ahmed, is it?' He laughs, proud of himself.

'Did you notice that mark on his skin?' She pulls back his jumper and on his forearm is a small black spot, like the splash of ink.

I run my fingers over it. 'Maybe it's a beauty spot. Was he born with it?'

'I'm not sure. Maybe I just never noticed it before. I hope it's nothing serious.'

For a minute, for a whole blessed minute, I forget about myself, become immersed in her concern.

'Ask your mother-in-law.'

'Yes, I will.' She removes the telephone cord from Ahmed's grasp. He has been chewing it.

I run my finger over Ahmed's arm. 'You're perfect, aren't you? Mummy is just fussing over little faults in you.'

He chuckles and turns to gaze at his first love. She looks at him with possessiveness and an ache I don't understand.

She sighs, 'Come on, Najwa. Let's pray so we can go to sleep.'

She leads because I am not up to it. Her gentle voice calms me down; it is easy to focus on the words she is hesitantly saying. Ahmed climbs on her back, he hangs on to her neck and makes it difficult for her to stand. My concentration breaks. I almost laugh at his antics and then the words come again, pulling me back. No matter what, I will return. This is my base and goal; everything else is variable.

We sort ourselves out for the night. Shahinaz and Ahmed on the couch and I on the floor. I lie awake, listening to her breathing. I am amazed to discover that Ahmed, baby Ahmed, snores. There is a taxi outside. I know it is a taxi by the sound of its brakes. They took a taxi to Heathrow this morning. They kissed Lamya and Mai goodbye. I see myself standing at the door of the flat saying goodbye to Doctora Zeinab. Tamer and I are helping her with the suit-cases. He looks at me. This is not a dream; this is a replay of the time his mother left London to go to the confer-ence in the States. She hands me a crisp ten-pound note, a tip. I take it as I am meant to take it, as a maid takes from an employer, but I am flustered because he is standing next to her, because he is watching me put the money away.

Shahinaz says, 'You took the money, so it can't have been love.' I must be falling asleep and her voice a dream, because she wouldn't say that in real life. It is not something she is likely to say. I am not well. I have a fever and I need my parents' room. I need their bed; its clean sheets, the privilege. I climb dark steep stairs to their room and there is the bed I have been fretting for. My mother's voice, her cool hand on my forehead. She gives me a spoonful of medicine, delicious cough syrup that burns my throat. Omar is sulking. He is jealous because I am ill and important. He wants something from me and Mama says, 'Leave her alone, can't you see she's burning.' I look up into my father's anxious face, his warm hand on my cheeks. I smell his cologne. He shouts at my mother, 'Put her on a course of antibiotics, you can't leave her like this!' I roll over, luxurious, sure that they love me. Around us, beyond the bed, the room is dark and cluttered, all the possessions that distinguish us in ruins. I am not surprised. It is a natural decay and I accept it. Carpets threadbare and curtains torn. Valuables squashed and stamped with filth. Things that must not be seen, shameful things, are exposed. The ceiling has caved in, the floor is gutted and the crumbling walls are smeared with guilt.

A NOTE ON THE AUTHOR

Leila Aboulela grew up in Khartoum and moved to Britain in her mid-twenties. She is the author of a novel, *The Translator*, which was longlisted for the Orange Prize, and a book of short stories, *Coloured Lights*. She is a winner of the Caine Prize for African Writing.

A NOTE ON THE TYPE

The text of this book is set in Linotype Sabon, named after the type founder, Jacques Sabon. It was designed by Jan Tschichold and jointly developed by Linotype, Monotype, and Stempel, in response to a need for a typeface to be available in identical form for mechanical hot metal composition and hand composition using foundry type. Tschichold based his design for Sabon roman on a font engraved by Garamond, and Sabon italic on a font by Granjon. It was first used in 1966 and has proved an enduring modern classic.